Debra Kent has been writing about marriage, infidelity, sex and family relationships for the past fifteen years, in *Mademoiselle*, *Redbook*, *Cosmopolitan* and *Family Circle*. She has also written a column, *The Diary of V*, for the website Redbook/women.com since 1997.

Wife Living Dangerously

DEBRA KENT

First published in Great Britain in 2006 by HEADLINE REVIEW
An imprint of HEADLINE BOOK PUBLISHING

First published in paperback in 2006 by HEADLINE REVIEW
An imprint of HEADLINE BOOK PUBLISHING

1

ISBN 978-0-7553-4014-9

Printed and bound in Great Britain by
Clays Ltd, St Ives plc

Headline's policy is to use papers that are natural, renewable and recyclable products and made from wood grown in sustainable forests. The logging and manufacturing processes are expected to conform to the environmental regulations of the country of origin

HEADLINE BOOK PUBLISHING
A division of Hodder Headline
338 Euston Road
London NW1 3BH

www.reviewbooks.co.uk
www.hodderheadline.com

For Alisa,
who brings me the beach.

Acknowledgments

It all begins with the beach, which means it all begins with my gracious, generous and beautiful friend, Alisa Sutor, and her dear parents who have opened up their magnificent home to our forlornly landlocked group. I am grateful to Anne Fuson, Nancy Barlow, Jennifer Forney, Ann Whitlatch, Lisa Deinlein and Kim Gibson, my companions for sunbathing and dolphin watching and discussing the mysteries of Mormon underwear. I could not have made vital revisions to this book without Vicki Minder, who taught me about desire and desirability. Much gratitude goes to my patient editors, Beth DeGuzman and Karen Kosztolnyik; my brilliant agent Sandra Dijkstra; the talented Candace Decker; the gifted Lauren Robert; Linda Alis, who showed me how to turn on the light; my mother Martha and my father Donald, a writer who left this world too soon; Hy and Sylvia Isaac; my friends Donna Wilber, Lorraine Rapp, Lisa Kamen, and Jason Vest. I must acknowledge my treasured Indiana family, Andy and Jane Mallor, Carolyn Lipson-Walker and George Walker, Julie Bloom and Richard Balaban. I thank my ex-husband and special friend Jeff Isaac for his tireless encouragement, and my children Adam and Annelise for being funny as hell and great kids too. And I thank Jamie Willis, artist, friend, playmate and partner.

Chapter ONE

It starts benignly. Mixing glass bottles in with the plastic, dropping a year off my age, fudging on my expense report. I download Joni Mitchell off the Limewire, not just one song but a whole album. I stop correcting cashiers when they make mistakes in my favor. I read a copy of *Good Housekeeping* from cover to cover in the café at Borders, accidentally stain page 31 with coffee, and never pay for it, just put it right back on the shelf and walk out of the store. By the end of the year I'm having sex with a professor of medieval literature who thinks that my husband is a fool.

How do I go from *Good Housekeeping* to good sex with Evan Delaney? I wish I could say I am pulled into this vortex of moral delinquency by some gravitational force beyond conscious control, but that would be a lie. I know exactly how I got here.

•••

This is our third trip to Frankie Wilson's beach house on Ocean Isle in North Carolina. We call ourselves, with only a little irony, the Beach Babes. All of us live in the same Indiana college town, in the same suburban subdivision, all are married, all are mothers, all of us hovering apprehensively near our fortieth year. It is 1:34 in the morning and after too many Tequizas, tortilla chips, and peanut M&M's, it is time for the game Annie Elliot has named Dirty Deeds. I'd rather play Pictionary, to be perfectly honest.

"I light the Candle of Truth," intones Annie, lifting a lit wooden Strike 'Em Anywhere match to the thick celadon pillar. The blue-gold flame swiftly engulfs the match head and races toward Annie's fingertip but just as it's about to make contact with skin she drops it into a wet saucer where it lands with a satisfying sizzle.

Annie Elliot was the only neighbor in Larkspur Estates who marked our arrival with any fanfare. My immediate next-door neighbors hadn't even waved or lifted their eyes when our old blue van pulled up to the curb behind the Greenway moving van. The Skaffs to the west kept on digging out crabgrass. To the east the Gilchrists continued hosing down the driveway though in truth there was no dirt to hose away, just clean Irish brick the color of desert clay. Hosing driveways, I have since discovered, is a popular pastime in Larkspur Estates, a hypnotic activity that holds homeowners in its sway for thirty or forty minutes at a time, long after the work of clearing debris is done. It is like masturbation with no climax or reward except perhaps for the deep black shine of the wet asphalt or, in the case of the Gilchrists' four-thousand-dollar driveway, the glow of red Irish brick.

But Annie Elliot sprinted all the way from Azalea Lane to personally welcome me. Nearly six feet of lean muscle with merry blue eyes and a smirky kind of smile, Annie had apologetically handed me a thermos of Starbucks coffee and a box of Little Debbie snack cakes, explaining that she hadn't had time to bake anything from scratch but thought it would be wrong to ring my doorbell empty-handed.

"We moved here last year and nobody even stopped by." She thrust the snack cakes toward me, Little Debbie's cherubic yet oddly authoritative young face grinning up at me. "I figured, if your neighbors are anything like the misanthropes on Azalea, you'll need all the friends you can get. And don't worry about returning the thermos, I have a million of them. I buy them at yard sales. Thermoses and picnic baskets. I don't know why considering we never go on picnics. My husband isn't a big fan of the great outdoors. Last time we went on a picnic we drove out to Maplewood State Park and ate lunch in the van. My kids were like, Mom, why can't we sit outside in the grass like the other people? I said, Your father hates nature. You know that. Good grief. Anyway. Welcome to the neighborhood." She gestured toward the box. "I stuck my number in with the Little Debbies. Call me when you need a break from unpacking or whatever."

I did, the very next day, and we have talked almost every day since then.

Annie lowers her voice and assumes the exotic tone of a fortune-teller. "When the Candle of Truth is passed to you, please reveal something you wouldn't dare admit in any other context but this one." The lush scent of sandalwood lifts and blends with the briny air. "As always, nothing leaves this room."

The room in question is a sprawling expanse of white pickled maple and white leather perched above the Atlantic Ocean, with extravagant windows and two sets of sliding-glass doors that open onto a sun-bleached wraparound deck and the twenty-six evenly cut cedar steps leading to the beach. A sandstone hearth embedded with shells and sea creature fossils sits at one end of the room and at the other, an extravagantly large entertainment unit with the biggest screen TV I've ever seen, but why would anyone want to watch it when the best view is right out the window?

The water is as black as the sky now, waves thwacking rhythmically against the hard-packed sand. As a landlocked Midwesterner who must settle for Lake Michigan or, embarrassingly, the Big Kahuna Wave Maker at Willy's Water Park, I enjoy no greater luxury than these brief, voluptuous vacations at Frankie Wilson's beach house. I love everything about it, everything except this game.

Annie edges the candle toward Frankie, who is about to snap off the last of her New York Naturals glue-on French-tipped fingernails. The pile of discarded plastic nails looks like a mound of onion slivers in the thin light of the dimmed-down candelabra.

"God, how I hate these things," she says, prying off the pinkie nail and flicking it to the heap. Frankie's real fingertips are gnawed beyond the quick. They have the flat, pliable look of frogs' toes. "Someone needs to make fake nails that don't make you feel like you slammed your fingers in a car door, you know?"

The first time I noticed Francesca Cavendish Wilson she was staffing the pop bottle ring toss at Twin Pines Elementary's annual school carnival. She had black curly hair and black eyes and she was wearing a black T-shirt that proclaimed in bright yellow letters: I EAT CARBS. SO SUE ME. Frankie, I came to discover, is queen of failed business ventures such as her unself-conscious magazine for plus-sized women called *Fat Lady* (she misjudged her audience's willingness to claim the title with pride), her disposable frying pan liners (which were great, except for the bursting into flames part), and Pet Pebbles (like pet rocks but smaller).

I finally introduced myself to Frankie at the Cambridge County Women's Leadership Club, a sort of alternative Rotary for "professional gals." Phyllis Bagley, president of First Cambridge Bank, had started the group because she was tired of being snubbed at the testosterone-laden Rotary events. Bagley's intent was to create a network of savvy businesswomen who could break the good old boy tourniquet on this town. Unfortunately Bagley hadn't realized that all the arteries of influence here lead to the same hardened heart. This calcified organ wasn't the university as many self-inflated academics would have you believe, but Copley Machine Parts and its thirty-five subsidiaries, founded, built, and managed by fifty-three-year-old Arnold Copley who has no heirs but many foot soldiers who serve on every significant board, foundation, commission, and council in the city. It has been said that no new project, however worthy, will succeed without Arnold Copley's blessing—and money. Phyllis Bagley set out to disprove the theory. So far she has not succeeded.

I was plucking pale lettuce leaves from the lunch buffet when Frankie appeared at my side and heaved a fat slice of strawberry cheesecake onto her plate.

"I only come for the dessert," she said, ladling extra strawberry compote on top of the thick wedge.

She joined me at my table and I marveled at the unselfconscious way she enjoyed her food. She pressed her spit-moistened finger to the plate to gather up the last of the graham cracker crumbs and bring them to her mouth.

At some point in the middle of Phyllis Bagley's exhortations, Frankie passed me a note: "Do you have a kid in Twin Pines?"

I nodded.

Next note: "Me too. Where do you live?"

I took her pen and wrote: "Larkspur Estates." I passed the pen and paper back and waited for her response, already burbling inside because I knew I was making a friend.

"Me too! On Periwinkle," she wrote. And then: "Do you hate living there as much as I do?"

I made a face and by tacit agreement we slinked out of the meeting room and regrouped at the Starbucks next door where we spent the next hour drinking the house blend and complaining about our neighborhood.

Frankie stares into the flame and I can see that she's sorting through her options. The last time we played this game she admitted to spying on the housepainter as he played with himself behind the garage. He was on a lunch break and apparently had packed a copy of *Great Big Butts* along with his tuna sandwich.

"Category, husbands." She runs her fingers through

her capriciously coiled hair. "Oh, boy. You guys are going to think I'm crazy."

"Nobody's going to think you're crazy," says Annie. "Remember? No shame, no blame."

Frankie darts her eyes to the vaulted ceiling and sucks in her breath. "I convinced my husband that Angelina Jolie is really a man."

We stare and wait for details.

"Jeremy has always had the hots for Angelina Jolie. He thinks she's a knockout. The boobs, the lips, whatever. Okay. So I told him that my mother's cousin Denise was the head surgical nurse during Angelina's—I mean *Angelo's*—sex-change operation. I threw in a bunch of believable details—the name of the surgeon, the brand of collagen they used for her lips, her first words when she came out of anesthesia."

"Which were . . . ?" I ask.

"Which were, 'Can I see my penis one more time before you throw it out?' Okay. So. Now Randy thinks Angelina Jolie is some kind of freak. And I never have to hear about her again." She smiles exultantly. "Do I pass?" Everyone agrees that Frankie's confession qualifies.

It is Annie's turn. "Oh, this definitely falls under the miscellaneous category," she says, putting her knuckle between her teeth. "Oh, God. I hate to admit this. Please don't think I'm awful."

"Just say it," Frankie demands.

"Okay. Here it goes." She takes a deep breath and cringes in anticipation of our response. "I don't pick up after Schatzi. Ever."

"Wait a second. I've *seen* you pick up after your dog,"

I say. This really was a revelation. All residents of Larkspur Estates are bound by a subdivision covenant that states, explicitly, that you've got to clean up after your dog. Other regulations include the proper storage of trash cans (out of view), parking of cars (never on the street), use of yard signs (prohibited except for the two-week period before election day). Annie was president of the neighborhood association for three years straight. She knew the dog poop rules better than anyone.

"No, you've seen me *pretend* to pick up after my dog. I just bend over and move a tissue around here and there so it *looks* like I'm picking something up but I always just leave it there. Oh, big deal. He's a miniature dachshund. You can hardly see his shit. Besides, it's all organic, isn't it? Well, isn't it? Will someone say something? Oh, God, I'm horrible!" Annie sighs heavily. "Well, friends. There you have it."

"Good grief," says Frankie, "this game used to be *fun.* Dog poop, Annie? For the love of Jesus and Mary." She tears open another bag of peanut M&M's. "Julie, please tell me you can do better than dog poop." The candle's small flame wavers as a sudden warm gust muscles through the screen door.

"Don't be so sure." I search my memory in futility for some transgression that might satisfy my friends but what's the point when I have never had an overdue library book, when I always correct cashiers when they make mistakes in my favor, and I don't lie, unless you count the white ones like telling Lala Townsend she looked great after she'd lost all her hair from chemotherapy. I had preserved my virginity until Michael and I were engaged, and even then I felt a little guilty. I suppose I could mention the time I told the pizza guy that yes, my eyes really were that green when I knew it was the tinted contacts that impressed him. Or I could tell them about the time I switched a store-bought pecan pie from its original foil tin into my own glass pie dish so other parents at the Brownies pot luck might think I'd baked it myself (although if anyone asked I would have told them the truth).

"I've got one," I say, finally. "Category: sex. I guess." I dip my pinkie into the hot wax that pools at the top of the candle and watch it harden on my finger. I am stalling. "Well, it was a Wednesday. No. Thursday. I was expecting a UPS delivery. My mother had told me to expect a packagc, some gifts for the kids. So, you know that UPS guy. The cute one?"

"Yes. The one with the ponytail," Frankie says.

"And that amazing ass." Annie smiles beatifically.

"Uh-huh. That's the one."

I ask you, is there a woman in this town who *doesn't* know this particular UPS driver? His hair is the color of butterscotch syrup, the ponytail unexpected and thrilling. He wears shorts even in the winter and the curly blond hair on his legs shimmers in the afternoon sun as he races up the walk and you wish he'd slow down just a little as he jogs back to the truck. Sometimes he waves as he's pulling away from the curb. No one knows his name.

I pick out four blue M&M's that, contrary to popular belief, will absolutely melt in your hands if you are nervous enough.

"As I was saying, I knew he'd be coming sometime that day, so . . ." My friends lean in. The room is quiet as a mausoleum. "I'm *saying* I made a special *effort* to look *nice.* I looked like crap all day but when I knew he was coming I put on makeup. Just for *him.* That's a big deal for me, you know? I'm *married,* remember?"

Annie is shaking her head as if I am the most pathetic excuse for a woman she has ever known. I blow out the candle. "Game over. I don't know about you guys but I can hardly keep my eyes open."

"That's it? That's your whole story?" Frankie is frowning.

"What else did you want to hear? That I met him at the door wearing a swimsuit? That I told him I liked his package?"

"That would be a start." Annie sucks an ice cube into her mouth and pops it back into the glass. "Were you thinking you might try to seduce him?"

Why would I want to seduce the UPS guy when I've got a husband whose lovemaking is as much an expression of adoration as it is an act of sexual impulse. Michael knows my body's idiosyncrasies the way Yo-Yo Ma knows his cello, approaching me with intuition, touching me with devotion and also precision. It's true that Michael and I haven't found much time for sex. He seems to be toiling longer and later at work and sometimes we go full days without more than a few words between us, let alone physical contact.

"It's just that," I continue, lamely, "I think he's good-looking. And I wanted to look nice when he stopped by."

"Why?" Annie asks.

"I don't know. Just because he's cute, I guess."

"Let's review the facts as we know them," Frankie

says. "You put on lip gloss so you'd look nice for the UPS guy. He gives you a package, you sign for it, you close the door. End of story?"

"Not just lip gloss. Blush too."

"Jesus, Julia, you are a fucking bore." Annie delivers this line with the finality of a game show host. I'm sorry. That's incorrect. You're out of the game. Annie has always said that I give off clear and indisputable married vibes. Even the meter-reader, widely known in our neighborhood for his glib lechery, will not flirt with me. "You work for the Bentley Institute, for Christ's sake, and this is the best you can come up with? Good God, woman."

Yes, that's right, I work for the Bentley Institute. As in, Eliza A. Bentley, the first American scientist to study, quantify, and demystify human sexual behavior. As in "The Annual Bentley Report on Sexual Behavior." As in the Bentley Museum, the world's largest collection of erotica and sexual artifacts, available for viewing by appointment only, and only if you have the appropriate academic credentials. You can't just walk in off the street and ask to see the Egyptian dildos.

"I think what Annie's trying to say," Frankie injects, gesticulating imploringly, "is that it wouldn't kill you to live a little dangerously. You don't have to do everything by the book, Julia. You need to get yourself some joie de vivre."

Not exactly a news flash. I've walked a circumscribed and sanitary path my whole life. My mother never had to ask me to wear a coat over my Halloween costume because I insisted on it. I never went on roller coasters, refused to play Seven Minutes in Heaven, never peeked at my presents before Christmas Eve, actually came straight home after the senior prom. I was a hall monitor, a junior crossing guard, and named "most reasonable" in my high school yearbook, a category I think they made up just for me. While my roommates in college rolled and passed around joints, I sipped diet soda and studied for finals and wore earplugs to muffle the sound of the stereo and their silliness. But for all my righteous living I am suddenly willing to admit that my friends have something I lack, a carefree and playful quality I strongly suspect men find sexy. I suppose it was that same quality that drew my husband to Susie Margolis but I'd rather not think about that right now.

My mother has joie de vivre. My mother was also a barmaid who drank freely on the job, divorced my father before I was born, brought lovers to our tiny apartment, and regularly wrote checks in amounts well above our bank balance. For years I thought that "Rules were made to be broken" was a phrase my mother herself had coined. Trina McElvy showed me how to sneak into the movies, steal your neighbor's newspaper, and switch price tags on sunglasses. She did all these things with the certitude it was her God-given right as an American to flout the rules. She encouraged me to forge her signature on school forms. ("What's the big deal? You know I'd sign it anyway.") When she bounced a check she always insisted she was just a crappy bookkeeper, that's all.

My mother was staffing the beverage table at a Girl Scouts ice cream social when the police came for her with charges of bank fraud. She kept her head bent and continued pouring lemonade into Dixie cups even as the two police officers approached the table and made clear their intent to arrest her.

"There are forty-five thirsty Girl Scouts in this room, sir, and I'm going to make sure every one of them gets a lemonade," she said, not once looking up from her pouring.

The cops were two ruinous ink blots on a perfect canvas of Easter pastels, of mothers and daughters in long sweeping skirts and ruffled blouses, yellow daffodils on every table, pink and baby blue crepe paper streamers twisted from one end of the room to the other. My mother glanced toward me and asked if they wouldn't mind skipping the handcuffing part and they agreed. The bald one grabbed a cup of lemonade on the way out. I sat with Katie Lender and her mother for the rest of the event except for the half hour I spent throwing up in the bathroom. Sour, regurgitated chocolate ice cream spattered on the toilet seat and across the scalloped white collar of my new dress. My mother promised me that she would be home by dinner and somehow she managed to make good on her promise. I was in third grade and I refused to go back to school so she found another rental fifteen miles away and I enrolled in a new school district. Every day for nine weeks she drove back to town to fulfill her community restitution sentence, picking up trash along the highway with other reprobates in bright orange vests. I wondered whether any of my friends would spot her as the school bus traveled along 37 South.

For the rest of my childhood and throughout my adult years, I shaped and defined myself as an inversion of Trina McElvy. If she had many lovers, I would have none.

If she had a tenth-grade education, I would get a master's degree. If she was unmarried with one child, I'd be married with three. But in avoiding the worst in my mother, I'd also denied myself her best. The inescapable truth about Trina McElvy was this: She was concupiscible, carnal, spontaneous, and, above all, happy.

Annie grabs the box of Strike 'Em Anywhere matches and relights the candle. "Julia, please raise your right hand and"—she tilts her chair backward to grab a copy of *Oprah* magazine off the end table—"put your other hand on the Bible." I do as I'm told, aware of a crazy little giggle percolating in my throat. I keep my lips clamped for fear it will escape, turn into something bigger and more frightening and impossible to constrain. "Julia Flanagan, from this day forward, you agree to live dangerously. Go forth and do something bad."

I don't know if it's the lateness of the hour or the alcohol or the reluctantly conjured memory of my husband and Susie Margolis, but I can feel a new resolve flood my bloodstream with all the force and conviction of a born-again conversion. On this night I decide that I will take my friends' advice and live dangerously. To heck with being good. And damn that Susie Margolis.

As predictably as the tough-stemmed dandelions that commandeer our lawn in April, puppy lust overtakes our family once a year. Someone in the neighborhood will appear on the street with a tiny thing trotting weightlessly at the end of a bright new nylon leash on tiny puppy feet and we are filled with desire. Caitlin, the eleven-year-old, will draw pictures of dogs and slip them into Michael's briefcase. Lucy, who is nearing her seventh birthday, will complain of vague physical ailments. ("I think I have a caterpillar stuck inside my head and it itches me. I think a puppy would make the itching go away.") Four-year-old Jake, Caitlin's apprentice in the art of parental manipulation, will tie a rope around his stuffed Dalmatian Benny and drag it forlornly through the house, bumping it up and down the stairs, scraping it along the sidewalk, propping it up on the kitchen table next to his cereal bowl. And he will look up at his father and ask, "Please, Dad? Can't we please get a dog?"

Michael has implored me not to bring home any animals and given that it was one of his only premarital requests, I felt obligated to comply, especially when his other demands were so benign—I had to promise I'd never throw him a surprise party, that we'd never go to sleep in a fight, and that I'd kiss him first thing every morning, morning breath be damned.

Besides, it wasn't Michael's fault that he balked at getting a dog. Kathleen and Jim Flanagan taught their sons that cats and dogs occupied the same category as used hypodermic needles: dirty, disease-bearing, menacing. They didn't allow their sons to have Play-Doh either, for fear it would attract "vermin." At some point, one of Michael's brothers secretly hid a moth in a box in the basement and actually managed to keep it alive for over fifteen days, but little Michael stopped asking for a dog and at an early age, probably more out of despair than anything else, finally acquiesced and absorbed his parents' opposition.

I didn't grow up with animals either, but only because our landlord prohibited all pets except fish and after the first goldfish came down with the apt-named ick and died, I couldn't bear to ask for another one. Katie Lender once managed to smuggle a chicken into her rental by successfully incubating a fertilized egg under her father's high-intensity desk lamp. She figured she could always claim ignorance: how was she to know that the egg would turn into a pet? A spiteful neighbor called the landlord and that was the end of the chicken. Katie's parents insisted they'd sent Lester to live with a nice elderly couple on a big farm, but Katie and I always suspected they just dumped her in the grass behind the JCPenney parking lot.

Even after the kids have given up all hope of getting a dog, I am still attached to the idea. Annie insists that I just need to have more sex but I'm sure it's not the lack of sex that drives me but the authentic desire for a dog who will curl up on my lap and snooze while I read the paper in the morning, who will give me slickery puppy kisses, who will watch me worshipfully while I'm dressing for work, and who will never ask me if I'm ever going to lose my post-pregnancy poundage.

I set out to soften my husband's resolve. I cook his favorite dinner—chicken fried steak, mashed potatoes with garlic and cream, and a dark ale served in a frosted stein. I iron the two striped oxford shirts that have been balled up in the laundry room for six and a half months because I never iron except in emergencies, always without an ironing board, frantically on my knees on the bedroom carpet.

After chicken fried steak and ironing, there is only one honeyed arrow left in my quiver. As Michael sits in the brown velour recliner and watches the basketball game, I massage his feet and make my appeal during the commercial breaks. By the time the massage is over, Michael has agreed to one small cage-restrained mammal. Specifically, a guinea pig. There are conditions: he prefers not to see it, smell it, touch it, clean up after it, or dispose of it in the event of its death. I am surprised to learn that my pet-averse husband has always had a soft spot for guinea pigs because his older cousin—the cool one, Edward, who had an electric guitar and Carlos Santana's autograph—owned two guinea pigs, Hendrix and Morrison.

Thank you, Edward, wherever you are.

It is my first ever visit to Pets-a-Poppin and I am stunned. The scale of the place, the breadth and depth of its offerings, the fact that entire aisles are devoted to cat food and dog biscuits and bird toys—the total effect is both dazzling but also troubling. In some parts of the world you can't even find a can of evaporated milk for humans and here were frozen liver popsicles and rawhides shaped like size nine moccasins. A sullen girl with no chin points me toward the "pocket critters" near the back of the store where the Muzak is nearly drowned out by the constant whirr of metal exercise wheels as gerbils scramble in desperate futility.

I am staring at the guinea pigs, hairy and inert in their glass enclosures, when a burly woman in a Packers sweatshirt sidles up to me. "Guinea pigs are okay but rats are fantastic," she says. I try not to stare at the constellation of round, meaty growths on one cheek.

"Really? I always thought rats were, you know, ratty." Michael would have a stroke if I came home with a rat.

It's totally out of the question. "I didn't realize that rats made good pets."

"You'd best believe it." She runs her hands through her mullet. "Jeez, these little guys are smart. And clean? Most people don't realize that. They're thinking, you know, *eeewwww,* rats. Sewers and the like. But that's just a stereotype. Rats are cleaner than you and me. *And* they're affectionate. Like a dog. Just like a cute little puppy dog." She utters this last line in a lispy baby-talk way.

Now she has my attention. If I can't get a lap dog, at least I can get a lap rat. "Like a puppy? Seriously?"

"Honest to God. My little Joey is such a lover. He just wants to be snuggled all day. I swear he thinks I'm his momma." She scoops a small white rat from its cage and offers it to me. It takes a moment for me to overcome my revulsion to the creature's naked whiplike tail and then I am charmed. The rodent sits up in my palm, waggles his whiskers. He seems to be studying me. I return him to its glass tank. He looks up at me, surprised, maybe a little confused. I lift him out of the cage again, and let his whiskers brush against my nose.

"Julia!"

I turn to find Annie wheeling a shopping cart; in it, a ten-pound bag of food for overweight dogs and a bright blue squeaky toy made to resemble a mail carrier. I describe my rat vs. guinea pig dilemma.

"Good grief, Julia. You want the rat? Get the goddamn rat." Annie motions to the chinless girl. "Miss? My friend here will take the rat, please." Then she glares at me impatiently. "You only live once, Julia."

It has been fifteen days since the beach trip and I decide that it is time to make good on my promise. You Only Live Once, a concept as foreign to me as Rules Were Made to Be Broken, fully encapsulates the rationale behind the carefree conviviality I'd sought for myself. The concept was a color not apparently suited to my complexion but appealing in its own right; I try it on gingerly, apprehensively, hopefully, and I try not to remind myself that lurking just beyond joie de vivre's shining borders is its ugly twin, profligacy.

I would be lying to my husband if I brought home this rat. I thought of my children. They wouldn't want a hairy, nonresponsive guinea pig stinking up the house. I had promised them a real pet and that's exactly what they are going to get because I honestly believe that every child should know the joy of nurturing another living thing, and by living thing I don't mean a moth, but a companion capable of expressing loyalty and affection.

I bring the rat home and tell Michael it's a dwarf Norwegian flat-coated guinea pig.

"He sure is a cutie," Michael says, reaching into the cage to stroke our new pet. He lifts him out of the cage and, "But he kind of looks like a rat, doesn't he?"

"I know. Weird, isn't it?" Oh, my God; oh, my GOD, I am lying to my husband, lying about the companion animal he'd trusted me to choose for our family, the only four-legged mammal he has allowed into our home, the one that's supposed to be just like his cousin Edward's beloved pet, and instead I return with a red-eyed laboratory animal. Then I have the gall to insist that it's not a rat, it's some other creature I just made up in my head, like the time Jake told me he hadn't really shoved a peanut butter sandwich into the VCR, it was Mister Eugene Finkelopolis from Mexico. But I'd promised my kids a real pet and I wasn't about to break their hearts by bringing home a fat stinking pooping fuzzy slipper.

Michael names the rat Homer. Instead of feeling errant and remorseful, I am defiant and free. I saw something I wanted and I lied to my husband to get it and I survived. The bond that soldered me to Michael is a little looser today. Much to my surprise I actually like how this feels.

Chapter TWO

My neighbor's sprinkler looks and sounds like a machine gun turret, aggressive and off-putting. The whole family—William and Geneva Skaff, and their three children, Billy, Georgie, and Geena—are in the driveway conducting their semiannual garage deep-cleaning. The entire contents of the Skaff garage have been temporarily relocated to the edge of the driveway. William is scalding the cement floor with a pressure washer while Geneva, in clean denim overalls and pink paisley bandana around her neck, appears to be oiling a pair of inline skates. The children are wiping down their respective bicycles with Orange Glo and paper towels while Harley, their overweight and unusually quiet beagle, snoozes in the shade. The first time the Skaffs performed this garage clean-out, I sauntered over to examine a set of golf clubs, then asked them how much they wanted for their old push mower. It wasn't until William silently rolled the clubs back into the garage that I realized with great discomfiture that my neighbors weren't having a yard sale, they were just cleaning out their stupid garage. None of the Skaffs look up as I pull into the driveway, not a waved hand or head nod or any other indication of neighborly regard.

That's the way it usually is in Larkspur Estates. When Michael and I moved from our scruffy stone and shingle rental house near campus to this subdivision of culs-de-sac and driveway hoops, I thought we were moving into a happy place. Larkspur brought to mind pretty purple flowers and little birds and the whole "happy as a lark" business. I had visions of hearty greetings and fragrant gardens, block parties and kids playing tag in the yards.

We have lived here almost five years and have yet to meet most of this block's inhabitants. They drive away in the morning behind tinted windows and disappear into their garages at the end of the day, automatic doors descending behind them. I don't see my neighbors tending their gardens because they hire other people to do that work, just as they hire other people to rake in the fall and shovel in the winter. There are no Labor Day block parties because everyone leaves town for Labor Day. Kids aren't outside playing tag in the street because they're playing hockey or soccer or football or basketball somewhere else, or taking riding lessons or karate, or they're in advanced after-school science classes. Or they're inside playing video games and Instant Messaging.

Most of what I know about my neighbors I've learned from their trash. I am pretty sure that the people at the end of the street recently had a baby because I saw the empty Enfamil cans in the recycling tub on Tuesdays. The

Skaffs recently bought a new microwave oven, someone in the Gilchrist family is on Slim•Fast, and farther down the street, the Chapmans have replaced their mattress.

Annie once said that our neighborhood was doomed from the start because the developer had all the topsoil removed even before the first house was built. Earl J. Jackson hauled away all the rich loam and sold it for a neat profit, leaving behind only crappy red clay and rock. Now I know why even my most determined neighbors can't grow the kind of lush lawns you see in the less expensive subdivisions. "It's all about fertility," Annie would muse philosophically. "How can we expect our neighborhood to be anything but sterile when Earl J. Jackson took all the topsoil away, the bastard."

Everyone assumes that our family belongs here because my husband is an attorney with Wellman, Weimar and Bott, but that's a relatively recent development. Michael's heart is still with his old job at Legal Services, where he represented poor people and earned only a little more than our cleaning lady makes now but came home every day at 5:30 P.M. with enough time and energy to play with the kids and make love to me. Now he works until seven or eight and sometimes falls asleep in the family room with the remote control in his hand. But he wouldn't trade his Honda Civic for a dozen Escalades and refuses to hire one of those companies that sprays chemicals on your lawn to kill the weeds. Our front yard is, therefore, not as constrained as everyone else's but my husband doesn't care. "I'd rather have weeds than cancer," he's always said.

I don't fit here either. Unlike the women on my street

who donate their time as reading assistants in the school library or planning PTO fundraisers, I have my salaried job as assistant director of the Bentley Institute.

On most days I can say with all sincerity that I like my work. I am employed by the most prestigious name in sexuality research, which makes me extremely popular at dinner parties. My office is only twelve minutes from my house so I'm home by the time the children step off the school bus. I can work from my house when they're sick or snowed in. My coworkers are pleasant and undemanding. My job would be perfect, if not for my boss.

"You MUST work here," Leslie Keen coos a mere fifteen minutes into my job interview. Her office is a crisis of heaps and piles and half-empty coffee cups, ashtrays crammed with lipstick-smeared cigarette butts, cracked pots of philodendra in various stages of death. There is a bottle of non-acetone nail polish remover on her desk, more ashtrays, a stack of autographed glossy color head shots of Leslie Keen herself, a contract with WABC radio, and two half-empty cans of Diet Coke.

If her office is in desperate disarray, Leslie's body is a hard-shellacked package of camera-ready womanhood. Her cream-and-violet double-breasted suit fits her flawlessly and her violet Mary Janes look dyed to match. Her hair is a highlighted helmet of champagne, platinum, and honey gold. Makeup is fashionably matte and the sculpted nails are squared, too long for typing or any real manual labor, and judging by the way the bottom edge of the nail meets the cuticle—flush, no gap—I suspect they've been recently tended to, probably by the Vietnamese manicurists on the north side of town.

Leslie leans forward in her chair and clasps her hands prayerfully. "Julia, PLEASE tell me you'll take the job. You'd be PERFECT here." An egg-shaped secretary pokes her head in to say they're ordering pizza and does she want anything. "You KNOW I can't eat that crap, Lorena. Jesus." Leslie looks at me and rolls her eyes, as if we're already on the same team, the management team. "Nice lady but dumb as a box of rocks. I've already started advertising for her replacement. You know anyone?"

I shake my head and furrow my eyebrows in an expression of solidarity. I want to be on Leslie Keen's team. I want to be on anyone's team. I have to get out of my house and working for this double-breasted cyclone is exactly what I need to counter the stifling inertia of domesticity and whatever corrosive traces of Susie Margolis I continue to harbor, in spite of my vow to forgive.

Leslie gives me the VIP tour of the Bentley, taking me through collections that aren't normally accessible to the public. She shows me Nazi pornography, underground magazines like *Girls and Donkeys,* photos of J. Edgar Hoover in drag. Though her aim surely is to impress, the tour leaves me nauseated and apprehensive.

Back in her office, Leslie makes her final appeal.

"So. Julia." She leans back in her black mesh and leather ergonomically correct chair and touches her clasped fingertips to her chin. "You're smart, you're organized, you've got a GREAT vita. I checked your references. Everyone LOVES you. You're much beloved, Julia. Do you REALIZE that? Please tell me you'll work here, or I'll go home straightaway and SHOOT myself!"

She opens a carved box on her desk and pulls out a pack of French brown cigarettes. I can't make out the label. She shakes out a slim cigarette and slips it between her lips. She doesn't light up. "And let's face it. There isn't exactly an abundance of job openings in this town. Unless you want to work at Arby's. But for someone with your skills, you'd be hard-pressed to find anything this good. Good salary, GREAT benefits package, flexible hours. It's PERFECT for you, Julia. And you're PERFECT for us. So? What do you say, Julia Flanagan? Do I go home and SHOOT myself or can I show you your new office? I think you're WONDERFUL."

"That's very nice of you to say. Not the shooting yourself part. I mean, everything else." I smoothed my skirt primly and straightened my posture. I found myself drawn to Leslie Keen. Thrice divorced, feisty, and in perpetual motion, Leslie was a minor celebrity in the field of human sexuality. She had successfully marketed the Bentley as a brand name, extending its reach far beyond the enclaves of the academy and straight to the masses. She had her own call-in radio show and for a couple of years hosted a nationally syndicated TV program, *Let's Talk About Sex.* Though she is fifteen years my senior, she could pass at a distance for a college girl, thanks to Botox, a forehead lift, and a diet limited to whole grains and fresh greens. Once when we were working through dinner and ordered in Chinese, Leslie ate only a tiny plate of steamed bok choy, no sauce. When I asked how she could possibly be satisfied with such a small serving, she smiled confidently and said, "Julie, it doesn't take a lot of fuel to run this lean machine."

It does, however, take a lot of Dexedrine, as I discovered one day when Leslie asked if I'd stop by CVS on my way into work to pick up a prescription. When I handed her the bag she winked and said, "Let's keep this *entrez nous,* shall we?"

Working for a speed addict, I've come to learn, is like being one of those tornado chasers, ever watchful for foreboding cloud formations, always plunging into turbulence while everyone else is driving in the opposite direction. Leslie Keen is a rainmaker, the university's most successful magnet for grants and private donations, but she is also at the center of the university's most destructive storms. Three months ago she held a press conference to announce her endorsement of mutual masturbation as a form of safe sex for teenagers. At 2:00 A.M. over weak coffee in her catastrophically messy kitchen, I helped her craft a face-saving public statement when all she really wanted to say was, Fuck you, fuck that, fuck this whole fucking job; the following day I stayed late to field phone calls from angry parents, concerned politicians, and eager talk show hosts. And only last week I booked guests for her radio show when she was too wasted to make it to the office. "You're so good to me," Leslie sobbed into my shoulder, gin vapors wafting from her mouth. "I don't know what I'd do without you."

Michael and I are spinning in our own orbits these days, two planets in two entirely separate solar systems. Tonight he misses dinner with me and the kids, doesn't get home until 9:14, pauses to kiss me, then goes upstairs to tend to Homer's cage, which he'd moved last week from Caitlin's room to his study. (Caitlin, who'd lobbied hardest of all for a pet, hasn't even noticed that the rat is gone.) My husband checks his e-mail and spends the rest of the night in bed clicking through channels.

When Michael and I were still in that foggy-eyed stage of early marriage, we vowed that we would never retreat to solitary spaces. No matter what tumbled across our path, we would confront it together as allies. Other marriages became our antimodels. My divorced parents were one. His bickering folks were another. But the ultimate antimodels were Janet and Harry Hobart, veterinarians who lived across the street from our first apartment on Skerwin Avenue in Ann Arbor. After too many piña coladas at a block party, Janet admitted that she and Harry sometimes went for weeks without verbal communication. One frigid February morning, Janet slipped on the wet spot her husband had left after his shower, smacked her head on the bathtub faucet, and lay there unconscious for hours until she eventually choked on her own vomit and died. Harry didn't discover her body until 11:00 P.M. that night, when he went into the bathroom to floss his teeth. This was the cautionary tale Michael and I referred to again and again as we renewed our commitment to a long, happy, and communicative marriage. "Do me a favor," he'd joke. "If I'm not back from the bathroom in a half hour, come check on me, okay?"

As I fold laundry this morning, I come across my pink Victoria's Secret camisole with matching tap shorts and realize that Michael and I haven't had sex in seventeen days. Our sex wasn't as spontaneous as it had been before parenthood, but it was as sturdy and dependable as an Oldsmobile: once a week, usually on a Friday, between the kids' bedtime and David Letterman.

Michael likes to tell people I seduced him with my whistle and he's probably right. I learned how to whistle in seventh grade from Cathy Sinclair, who shared a desk with me in homeroom. Cathy was from New York and she said that everybody in New York knew how to whistle because how else would you call a cab? She showed me how to make a little circle of my thumb and forefinger, press back on the tip of my tongue, shape my lips around my fingers, and direct the breath in just the right way to produce a loud, strong, enduring trill. I used to be shy about whistling like this, full throttle with two fingers in my mouth. I thought it was vulgar and unladylike, something my mother would do. I also thought it was unnecessary since taxis don't cruise the streets here looking for passengers; anyone who needs "car service" would summon it with a phone call.

Over the years I've come to appreciate my whistling skill. People admire it, especially men, who turn their heads to find the source of this eardrum-puncturing sound and smile when they see it's coming from a girl. Whistling is also very handy when you want to express intense enthusiasm but don't have the energy to applaud, during the rousing curtain call of *Les Misérables,* for instance. The way I figure it, one or two good whistles are worth three minutes of steady applause and it won't leave you with sore palms.

I went to my first football game in graduate school, Michigan against Penn State. I'd gone with a fellow teaching assistant, Henry Cochran, who had only recently begun to wear his hair in braids because he learned that his father's great-great-grandmother might have been part Ojibwa. Henry had never been to a football game either and sat through the game grading papers. But I was quickly sucked into the crowd's excitement and when our team made a critical touchdown I jumped to my feet, pulled off my glove, stuck my fingers in my mouth, and let loose with a skull-shattering whistle.

A guy wearing a navy blue Michigan knit cap turned around and stared at me. "Did *you* do that?"

"Uh-huh."

"Can you teach me?"

Michael Flanagan was a third-year law student. I recognized him from student legal services where I'd gone for help with a problematic landlord—Sheba Horton refused to return my security deposit. Even though I'd left the apartment in pristine condition, she'd insisted that I'd violated the terms of the lease because I repainted the dingy walls. I was assigned to a hairy girl named Rebecca Turk and I distinctly remember wishing that I'd gotten the tall guy in the flannel shirt instead. With his face full of freckles and thick crimson hair he looked like someone who could slip into a McElvy family portrait and pass for one of my cousins. Considering that I had no cousins, and considering that I did not in fact have a family portrait, this boy's familiarity was profoundly appealing to me. I assumed I'd never see him again. But here I was, on this bone-cracking day, teaching him to whistle.

"Make a circle with your fingers. Like this." I touched the tip of my thumb to my forefinger.

"Like this?"

"Yes. You've got it." His enthusiasm for this endeavor made me laugh. I wanted to kiss his soft pink lips, wanted to touch every one of his freckles, run my finger over the slope of his nose. "Now put your fingers in your mouth, and sort of flip your tongue back and down."

"Like this?"

"Yes. That's right. Now tense your lips a little and blow." I produced one of my more restrained whistles; I didn't want to show off.

He kept his eyes locked on mine as he followed my instructions but what came out wasn't a whistle, just a hollow whoosh.

"What am I doing wrong?"

"I think it's the way you're holding your fingers." I stood on the tips of my boots and peered into his mouth. "And your tongue. You need to . . . here . . . let me show you . . ." As I reached up to adjust his fingers he took my hand and held it there with my fingertips resting against his cool lips. He gave me a look that seemed to say, *I could make your head explode if you let me.*

But I didn't, not for another year, not until we were married.

My new husband was an eager, adventurous lover who believed that sexual technique could be cultivated like any other talent, flying a kite, for instance, juggling, or cooking Indian food. He had been initiated at the tender and highly adrenal age of sixteen by a divorcée who had hired Michael and his brother Dave to care for her four parakeets whenever she was out of town. Both boys got fifteen dollars but only Michael received the bonus.

His lovemaking was intuitive and hungry and he was always pressing me just past my comfort zone, boundaries I'd arbitrarily set for myself in the absence of experience; I didn't know enough to know what I'd enjoy. But Michael was a persuasive teacher and I a willing student; my repertoire quickly expanded as he showed me that my body could be explored in ways I'd never imagined and all of it felt good. Sex was as natural as breathing but also a little bit naughty, exotic, and purloined. Michael would tease me while I was on the phone with my boss, slip a hand into my panties in the crush of a tightly packed elevator, flick his tongue against my cheek at a church picnic, which appeared as a polite kiss to anyone who happened to be watching.

I'm not sure when things began to change, maybe between kid two and kid three, or maybe when Michael moved from Legal Services to Weimar Bott. I'm just not sure.

I set the Victoria's Secret things aside for later, but Michael is asleep by the time I'm done brushing my teeth. I lie there a long time under the glare of my full-spectrum reading lamp and listen to my husband snore.

Inspired by an article in a women's magazine ("Twenty-one Ways to Keep Romance Alive & Kickin") Michael and I are going on a date. Our evening will be a study in marital compromise. He gets the action movie—in which a famous grizzled actor and nubile young actress survive a plane crash, detest each other, have sex, and get rescued—and I get sashimi. For the kids, I managed to snag über-babysitter Heather Cradduck who charges eight dollars an hour but comes equipped with a backpack full of diversions including her own Game Boy, which she handles with the virtuosity of a nine-year-old.

The movie is at the Superplex in theater six, the one that smells like sewage and tater tots. In the canvas tote bag I got for renewing our membership to public radio I have packed a box of Junior Mints purchased not at the movie concession but at the supermarket, along with two tangerines and two bottles of water. This is the first time in my life that I've sneaked food into the movies (not counting the Metamucil wafers I brought to the movies when I was pregnant with Jake and perpetually constipated). I feel like a heroin mule. Michael and I sit silently as a series of movie trivia questions appear on the screen. Which actor was a world-class tobogganer in high school? What movie featured Eddie Murphy and a talking schnauzer? Based on a quick survey of the audience, Michael and I are easily and predictably the oldest people here because that's what happens when you live in a college town. If we'd wanted to be among grown-ups, we should have seen the documentary about the migration of Canada geese.

"My, my, look at all this loot," Michael says, peering into my bag, pulling out the Junior Mints. "What *is* all this?"

"I'm living dangerously."

"You're what?" Michael slips his arm around my shoulder, fingers resting gently across my right breast. I remember how my husband enjoyed making out in movies. Actually, he still does but I'm always afraid one of the Bentley's student interns will be sitting right behind me. As I said, this is a small town. And I've never been comfortable with public displays of affection. Michael leans over and kisses me softly on my neck.

"Living dangerously?" he whispers, and kisses me again. "Sounds intriguing. Tell me more."

"Never mind." I know I'm supposed to be breaking all kinds of rules and I don't want to disappoint my friends, but the truth is, I regret bringing this stuff into the theater. I've read that theaters really don't profit from ticket sales, only from the refreshments they sell in the lobby. If all of us carried in our own snacks and soda, movie theaters would be forced to raise ticket prices even higher and eventually they'd all have to shut down, which would, in turn, put Hollywood out of business. I don't want to be responsible for the demise of the movie industry. I eat one of the tangerines, which seems to have filled the entire theater with its citrus scent.

I fall asleep right around the time the baggy-faced actor is kissing the twenty-four-year-old's creaseless neck. I don't wake up again until Michael gently nudges me with his elbow.

"Sweetie. Wake up. Movie's over."

I open my eyes to see the credits rolling and ushers sweeping out the aisles.

"What did I miss?" I wipe the drool off my cheek.

"Not much." Michael leans over to kiss my nose. "Here's an idea. Next time why don't we send the kids to the movies with the sitter so we can stay home and fool around."

"Sounds perfect." But what I'm really thinking is, unlikely scenario, my dear, hopelessly optimistic husband. The last time we had a couple of hours to ourselves at home was six months ago, when my in-laws took the kids to a concert in the park. Michael and I agreed to meet in bed after we'd checked our e-mail. We managed to get half our clothes off before we both fell asleep.

Tikumi is a Japanese restaurant in the Brewster Village Square, which isn't a square at all but a strip mall between two gas stations. The Japanese sushi chefs at the front of the restaurant welcome new arrivals with a half-hearted ritualistic greeting in their native tongue. The waiters are American college students, some of whom seem to have made an earnest effort to appear Asian, flat-ironing the hair, drawing eyeliner at an angle, speaking with a faint accent. Half of the tables in this wheat-hued room are low to the floor and have cushions for seats; it is understood that if you choose to eat in this area you will first remove your shoes. Michael prefers to sit at a "real" table because he doesn't like being sock-footed in public. Actually, neither do I.

Soon after we're seated beside a rice paper and black walnut screen, Michael spots Karen and Brad Merila in line near the door.

"Hey, guys," he says, waving them over. "Brad! Over here! Join us!"

"Sure beats waiting on line," Brad says, pulling the seat out for his wife and casually kneading her shoulder with one hand as she settles into her chair. Karen Merila is spry as an elf with short spiked hair and four diamond chip studs in one ear, a gold hoop in the other. She has a wide, flat ass and floppy, unfettered breasts. She's taller by a head than her husband, who is built like a bear and is almost as hairy.

Brad and Karen had also gone to the movies, it turns out, but they saw the French film playing at the art cinema downtown.

"That was one hot movie." Brad is fanning his face with his hand. "I didn't think we'd make it out of there with our clothes on." Karen playfully slaps her husband with her napkin and he leans in for a kiss.

"I'm surprised you guys are here at all," Michael says. "Shouldn't you be home in bed?" The Merilas have never been shy about discussing their sex life. Karen and Brad celebrated their fifteenth anniversary at Amoura, "the hideaway for lovers" off the bypass. The last time Michael and I had champagne and sex in a heart-shaped bathtub was on our honeymoon. Karen and Brad have no children, I feel compelled to mention.

"Why would we have to go home?" Brad throws a sideways look at his wife.

"Bra-ad," Karen whines in mock protest.

"Let me guess." Michael spears a chunk of steak teriyaki. "The car?"

Brad winks a bushy-browed eye. "Bingo!"

I hold up my hands in protest. "Please. Enough." This conversation is beginning to feel like group sex.

After dinner we cross the parking lot to Coneheads, where I order a double fudge sundae, extra nuts, hold the cherry. I could have been virtuous with a cup of the stuff so totally devoid of recognizable ingredients that it must be labeled, by law, "frozen dessert product," but I want the real thing.

"Has anyone ever told you that you look like a white version of Whitney Houston?" Michael asks the young woman behind the counter as he reaches for his sensible blueberry sorbet.

The girl smiles indulgently. "No, sir, I don't believe anyone's ever told me that." She deftly hits a few keys on the register. "And five-fifty is your change."

In the car on the way home, Michael turns onto Belmore and now we're stuck behind a spandex-clad cyclist who stubbornly insists on riding along our narrow and heavily pockmarked road. How I resent these cyclists, and not only because they have such well-toned thighs but also because they terrorize everyone else by putting themselves at risk cycling on roads meant only for cars and, like this lunatic, by driving in the dark. Our town isn't built for bike riders and despite the billboards urging me to "share the road," there's just not enough road to share. What if I hit one? What if I kill one? How will I live with myself knowing that I actually killed another human being and only because of his compulsive insistence on riding his stupid bicycle on a narrow road in the dark? Why can't these people ride on the sidewalks? Or join the real world and drive environmentally devastating cars like the rest of us?

Later that night in bed I lie awake with Michael snoring phlegmatically beside me and reflect on the way my husband flirted with the Conehead girl, the supposedly white version of Whitney Houston. It's quite a gimmick he's got, this look-alike thing. The cashier at Kroger is Michelle Pfeiffer but shorter. Jake's nursery school teacher is a dead ringer for Cindy Crawford except blond. The comparisons are always directed at women and are always fabulously complimentary. He has not, for instance, told anyone she looks like Eleanor Roosevelt.

But Michael's real chick magnet is his ear. My husband is an attentive listener, one of those men who is at ease navigating intensely emotional terrain. He consistently attracts women who are either newly divorced or seriously contemplating separation. Women talk openly about their marital situations, though he insists that this is only because they know he's a lawyer and they're simply fishing for free legal advice. Women I hardly know will stop me to say things like, "You've got a real gem there." To which I always answer, sincerely, "I know," or "Does he have any single brothers?" to which I always answer, just as sincerely, "Yes, but you probably wouldn't like them."

The thing is this: By the time Michael comes home to me, there's often not a lot of listening left in him and it's been a very long time since he compared me to a beautiful celebrity.

Michael sputters in his sleep and rolls over, mumbling something that sounds like "I ate the king of New Jersey." My husband talks in his sleep a lot. Sometimes I'll prop myself up and keenly listen, expecting to hear, I don't know what, some profound channeled message or intriguing tidbit I can tease him about in the morning, but usually it's just garbled work talk, as if he's litigating in his dreams. Sometimes he rouses himself just enough to tell me he loves me, wraps his arms and legs around me, then falls back to sleep.

In the frantic scramble to get ready the next morning, the kids miss the bus and skip breakfast completely and

I'm pretty sure Jake is wearing yesterday's underwear and Lucy didn't brush her teeth. I stop by the German bakery on Highpoint to buy them each a giant bowtie cookie encrusted with sugar crystals the size of half-carat diamonds. As they shove the cookies gleefully into their mouths, I feel like the world's most negligent mother and look over each shoulder to see if anyone has caught me feeding my children cookies at 8:45 in the morning.

On my way to work I get a call from Caitlin who wants me to know that I'd forgotten to sign one of her twenty-seven permission slips and as a result she won't be allowed to participate in the school's Peace on the Playground peer mediation program. I am drowning in permission slips. Permission to be photographed. Permission to use the Internet. Permission to go to the public library. Permission to participate in sex education. Permission to eat a special ethnic dish that may contain peanuts. Ten minutes later I glance in the rearview mirror and notice Jake's black and red nylon Spiderman thermal lunch bag on the backseat, which means that he has to eat school lunch, which means he probably won't eat anything today because he hates school lunch. I have already failed two of my children and it's not even 9:00 A.M. I am a hideously horrible mother. I must have been delusional to believe I could handle a full-time job and the full-time demands of motherhood.

I stop at Kroger's to pick up something for lunch. I want to be virtuous and get something from the salad bar, but I know I'll wind up with a seven-hundred-calorie heap of chow mein noodles, sunflower seeds, raisins, egg, cheese, French dressing, and maybe something green and leafy somewhere at the bottom. I finally settle on frozen linguini with marinara sauce and head back to produce for an apple.

"Excuse me, ma'am?" I look over my shoulder. It is the young produce guy, the one with the giant mole over his left eyebrow.

"Yes?"

"I hate to be the one to tell you this, but . . ." He doesn't continue. He just points to my back. I immediately assume that there has to be something gross stuck there, a cockroach, or worse, a bat, which is not as ridiculous as it sounds. Two weeks ago, a small brown bat had managed to squeeze through a crack in the roof. Shoppers all over the store ducked and dodged as the bat jagged frantically looking for a way out. Cashiers scrambled to capture it, first with an empty wooden fruit crate, then with a yellow nylon rain slicker they tossed futilely into the air, and finally, successfully, with a giant net attached to two mop handles.

Now I am certain that this same bat is clinging to me now.

"Oh, God, get it off me!" I am shrieking and flailing my arms. "Get it *off*!"

"Okay," the guy says, and reaches out to gingerly peel a brassiere off my back. Thanks to the magic of static cling (I ran out of dryer sheets), my size 36B WonderBra had attached itself to my sweater. How many shoppers had observed this spectacle yet said nothing? I'd already made it from frozen entrees to produce. That's twelve aisles!

The young man hands me my bra. To his credit, he is not laughing. "Here you go."

"Thank you," I say quietly. The missed bus, cookies for breakfast, an unsigned permission slip, and now the bra: I try to ignore the itching suspicion that the world I've worked so hard to structure and bridle is careening out of control.

In the category of living dangerously: I take the cashier's gel pen, which fits comfortably in my hand and rolls so smoothly across the paper that I must have it. I tuck the pen into my purse and check the cashier's expression who shows no sign that she cares. I suppose she's accustomed to this.

The bra incident notwithstanding, I must admit, I do love this sweater. It's the only shade of orange that doesn't clash with my red hair. I actually thought I looked (dare I say it?) beautiful this morning and hoped Michael might notice. He didn't. Then again, he also failed to notice that I had a bra stuck to my back as I prepared breakfast. I am trying not to think about this as I pull into the parking lot on University Street and start hunting for a spot.

On a campus where the average male professor is frail or fat, rumpled and frayed, the man by the parking meter is a magnificent freak. He has the broad shoulders and muscular arms of a shipbuilder, taut haunches and long, solid legs. Most men around here look as if they'd been dressed by their mothers—high-waisted pants, slick polyester blazers, and dated neckties—but this one is wearing faded jeans, a white oxford shirt open over a white T-shirt, and well-worn hiking boots. The only professorial thing about him are his glasses, smudged and horn-rimmed and not the self-consciously fashionable retro kind; I suspect he has owned these since eleventh grade. Everything about his face is outsized, the nose, prominent and a little crooked, like a fighter's; full lips, strong jaw. Stubble suggests the beginning of a beard, his eyes are absolutely green and he glances up at me and I wonder if this is what they mean by bedroom eyes because, well, you know.

I slip my coins into the meter and watch him rummage through his front pockets, muttering as he searches. "I'm pretty sure I've got. Hmm. A quarter. In here. Somewhere." As he talks he's pulling various small items from his pocket and setting them on the hood of his battered black Jeep. A crumpled dollar bill. A wrapped stick of Dentyne. A movie ticket stub. Two pennies. I half expect him to pull out a pack of baseball cards and a frog. I will myself to look away from all this activity around the front of his pants.

He glances at his watch. "My class starts in three minutes." His glasses have slipped down his nose. His biceps bulge and I feel my face redden. I strongly suspect that he has no idea how good-looking he is.

"I'm positive I've got a quarter in here somewhere." He pulls something out of his back pocket, holds it up to the light, and smiles. "I've been *wondering* where this went. Found it on Delray Beach. Visiting my mother." He offers me the shell. It is smooth as gossamer, as soft and pink as a baby's fingernails and almost luminescent. "She lives in one of those gigantic retirement complexes. Last time I was there I brought her a cat from the animal shelter but they don't let the residents keep pets. *Bastards.*"

His mother, the cat, his resentment toward the condo association—these are small intimacies I wouldn't expect from a stranger. Is it arrogance or social cluelessness behind his presumption that I care about these details of his life?

"Wait a minute," I finally say. "I think I've got some quarters." Actually, I'm sure I do. I always keep several coin rolls in my glove compartment. I give him three quarters and the pink shell. He isn't wearing a wedding ring. He pushes up his glasses and his eyes focus as if he is seeing me for the first time and he smiles. His teeth are white and straight, his lips a deep rose. I am dizzy. He sticks out his hand, which causes a book to slip from his arms and onto the asphalt. *Early Works of Ovid.* He bends down to retrieve it, and on the way up extends his hand again. "Evan Delaney."

"Julia Flanagan. Nice to meet you."

"Likewise." He ducks his head so boyishly that I'm overcome by the urge to plunge my fingers into his hair. "Thanks again for the quarters. Not that my students would mind if I didn't show up. Midterms are due today. Half of them will wind up cutting class anyway." A sad look flashes fleetingly in his eyes, the look of a man forced to abandon idealistic notions about teaching eager young minds. The few times I agreed to guest lecture in human sexuality, I faced a room full of disheveled slackers who were sleeping, loudly chatting, or circling classified ads in the weekly *Trucks n' Cycles.* The only motivated student was a thirty-six-year-old woman from a tiny village in Southeast Asia who planned to open the first sexual dysfunction clinic in her hometown. She wore thin white anklets and clear blue plastic sandals. She called me Mrs. Lady.

Evan Delaney tucks the book into his worn canvas briefcase. "That's a great sweater, by the way. I mean, the color. Brings out your, you know. Eyes." He looks shyly away. "Well. Okay then."

For the rest of the day I don't think much about Evan Delaney, at least not consciously, but I am aware that his comment about my sweater rests lightly in the background all day, favorably, like the afterglow of a good massage. I was just offering a helping hand, that's all. Anyone in my position would have done the same. By the following morning, I have forgotten him.

I lived with the idea of Michael's cheating the way some healthy people live with the idea of cancer, that they're destined for it. So even in the flush of new marriage, when life was sunny and Michael was always kind, I was plagued by a morbid combination of suspicion and dread and also certainty in defiance of all the positive barometers of a successful marriage. How I developed this pessimism I can't say considering that I grew up without a father and thus never experienced the reckless turmoil and instability that cheating husbands or wives, for that matter, create for their children. My fear of infidelity was as ingrained and as inexplicable as a five-year-old's prodigious skill at painting in the impressionist style.

So all my life as an attached woman I have been hypervigilant for signs of an affair though Michael never gave me any, not until his relationship with Susie Margolis was over. Perhaps I missed the clues because in my imaginings about Michael and his inevitable extramarital romance I always pictured a woman who embodied my own fantasy of a feminine ideal. Michael's lover would be younger and taller than me, more confident, more intellectually engaged. She read the *Atlantic* and *Harper's* and possibly *The Nation* because she was passionate about politics and still young enough to be idealistic about the left. Michael's lover would have big white teeth and narrow hips and skin that tans, never burns. She would be a swimmer. A diver, actually. And he would sneak away to her meets and watch her lean diver's body arc into the pool like a dolphin's, propelled by sexual vigor, youth, and muscle. She would meet him at his office, damp and smelling of chlorine, and they would have sex on his desk in full view of the family photographs.

Susie Margolis was none of these things. She was like the nursery rhyme teapot, five feet tall with a barrel of a torso and knobby knees. Her hair was vaguely brown, shoulder length, parted to the left side, graying. Susie was a clarinet teacher who gave private lessons and played with the Cambridge Community Pops. I'd see her occasionally on Saturday mornings at the farmers' market, skinny legs crossed at the ankles and tucked under the black metal folding chair. For these performances she dressed in the customary dark skirt and white blouse like the other musicians, but ordinarily she wore her husband's T-shirts and sweatpants that strained across her buttocks and clung closely enough to reveal dimpling. Always practical, Susie chose function over form. Her eyeglasses, outdated in their enormity, gave her the widest possible field of vision but made her look owlish and old. Her best feature was her nose, straight and fine with sleek nostrils that flared imperiously when she was trying to make a point.

Susie didn't seem to worry about the things that worried me. Calories, for instance; her signature casserole was decadent with whole milk ricotta and melted mozzarella and slices of fried eggplant saturated with fragrant olive oil. Susie had a somewhat salacious gap-toothed smile; when she laughed she poked her tongue between her teeth and tossed her head back, surrendering her whole body. She wore shorts and sleeveless tops in the summer without self-consciousness, her full flesh glistening and aromatic with coconut oil.

Susie was David Margolis's wife and David had been Michael's best friend since seventh grade at Benjamin Franklin Middle School. Five years ago David had been diagnosed with amyotrophic lateral sclerosis and by the time doctors finally put a name to his symptoms, the disease had appropriated his body, progressing from fasciculations and pratfalls to muscle atrophy and incontinence.

Michael spent his weekend afternoons at the Margolis house helping with the household tasks David could no longer handle, putting up storm windows and hauling firewood and moving the TV from the family room into a downstairs bedroom where David was spending more and more of his time. When Michael stopped initiating sex I did not blame him. Who would want to have sex after spending all day with a dying man? It never occurred to me that Michael might be falling in love with the dying man's wife.

I sometimes entertain the notion that my husband didn't fall in love with Susie herself but with her distress and her appreciation. In that household under Susie's grateful gaze, Michael was a man of valor, a hero, a knight. Michael wedged himself into the cabinet under the kitchen sink to investigate and repair a leaking pipe. He dragged oxygen tanks into the bedroom and more than once carried David from one room to the other. Susie rewarded Michael with bespectacled eyes that shone with gratitude and respect. And later, as I imagined it, she rewarded him with her body, generous and unflinching.

It wasn't an act of sex, as Michael had explained it to me.

"It was more like an expression of relief. David was so sick. He suffered so much, Julie. And when he died, the suffering, it was finally over, you know? Jesus, honey, I can't believe it myself. I never did anything like this. I never even considered it. We were just so relieved and happy. For David. It was just that one time. Please. You have to believe me."

"You were happy for David so you had sex with his wife?" I pulled another tissue from the box of tissues impregnated with aloe. "Are you out of your mind?"

Three hours ago we were standing in the drizzle at David's grave site in Resting Slopes cemetery dropping handfuls of cold, damp dirt onto the pine casket as Rabbi Sheila Dumas recited prayers exulting God's glory. I watched as my husband took his turn with the dirt, and then, passing Susie Margolis, touched his hand to the small of her back. It happened so quickly I probably wouldn't have noticed had I not been watching Michael closely, studying his technique with the dirt before my own turn; I'd never been to a Jewish burial and was afraid I'd do something embarrassingly wrong.

When I saw him touch her that way, I knew at once that he'd had sex with her and I started bawling, which no one found odd given the context. In the car on the way home, I asked Michael straight out if he had slept with Susie Margolis and straight out he told me that he had. I felt Jake twist and kick in my womb.

"Let me out of the car."

"What? We're on the highway!" Michael hit the automatic door lock and gripped my arm. "Please. Julie. Look. Oh, my God. I'm so sorry! What I did was wrong. I'm not proud of myself. But you can't get out of the car in the middle of the highway. You'll kill yourself."

"I *want* to kill myself!" I screamed, crying, coughing up phlegm, wresting myself from my husband's grip.

"Why?" Michael screamed back. "Because I had sex with Susie Margolis? I'm the one you should want to kill. Are you CRAZY?"

Short answer: yes.

Never had I felt so overcome by an impulse so extravagantly desperate. I wanted to tear at my clothes, pull my hair, claw at my skin. I wanted to fling open the car door and leap into traffic. I felt fat and homely and I felt stupid for missing the indicators, all of which now seemed perfectly obvious. The long evenings and overnight stays, the chatty e-mails and phone calls at 10:00 and 11:00 P.M. I felt the weight of pregnancy, not just the pounds but the iron anchor of motherhood that would keep me stuck in that house with this man when all I wanted to do was fly away, light as a sparrow into the sky. I never thought I had anything in common with Susie Margolis but now we had this; my husband had fucked her and me both and it made me sick to my stomach.

"You've got to pull over. I'm going to throw up."

"You're not going to throw up, Julie. We're almost home."

I tried to swallow back the mass of eggs and sausage that had pushed its way up my esophagus but it was too late. Michael lifted his foot from the gas pedal and tried to kick a white plastic Walgreen's bag in my direction. With another fierce wretch I threw up on the bag as well as his foot.

"God, Julie. I'm so sorry."

Back at the house I raged against Michael and he absorbed all of it, slump-shouldered on the edge of our bed. I hated him for having a life outside the asphyxiating confines of domesticity, a life that included not just work and approbation of clients but now this: affection, appreciation, gratitude, and sex. I wanted every bit of that for myself. I decided then that I would go back to work as soon as I could enroll Jake into a good day-care program. It didn't even matter where I worked. I had to get out of my house. Three months later I held Jake to my breast with one hand and circled classified ads with the other. That's the week I got my job with the Bentley.

The Susie Margolis incident, as we would come to call it on those rare occasions when we called it anything at all, was treated as a malignant anomaly, a squamous cell carcinoma, caught and cut away before it could advance. Convinced by my husband that the affair was a singular and entirely unexpected expression of grief and release, I agreed to forgive. We would never mention the Susie Margolis incident again. Michael became even more attentive and affectionate. Susie married a tuba player a year later and moved with her new husband to Arkansas where they both found jobs with the Little Rock Symphony.

I spent the following year extracting my due; the balance of power had seesawed in my direction and I planned to make the most of it. While my husband worked relentlessly to regain my respect, I spent enormous amounts of money, ordering new bedding, shoes, and shearling coats from catalogs, a home theater, new living-room furniture. I felt entitled to detach at will, offering minimalist responses, initiating nothing. I allowed myself great expanses of masochist rumination; details Michael refused to provide I fabricated for myself: the movement of Susie's soft body, his hands on her hips, the feverish rocking, the way he held her afterward.

Then one day, in the middle of breakfast at Denny's as Michael buttered an English muffin and the kids chased each other around the table, I realized that I would never leave my husband. We had three children and I had no intention of being a single mother and besides, I loved him deeply despite everything. I felt something inside me click back into its default position. I was done living my life in reaction to the Susie Margolis incident. My husband was a good man. It was time to forget.

Now I realize that I had never really forgotten, just pushed the episode back deep beyond the temporal lobe, beyond the stubbornly nostalgic hippocampus and into an area of my brain that was eager to forget or to begin with had never possessed the capacity to remember. Denial served a vital function for me that year, and not just because it enabled me to love my husband again. It gave me the stamina to impel myself out of bed every morning, feed my children, and function at work. Denial was my ally and constant companion, my most reliable hedge against self-pity, and I welcomed it into my life, until that night at Frankie's beach house, when I'd taken the oath to live with more joie de vivre.

Now a new memory comes paddling up to the surface. It is mid-July, a week before David is diagnosed. Susie and David are at the house for a barbecue. After they leave, I mention, albeit unkindly, that I'd love to give Susie a makeover.

"She's a real Glamour Don't, you know?"

Michael shrugs. The "Glamour Don't" designation means nothing to my husband, but he gets the gist of it.

"I think she's just fine the way she is. She's no fashion model, but she's got joie de vivre."

Chapter THREE

Sunday, 6:49 A.M. At first I think it is the miserable honk of a clogged carpet sweeper, then I discover it is Michael on the saxophone. He has lugged his old instrument from the upstairs crawl space where it had languished for the last thirteen years alongside my stationary exercise bicycle and the knock-hockey game we bought because we thought it would be fun to play together. (It wasn't, by the way. Michael and I don't do games very well. He is too competitive and I take things too personally.) I count three more honks and propel myself out of bed. The family room is still dark and the saxophone case lies open at Michael's feet as if he is inviting spare change.

"What's going on, sweetie?" I ask, squinting at my husband through my grainy, sleep-deprived eyes. Michael stands barefoot in his saggy white underwear and the Super Dad T-shirt the kids bought him for Father's Day two years ago, his tarnished alto saxophone suspended from a black leatherette strap around his neck.

"I'm thinking of joining a band." His eyebrows are raised hopefully, an embarrassed smile plays at the corner of his lips. "A rock band."

"That's nice, honey," I say, hoping I don't sound as skeptical as I feel. "Which band are you thinking of joining?"

"They call themselves Past the Legal Limit. Curt Cartwright started it with some other guys at the firm. Barry Sanders, Joe Patterson." Michael lightly fingers the keys on his saxophone, producing the dull tap of felt on brass. "They used to play big band music at nursing homes and the VFW, but now they're into classic rock and they're getting better venues."

"You mean bars?"

"Bars, clubs, that sort of thing. They play once a week wherever they can find a gig, and they host the open mike every other Wednesday at The Rock Barn." He gives me a moment to digest. "Anyway, they're looking for a sax player. I ran into Barry Sanders in the men's room and he asked me if I'd consider playing and I told him I'd think about it. I mean, I know it's been a while since I played, but it shouldn't take me too long to get up to speed. What do you think?"

I look at my husband with his thin arms and pale spindly legs and I suddenly feel such sorrow for him. Michael works hard for our family and asks for so little in return. I've wondered at times if he might have anhedonia, a clinically diagnosable aversion to pleasure. My husband takes the dark meat, the chipped plate, the broken umbrella, the store brand shampoo. He gave up tickets to a playoff game to cover for Joe Patterson in court (while Joe was getting a hair weave). It was Michael who held our place in line for Pirates of the Caribbean at Disney World so the rest of us could eat lunch. When the other lawyers go out for drinks after an especially difficult victory, Michael always comes home to me and the children. He has never known the joy of driving a brand-new car, has never had a professional massage, has never accepted a gift or compliment without resistance.

He fiddles with the mouthpiece and looks at me. "So? What do you think?"

In other words, Can I go play with the other boys? Can I? Can I? Huh? Huh? Pleeeeeeeese?

"Absolutely," I say, and I mean it. For years I've pestered Michael about carving out some leisure time for himself and I know he regrets giving up the saxophone. "When do you start?"

"They've got a gig this Saturday and they asked me to sit in for a set."

Gig? Sit in? Set? Already he's using the jargon. I want him to do this, I really do. But I am also aware of an uneasiness tugging at me. What am I worried about? I suspect I'll figure that out in due time.

"Sure. Do it, Michael. It'll be fun!"

He grins happily. "You really think so?"

I stand up on tiptoe and kiss his stubbly face. "Yes. I really do."

He bends to rest the saxophone gingerly against the sofa and takes me in his arms. He is hard as a brick and insistent through his Hanes and just as quickly I am ready for him. He tosses the cushions off the couch and pulls me on top; we try to move quietly so as not to wake the kids who normally sleep late on weekends but not always.

It has been three weeks since Michael announced his intent to play with Barry Sanders's band and tonight is their first gig at The Rock Barn, literally, a metal pole barn on what was once the Pibley Goat Farm, all of which was bought by Copley Machine Parts' real estate division, parceled and sold off to various loud, clanky, greasy businesses: a transmission repair shop, an industrial plumbing supplier, a tire store. The barn itself was purchased by the enterprising young Connelly brothers; Bert and Bart had announced at a city zoning meeting that their place would be a "showcase for local performers." While it fulfilled the latter goal—no one of any national fame would consider playing there—it also failed at the former given that "showcase" suggests a significant audience and The Rock Barn never pulls more than a handful of listeners, mostly sodden townies who come for the cheap beer by the pitcher. I can still smell the goats.

I peer into the smoggy darkness.

"Julia! Over here! I saved you a seat!" Stacy Sanders, Barry's wife, waves me to her table by the stage. Stacy is not yet forty years old but she already looks like someone's grandmother with her shelflike bosom and putty-colored orthopedic shoes. I see Stacy at the occasional Weimar Bott gathering and we always wind up sitting together though we have had nothing in common until now. Now we're both with the band.

I order a Diet Coke and Stacy asks if they serve tea, which they don't, so she politely requests a bottle of water. I see that my husband is wearing his prescription sunglasses, a prop he chose at the last minute because "I need a trademark. I can't just go on stage like this, looking the way I always look."

Barry steps up to the microphone. "Hel-*lo,* ladies and gentlemen. It is my great pleasure to welcome you to classic rock night at The Rock Barn. I'm the Buzzard, and *this,* my friends, is Past the Legal Limit!" He thrusts his fist above his head and the band careens into its first number, a decent rendition of Led Zeppelin's "Black Dog" which has no part for a saxophone but Michael plays along anyway.

"Let me tell you something," says Stacy, leaning close and literally screaming into my ear so I can hear her over the music. "This band is the best thing that could have happened to Barry." She pulls a ball of yarn and two long wooden knitting needles from a quilted tote bag. "Makes him feel like a teenager. And not just onstage, if you know what I mean. Better than Viagra."

I try to block the mental image of Stacy and the Buzzard in bed but it's too late. The band stops for a break between sets. All the husbands find their wives except for Michael who stays onstage to fiddle with the amplifiers. He grins at me and I give him an enthusiastic thumbs-up. In truth, his saxophone croaked like a thirteen-year-old boy heading into puberty, but I believe it is my responsibility as his wife and best friend to encourage him.

"Barry, you're sweating," Stacy says. "Should I get you some water?"

"I'm not Barry," Barry whispers. The armpits of his gray FUBU T-shirt are heavily ringed with sweat. "I'm the Buzzard. I *told* you."

"Right. Sorry. Buzzard." Stacy smiles patiently. "You want some water?"

"I like the earring, Buzzard," I say, touching my own earlobe. "Very cool."

"It's magnetic," Stacy whispers. "Barry would pass out if someone stuck a needle in his ear."

Barry glares at his wife. "Do you have to do that here?"

"Do what?"

"What do you think?" He looks around. "*Knit.*" He lowers his voice. "It's not *appropriate.*"

Stacy waves away his complaint with a patient smile and continues working her needles. "It's a great ego boost," Stacy tells me later, once our husbands have re-assembled on stage for their second set. "Just look at them up there. They even have groupies."

She smirks and I follow her goggling eye to an old hippie shuffling barefoot on the filthy floor. She is wearing a black tube top and a ruffled patchwork skirt, dancing near the edge of the stage with a beer in one hand. When the song is done, she claps, spills the beer on her chest, and says, "Aw, fuck." Michael looks at her, then at me, winces, and smiles a private kind of smile, a husband-to-wife kind of smile.

Somewhere in the middle of a groaning rendition of "Free Ride," I feel a hand on my shoulder. "Is there room for one more at this table?"

"Annie! What are you doing here?"

"I thought you could use the moral support."

Annie pulls up a stool, introduces herself to Stacy, and orders a beer. She's wearing a dark denim jacket over a white camisole, flared jeans, and cowboy boots. She looks up at the stage and smiles. "Well, look at *him*. A regular rock star."

"Not quite," I say, grimacing.

She slaps me lightly on the hand. "Be nice, Julia. He's"—she curls her fingers into quotation—"following his bliss." She slides over and undoes the top two buttons of my blouse.

"What are you doing?"

"What do you think I'm doing? You're with the band now. You need to dress the part."

I redo one of the buttons. Even in the dim lighting I can see Annie scowling at me. "What?"

"You know what. Loosen up, Julia. You're in a bar, you're a grown woman, the kids are with a sitter, your husband's up there rocking and rolling. Or whatever. Just have fun for a change, okay?"

Michael joins us when the set is done. "You've got quite a following," I tell him, tilting my head toward the beer-soaked woman in the tube top. "Should I be jealous?"

He smiles. "Absolutely. How could you possibly compete with a woman of her beauty and grace?" He takes a sip of my Coke. "So how did I sound up there?"

He sounded like a goose struggling to free itself from an oil spill.

"Fantastic, honey," I tell him. "Amazing."

"You really think so?"

"Yes, I really do." Michael is beaming now and except for the bald spot he looks exactly like the boy I fell in love with.

Priapus, the son of Aphrodite, has an erection the size of a baseball bat. I am looking at a photograph of a fresco fragment from the House of Vettii in Pompeii. Obviously I can't get the fresco for the exhibit, but I can probably get a good reproduction, printed onto a slab of stone. I make a note to call Jodi Mattson at the Field Museum.

I'm in the Whole Beanery trying to get a head start on the ancient sex exhibit, a collection of art and writing from the Greco-Roman period slated as the centerpiece of the Bentley's seventy-fifth anniversary celebration. It will be a sweeping exhibition with depictions of the promiscuous Zeus, who routinely transformed himself into a swan or bull or eagle to gain sexual advantage over women and boys; the *hetaerae* of Greece, the elite among prostitutes known as much for their intelligence as their sexual expertise; Aphrodite, the patron goddess of the *hetaerae,* ruler over lust, capable of sending victims into destructive sexual frenzies; and Bacchus, the famed god of ecstasy and wine who inspired drunken orgies so wild and lawless that authorities found it necessary to arrest participants by the thousands.

"You work at the *Bentley* Institute?"

I turn to find a man at the table beside mine smiling as if he knows me. It is the man from the parking lot, the professor with the pink shell and three pennies and bedroom eyes. Evan Something.

"Yes," I say, aware of a warm flush that has something to do with my pride in the Bentley and something to do with this man's lips. "I'm the assistant director."

"Julia Flanagan. I remember. I'm Evan Delaney. I'm, uh, the guy who was in desperate need of change. For the meter, I mean."

"Yes." I am abruptly aware I've got pictures of naked Greeks and Romans scattered about the table. I sweep everything into my briefcase.

"You don't have to stop on my account."

There is the beginning of a sly grin and I know what he is thinking. Everyone assumes that if you work at the Bentley Institute you must have an Olympian sex life.

"That's okay. I was just finishing up anyway. There's only so much of this I can take in one sitting."

Why did I say that? It wasn't true. I have been known to sit in one place for six hours consecutively until my work is completed. Leslie hired me because I'm a workhorse and we both know it.

Evan asks about my job and I hear about his frustrations teaching medieval literature to nineteen-year-old students who would rather be back in their dorm rooms, sleeping or getting stoned or playing with their pet ferrets.

I notice the book on his table. "Ovid?"

He doesn't say anything for a moment, just gazes at me in a way that makes me feel vulnerable and shy. "Publius Ovidius Naso. One of the greatest writers of classical antiquity. Exiled to the shores of the Black Sea. A poet. A lover. A soul in pain." He opens the book and turns to a page somewhere toward the end. "This is one of my favorites. From 'The Art of Love.' "

Evan reads aloud, unself-consciously, in a mild and matter-of-fact way. Occasionally he lifts his eyes to meet mine, not salaciously, but engagingly, and every time he looks at me I can feel my heart clench.

"In Cupid's school, whoe'er would take degree
Must learn his rudiments by reading me,
Seamen with sailing art their vessels move;
Art guides the chariot: art instructs to love.
Of ships and chariots others know the rule;
But I am master in Love's mighty school.
Cupid indeed is obstinate and wild,
A stubborn god; but yet the god's a child:
Easy to govern in his tender age,
Like fierce Achilles in his pupilage:
That hero, born for conquest, trembling stood
Before the centaur, and receiv'd the rod."

I realize that this is exactly what I need for my exhibit and tell him so. "It's on the sexuality of ancient civilizations. Greco-Roman period. Art and poetry. For the Bentley's seventy-fifth anniversary. Very big."

"Really?" He has completely shredded his paper napkin. "Huh. Wow. Hmm. Well. I'll tell you what. How about if I Xerox this and pop it in campus mail? You'll have it by tomorrow."

"That'd be great. Thanks."

I have never been one for artistic abstractions and prefer a page of news analysis over a paragraph of poetry any day, but I know enough to understand there is sex and longing in Ovid's words and that there is something obstinate and wild in my own heart, something I've worked very hard to restrain. I also I know that the tectonic plates of my stable life are beginning to shift beneath my feet. I don't like it.

Why is it that my house looks fine until we're expecting company, at which point every flaw is in urgent need of remediation? The drippy faucet in the kitchen, the overgrown ivy by the front door, the missing handle on the bathroom vanity. I am making brunch for Michael's senior partner Rick Wellman and his wife Lanie. If Lanie wants a tour of the house, the kids' rooms will have to be off-limits. In fact, the whole upstairs had better be off-limits. I can't risk having either of them correctly identify Homer as a rat.

While I race around to clean, Stan the Handyman is here to fix the broken cabinet door on the entertainment unit in the family room. Like many local fix-it men, Stan came to town to study philosophy and couldn't find a job even remotely connected to his scholarly interests so he invested in some power tools and started hiring himself out to mechanically inept white-collar families like ours and there are enough of us to keep him busy for the rest of his life. I don't know much more about Stan except that which I observe: he shaves his legs, eats teriyaki soy jerky, is slightly cockeyed, hums tunelessly when he works. I also know that his mechanical skills are only a little better than the average person's. Stan swears when he stabs his thumb with a Phillips screwdriver for the second time and I vow never to hire Stan again. If I want someone who screams SHIT! every ten minutes because he can't get the screw holes to align, I'll just give the job to Michael.

As the strata primavera bakes in the oven, Michael and I pull everything off the refrigerator—the kids' artwork and Personal Best ribbons, the photos, coupons, receipts, newspaper clippings. The telephone table is stacked with junk, so I swipe everything into an empty Kroger bag for future sorting. As I do, I am horrified to see the Ovid poem that I'd carelessly left out for anyone to see. I forget that the poem has every legitimate reason to be there. I am, after all, using it in an exhibit.

The house is immaculate by the time Rick and Lanie arrive for brunch, and the table looks like something out of a magazine spread, with my grandmother's blue and white dishes, a big bouquet of daisies, a glass pitcher of fresh-squeezed orange juice, and cloth napkins folded and fanned out in goblets.

"Delicious meal, Julia." Michael's boss has me cornered in the kitchen while my husband chats up Lanie in the dining room, telling her, I imagine, that she looks exactly like Elizabeth Taylor only younger and slimmer. I decide that Rick Wellman would be handsome except for the distinct absence of vitality in his face that makes him look gray and brittle like an old wooden puppet. It is as if someone stuck a hose in the side of his head and sucked the life out of him.

"Michael never told me," he says, moving so close I can see his bridgework, "that his lovely wife is a gourmet cook." Is my husband's boss flirting with me? Or does he need to be near because of a hearing impairment?

"Oh, thanks," I say, "but all I did was follow the recipes. Right out of the magazine. I'm so glad you enjoyed it."

"I can't wait for the pie," he growls and suddenly I feel Rick Wellman's hand graze my buttocks. Now I'm quite certain that he is flirting with me.

I tell Michael about this incident after Rick and Lanie have left, as we're loading the dishwasher together. Michael is doubtful.

"I just don't see it happening, hon." He shoves the dishes haphazardly into the racks and I'm right behind him, repositioning. He's rushing because his band is playing at The Rock Barn again tonight and he's anxious to rehearse before the gig. "I really don't think Rick would come on to you."

"Is that because he's not the kind of man who flirts, or because I'm not the kind of woman a man would want to flirt with?" I'm alarmed by the sudden rush of hostility I feel.

"Both. No. Wait. I didn't mean that. You're a beautiful woman. I just—"

"It's okay. I know what you meant." I slide the last plate into the dishwasher and go upstairs. Behind a locked bathroom door, I stand before the mirror, studying my face. Michael is probably right. I'm not that kind of woman.

I don't make a big deal of my dreams the way some people do. I don't believe they're symbolic or prophetic or necessarily special in any way. Maybe some people dream important things, emotional insights, cultural archetypes, solutions to profound questions, but my own dreams are just the silt runoff of my brain, meaningless fragments, flashes, bits of nonsensical dialogue, useless images. I dream of tomato seeds, broken lightbulbs, chicken fat, trowels, tire treads, strangers. I put no stock in my dreams. So when I dream of kissing Evan Delaney in the basement of the Bentley Institute, on the rumpled blue silk sheets of a bed that just happens to be there, I am, as you can imagine, alarmed. In the dream I am in the archives, standing at a file cabinet, my back to the rest of the room. I am looking for something, some kind of legal document, and I am completely focused on my task. I don't hear the door open or the footsteps behind me. Then a strong arm wraps around my waist, and I am pulled close and tight against this man, and feel him swelling and hardening. I loll my head back and feel his hot breath against my neck, his lips and tongue, and then we are on this bed, this soft, beautiful bed that has materialized amid the bookcases and filing cabinets. Now he is over me, kissing me, licking me along my neck, breasts, belly, moving his head between my legs. I sense that someone else is in the room and turn my head to find my mother sitting at a big oak desk. She is serving lemonade.

I wake up gasping for air.

Michael stirs. "Bad dream?" It is four in the morning. He'd stumbled into bed only two hours ago smelling of beer and smoke.

I am acutely grateful for the fact that my dream hadn't

been projected onto the ceiling above our bed but remains locked in my own skull.

"Yeah. Awful dream." I am still mad at him for insisting that his boss couldn't possibly have been flirting with me.

Michael rolls onto his side and pulls me against him. "Go back to sleep," he whispers into my hair. "I love you."

Chapter FOUR

Husbands in Victorian England were implored to show sexual self-restraint unless the intent was to procreate. Wives were instructed never to move during the act of sexual congress.

I know this because one of our research interns has proposed an exploration of Victorian class-based sexual behavior during a time of public prohibitions against sexual expressiveness and the private flourishing of prostitution and pederasty. While aristocracy brazenly flouted sexual freedom—the Prince of Wales's well-publicized affair with Lily Langtry was among the most notable sex adventures of the time—the middle class pursued sexual restriction, even in marriage. Given the state of sexual activity in my own marriage (our family room interlude was the last time we made love) I think Michael and I would fit quite nicely in Queen Victoria's England.

I scan the intern's list of proposed exhibit materials:

posters and pamphlets decrying the danger of onania, the heinous sin of masturbation named for the biblical character who spilled his seed in defiance of God's command to be fruitful and multiply; excerpts from an authentic diary describing the frustrations of a semicelibate marriage; writings by the Swiss physician Tissot, who warned of the physical dangers of sex, chief among them: insanity caused by the blood rushing to thc brain. I'd told the intern I'd help if she couldn't find everything on her list; I've already put through two calls to Tissot's heirs, and another to the British Library in London.

As I'm studying the proposal, Leslie leaps into my office to ask if I'll serve on something called the Mendelsohn mural committee.

"I just can't be bothered with this now," she tells me.

And I can? I'm the one with three young children and the Bentley Greco-Roman anniversary extravaganza on her docket.

"Please, Jules, be a sweetheart and fill in for me. Please? Pretty please with sugar on top? I'll be your best friend for life."

I close my eyes as a migraine encroaches and nod grudgingly.

"I ADORE you!" She grabs me by the shoulders and plants a lipsticky kiss on each cheek. "I owe you one, Julia." Actually, she owes me six hundred and forty-seven. Repaying debts isn't Leslie Keen's style. "The first meeting's today, by the way. Four P.M., Whitehead Hall."

Truth is, I could probably use the distraction. I'll do anything to keep my mind from meandering to Evan Delaney. In unguarded moments I have found myself speculating about whether he has ever dated a redhead, what he looked like as a little boy, and how he spends his leisure time, all because of two brief conversations and one silly dream.

No time for those musings now that I am on the Mendelsohn committee. A poor man's Caravaggio, Mendelsohn achieved some fame in the early 1920s for his sensationalistic blend of sex and violence. This particular painting was bequeathed to the university by George "Jelly" and Alma Bean, a local couple with bad taste, a lot of money, and no heirs. The mural depicts a plump, bare-breasted blonde with her arms bound behind her back, stoic under the salacious leer of her captor. Most of the scene is thrust into darkness, with one broad beam of light raking across the girl's body and another illuminating a wall of big game trophies, bears, lions, and leopards who seem to gaze sympathetically at the latest victim.

Campus animal rights activists have managed to collect 2,548 signatures on a petition demanding the painting's immediate removal. I'm not sure where I stand on the issue. Should the mural be removed simply because it offends the sensibilities of a special interest group? And do I really care? I'd much prefer to be home with my husband and children tonight, eating crock pot chicken stew and playing Candyland.

I call Michael to let him know I'll be late and ask if he can be there when the kids get home from school.

"Sure. Oh, no. Wait. Today's what? Monday? Oh, sorry, honey, no can do," he says, between bites of what sounds like a big, sloppy burrito. "Got an ex parte meeting with

Judge Block. Can't reschedule." Pause. "What kind of committee is this, anyway?"

Though I'm sure he means no offense, Michael's question irritates me for the following reasons:

(1) It indicates that he wasn't listening two weeks ago when I told him about the whole Mendelsohn controversy.

(2) The question has a subtext. It is Michael's way, conscious or not, of diminishing my work on the committee; the hidden word is "nutty," as in "what kind of nutty committee is this anyway?"

Though Michael says he's proud of my career, I sometimes wonder whether he believes that his commitments are implicitly important while mine are more like hobbies and inherently dispensable. This has been a live issue between us since we were newly married. While my husband was in law school, I worked at a school for dyslexic kids during the day and taught English as a second language four nights a week, yet I was the one expected to stay home and wait for the electrician.

"Never mind," I say. "I'll put the kids in extended day."

"Okay, sweetie. Catch up with you later." Pause. "Hey, listen. I'm thinking, maybe we can get the kids to bed early tonight. How does that sound?"

It sounds like a fine idea in theory but nearly impossible given my older daughter's circadian rhythms that invariably manage to foil our sexual intimacy. Only after 10:00 P.M. does Lucy ponder the existential questions: Why was I born? What happens after we die? How long before I can get my ears pierced? Only after 10:00 P.M. does Lucy feel motivated to sort all of Flatsy Patsy's tiny flat plastic accessories, or plan her next birthday party, or examine her body for birthmarks—all of which somehow require my counsel, admittedly given freely while my husband sighs and waits and, eventually, falls asleep.

By 4:00 P.M. I am climbing the steps to Whitehead Hall, wondering if my marriage is disintegrating or I'm just in the throes of premenstrual syndrome. I tell myself: I'm happily married. I'm happily married. I'm happily married. I'm happily married. I'm happily married. The mantra bellows in my head as I walk down the waxed tile corridor that smells strongly of Pine-Sol and old wood, as I heave open the heavy door, as I step into the cavernous conference room, as I see Evan Delaney sitting at the table, smiling at me. **DEAR GOD, I'M HAPPILY MARRIED.**

Evan jumps to his feet when he spots me and gestures for me to sit beside him. "You got roped into this too?" he whispers, and I can feel his warm cinnamony breath on my neck.

I see that he has been doodling, not the assertive squares within squares that my husband draws in the white space around *The New York Times* crossword puzzle, but little cartoon faces, the kind you learn to draw when you're a kid. A puppy with big floppy ears and whiskers. A bald-headed guy with horn-rimmed glasses and bulbous nose. I can't explain it, but these silly little pictures make me want to kiss him. I'M HAPPILY MARRIED. I'M HAPPILY MARRIED. I'M HAPPILY MARRIED. I'M HAPPILY MARRIED. I'M HAPPILY MARRIED. I'M HAPPILY MARRIED.

"Yeah, they roped me in too." I try to sound resentful of this new obligation, but suddenly I am not sorry that I agreed to serve on the Mendelsohn mural committee. I suspect that Evan Delaney isn't sorry either. He eases back in his chair and moves his arm a fraction of an inch closer to mine; he isn't touching me, but he is definitely in my air space, and I think I can feel the heat radiating off that sinewy arm, though I may be imagining it. It may just be my own heat, is what I'm saying. I don't let myself inhale the scent of him. I don't let myself see how his dark curly chest hair peeks above the crew neck of his soft gray sweater, don't let myself notice his strong fingers, the raised bumps where he'd shaved his jawline this morning, the flecks of gold in his softly hooded green eyes, the fringe of dark lashes. No, I do not notice anything at all about Evan Delaney.

Art history professor Donatella Pope, who has a mustache and smells like chicken salad, stands at the head of the long, highly polished walnut conference table and explains the procedure. The only makeup she's wearing is a swipe of bright red lipstick, which, along with the mustache, gives her an almost hip but ultimately unattractive Frida Kahlo wannabe effect.

"I want you," Donatella calls out, "to partner with the person to your left. Take a half hour, process your thoughts. We'll reconvene to share and synthesize." She claps her hands briskly. "And remember, our goal here is to be sensitive to the students' concerns. But let's remain cognizant of the university's mission too, you know?" She claps again. "Okay, people, let's get rolling!"

At my left is Vernon Blankenship, professor emeritus of mathematics who has age spots as big as my whole head and weeping sores on his elbows. I am grateful when Evan ignores the person to *his* left, a petite blonde from East European Studies, and leads me toward the back of the room. I'm also grateful that this conference room is lit the old-fashioned way, with skin-flattering tungsten lamps and sconces shaped like Easter lilies. We just sit there for a moment, not saying anything. He seems so awkward and happy.

I surprise us both when I reach for his eyeglasses. "May I?"

I gently remove them before he can answer, mist the lenses with my breath, and use the edge of my cotton blouse to wipe them clean. He looks a little lost without his glasses, but his eyes are bigger now and even more vividly green. I hand them back. "Better?"

He blinks and smiles. "Much. Thank you."

I can hear my pulse hammering in my ears. "I'm sorry. I can't believe I just did that. I didn't, I mean, I'm sorry if that was rude."

"Not at all, Julia."

I see my name leave his lips in slow motion. I see his tongue linger behind his teeth when he reached the "lee" in Ju-lee-ah, and my name is suddenly so much more than the appellation by which I'd been known my whole life, but a bit of lovely music, or the name of a soft pink flower.

"Maybe we should talk about the mural," he says, and I notice a deep flush moving up his neck, crimson against his olive skin. "Um, here's what I'm thinking. On one hand, the students have a point, I suppose. If you like animals, and I do, very much, the mural is, well, it is offensive. It's also not very good art. I'm not sure anyone would suffer if they hauled it away."

I nod my head. I am not even listening. I am replaying the eyeglass-removal scene in my mind and wondering if he's doing the same.

"On the other hand," he continues, "what is a university if not a place for the exchange of free ideas? Here's an opportunity to talk about art—or bad art as the case may be. Let it be a vehicle for debate and learning. Is the university expected to capitulate just because one group or another declares something offensive? It's an unhealthy precedent, I think. Don't you?"

"I agree," I say, wishing he would say my name again. "An unhealthy precedent." I feel drugged. I have to get out of here.

"Good. I guess we're done then."

"I guess." I begin reluctantly to rise from my seat but Evan isn't moving.

"The truth is I only agreed to this committee because my chair says I need to boost my service record. Before they'll promote me to full professor. Apparently I'm not enough of a team player. I've only been on two committees since I joined the faculty."

"How come?"

He shrugs. "I guess I've been too busy working. A professor who's too busy to serve on the bake sale committee? Scandalous."

"Come on, your department doesn't really have a bake sale committee." I pause. For a moment it seems plausible. "Does it?"

He smiles with those twinkly eyes and mumbles something that sounds like "charming."

"So what's your excuse?" he asks, leaning back and

wrapping his arms around the chair back to stretch, shoulders enticingly well defined.

"What do you mean?"

"You know, why are you here? I'm sure there are far more important things demanding your attention."

Do I admit to an overbearing boss, bouts of insecurity, my unrelenting need for approval, a husband and children at home? I consider the tacit hierarchy of conversational intimacy; the levels of truthfulness one scales, degrees of information one allows, as a relationship develops.

"My boss asked if I wouldn't mind standing in for her."

Evan smiles. "You're a Girl Scout, aren't you, Julia Flanagan?"

I stare at the legal pad in my lap and say nothing.

The committee regroups and votes to keep the mural but also agrees to give the activists a four-by-six-foot wall space in the same lecture hall on which to present their views. Our group's next charge is to develop guidelines for the student display. This will require yet another meeting.

"To save time," Donatella Pope calls out, "I'd like partners to meet once more before our next meeting. Okay, people?" More claps.

"Best idea I've heard all day," Evan whispers. "Listen. Julia. As long as we have to meet again, why don't we do it, you know, over, uh, dinner? Um, how do you feel about Italian? Sotto Voce? Three weeks from this Friday? That would be . . ." He pulls a battered black date book from his back pocket. "The twenty-sixth. Would that work for you?"

Whoa, Nelly. First of all, night is *night.* I was thinking

maybe coffee at 10:00 A.M., preferably in the faculty cafeteria. Second, Friday night is a *date* night. And Sotto Voce isn't just a restaurant, it's a *romantic* Italian restaurant, so named for its hushed, almost conspiratorial ambiance; every table in that place seems to be a table for two in the back.

"Okay," I hear myself say, and immediately catch a look of relief, possibly gratitude in his eyes.

"It's a date, then," he says, and I think, Please don't use that word. This isn't a date, Professor Delaney. It is a business meeting.

The following day I decide to work from home, if for no other reason than to avoid Evan. Working from home has other advantages, of course, the absence of Leslie Keen being chief among them and the chance to stay in pajamas all day being another.

But working at home is also an isolating experience; I go out for the mail or just to breathe the unair-conditioned air and see nary a soul. Then again, Larkspur Estates is nary a neighborhood of people. It's a neighborhood of cars. Big, shiny luxury trucks and zippy little imports, black Hummers and cobalt blue Roadsters and creamy Lexus convertibles. The house diagonally across the street has four vehicles, yet, confoundingly, there are only three drivers in the family. Given that I've never actually seen anyone leave or enter the house, the various configurations of these vehicles are like crop signs: spontaneous, mysterious, inexplicable.

6:00 A.M.: Corvette in garage, SUV and van on driveway, Thunderbird parked outside house.

9:45 A.M.: Thunderbird gone, Corvette on the driveway, SUV in garage, van on street.

3:00 P.M.: Corvette gone, Thunderbird in garage, SUV parked on street, van gone.

6:00 P.M.: All four vehicles gone.

10:00 P.M.: Corvette in garage, van gone, Thunderbird on street, SUV now parked across the street.

Why?

And why am I standing at the bathroom window staring at my neighbor's driveway when I should be working? Why am I finding it nearly impossible to find my copy of a 1940s sex manual entitled *A Modern Guide to Marital Happiness,* a book one of the graduate students has agreed to read and index for me? Why haven't I called my husband at work, just to say hello, as I've done almost every day for the last eleven years?

Michael does eventually phone me to tell me he loves me and remind me that his new glasses will be ready at Goggles this Saturday and I should remind him to pick them up.

Goggles is more than an optometry shop, it's a cross between Hooters and *Charlie's Angels,* a brilliant marketing ploy geared toward attracting upscale male myopics. Optometrist Tim Larson employs three female assistants, an elegant blonde, a vivacious and chemically enhanced redhead, and a raven-haired knockout. Rather than having them wear those fake lab coats (we all know they're not doctors, not even close), Tim has his girls dress in evening wear—sparkly tops with plunging necklines, slinky skirts, strappy sandals. All three wear glasses. I suspect they don't need to. That would be another of Tim Larson's marketing ploys. You see? Men *do* make passes at women who wear glasses.

As much as the place irritates me, I will never say anything about the Goggles girls and I can thank my mother for my self-restraint. "Men hate a jealous woman," she'd say. This was perhaps the most important of the handful of tips my mother had dispensed. Tighten your bra straps so your boobs don't droop. Tight ponytails will give you headaches. A Wal-Mart checkout line with three men will always move faster than the line with one woman. Don't cry in public. Don't eat spinach salad on a date.

And never, ever, *ever* let a man know you're jealous.

When I was in high school and miserable because I spotted my boyfriend driving around town with the exceedingly busty Pamela Newton, my mother said, "If Jesse McNamara wants to drive around town with another girl, get over it or cut him loose." A Newport hung perilously from her lip as she hemmed the bottom of my prom dress. "Nothing in this world's uglier than an insecure woman. All clingy and whiny and shit. Men hate that. Believe me, Julie-bell, it's about as sexy as a housedress."

When my husband was nearing the end of law school and preparing himself for job interviews, he determined that it was finally time to switch from his gold aviator glasses to contact lenses. He excitedly returned home from the ophthalmologist with a bag full of stuff, special storage cases and cleansing solution and, of course, the lenses themselves, packed into a tiny white cardboard box labeled with Michael's name and prescription. It was the first time I'd actually seen a contact lens up close. I couldn't believe there could be so much precision and corrective power in something so small and flimsy. It was a miracle, really.

Michael spent two hours trying to get those little miracles into his eyes. He reached around his head with one hand like a yogi to pry his eyelid open, and with the other hand struggled to stick the thin plastic disc onto his eyeball. Again and again he assumed this position, always with the same results. Either he couldn't get the lenses off his fingertip or he couldn't get it centered on his eye or he'd drop it into the sink and have to start from the beginning, rinsing and reaching and prying and sticking, to no avail. He finally got them in and hated the sensation.

"It feels like I have a fucking piece of Saran Wrap in my eye," he yelled from the bathroom. "How does anyone LIVE like this?"

"People live like that all the time," I yelled back. "Didn't the doctor tell you that you just have to get used to it?"

"I'll NEVER get used to it. I HATE this."

"Fine. So don't wear them. You look cute in glasses."

"You really think I look cute?" He was standing in the door frame now, glasses back on, smiling and trolling for more compliments.

"Better than cute. Sexy. Like Superman."

"You mean Clark Kent," he said, unbuckling his belt with one hand, groping under my blouse with another. "Clark Kent was the one with the glasses." This was before we had real jobs and children and a mortgage and soccer games and piano lessons. We had each other. We had sex.

Today is Saturday and Michael's new glasses are ready. When we walk into the lushly carpeted "visionary boutique," which is how Tim Larson advertises his place, we are immediately approached by Marguerite, the trio's buxom redhead. "You're looking dapper today, Mr. Flanagan," she murmurs, with all the finesse of a seasoned courtesan. She picks a bit of fluff off his collar and I want to kick myself for not picking it off myself when I noticed it back at the house. "What's your pleasure this afternoon?"

The last time we were at Goggles we happened to have Michael's parents with us and my father-in-law took me aside and whispered, "Is this an optometrist or some kind of whorehouse?" Michael's father is from the Bronx and he pronounced the word "hoor-house." I made a face as if I was deeply offended but I agreed with him. After Marguerite had presented us with the bill—$490 for one pair of glare-free, solar-sensitive designer spectacles—I began to understand the method behind Tim Larson's hoor-house madness. I have yet to grasp, however, how this approach could possibly appeal to female customers. When and if I need reading glasses of my own, I'm going straight to Target.

"And you're looking rather dapper yourself," Michael says, glancing quickly away from Marguerite's décolletage. "Hey. Has anyone ever told you that you look like Nicole Kidman, but shorter?"

I shudder. "Can we pick up the pace a little?" I say. "Jake has to be at a birthday party in forty minutes."

By the time we leave Goggles, our checking account is significantly diminished but Michael is florid and fribbling after Marguerite's lavish attentions. He made a point of inviting her to Legal Limit's next performance.

"I know they're expensive," he begins, checking his reflection in the rearview mirror as he buckles his seat belt, "but I think they're worth it. I mean, there's no one else in town with this kind of quality. You know?"

I say nothing.

"And the service is just phenomenal. Don't you think?"

I grunt.

"Jules? Honey? Is something wrong?"

"Not at all," I lie. "I'm just anxious to get Jake to the party in time."

"Hey listen," Michael begins. "About tonight. I know we've got a sitter lined up but I've got to go back to the office. It's the antitrust case. We've got to get our depositions wrapped up by Tuesday morning and I'm behind the eight ball. I'm so sorry, honey."

"It's okay."

"Really?"

"Really."

"You're not just saying that?"

"No, Michael, I'm not just saying that."

I am suddenly overcome by the bleakness of the situation. My husband works too hard, he doesn't think I'm attractive enough to provoke flirting, and it has been too long since we had sex. As we drive home together in silence, I promise myself that I will find a marriage counselor. Something ominous is happening to our marriage and we've got to confront it before it gets worse.

Chapter FIVE

Instead of a marriage counselor I decide to go for something cheaper and faster. A new haircut. It is my mother-in-law's idea, actually. Last week, while Michael and his father are in the basement watching the game and well out of earshot (that's her modus operandi—no witnesses) Kathleen leans forward and says, "If you don't mind me saying so . . ."

I should have shouted: FREEZE! PUT YOUR HANDS IN THE AIR AND STEP AWAY FROM YOUR MOUTH! Experience has taught me that my mother-in-law always prefaces her helpful suggestions with one of the following:

- "If you don't mind me saying so," as in, "If you don't mind me saying so, Caitlin is getting a little chubby. What do you feed her?"
- "No offense, but . . ." As in, "No offense, but you really need to hire a cleaning service, honey."

- "It's really none of my business," as in, "It's really none of my business, but if you keep picking up the baby every time he cries you're going to end up with a spoiled brat."

"Yes, Mom?"

"Have you ever thought about cutting your hair?"

"No, Mom. Why do you ask?"

I know why she asked. Because for my dear mother-in-law, a day without criticizing Julia is like a day without prune juice. She just doesn't feel like herself until she's gotten all her crap out.

"Oh, honey, I don't know. It's lovely hair. It's so lovely you could probably make a wig out of it. For cancer patients. A Chinese girl in my aerobics class did that. So interesting. Your hair has to be something like a foot long. Have you ever measured your hair? I think they say it has to be ten to twelve inches, I'm pretty sure. It has to be clean, obviously. You just make a ponytail, lop it right off, stick it in a plastic bag, and off it goes. Some place in Ohio. And not just cancer patients. Burn victims, people with that balding thing, what do they call it, aloicious—"

"Alopecia."

"That's it. So you mail your hair to them, and then they soak it in this chemical to sanitize it because of course you don't want to be sending germs to these poor people, they're sick enough already, you know? God, it's like when my cousin Roseanne made me a casserole after my hysterectomy and I got deathly ill two days later and then she tells me that she was sick and she sneezed all over it and when I said, Rosie, how could you DO that? She had the nerve to hang up on me, can you BELIEVE it?" Kathleen pops a piece of celery into her mouth (as opposed to helping me chop it, I should point out). "Anyway, Julia, I was thinking, your hair is just so, I don't know, *bland.*"

Ouch. I always liked my hair. It's obedient; it curls when I wrap it around a hot iron, lays flat and smooth when I use a blow dryer and paddle brush, and I don't have much gray. But I suppose my mother-in-law is right. My hair doesn't have any particular style. I usually pull it back in a ponytail or headband, same look since high school. I finish chopping the salad and resist the urge to dump the whole thing down the garbage disposal. Instead, I tell my mother-in-law that I have found many occasions to wear the green plastic necklace she gave me when in truth I handed it right over to Lucy for playing dress-up.

Michael and his father emerge from the basement. "Hey, Miss Julia. Do you know why the Dairy Queen got pregnant?" Jim wisely doesn't wait for an answer, because by now he knows that an answer is not forthcoming. "Because the Burger King forgot to wrap his whopper!"

Meet my father-in-law, Jim Flanagan, the towering Irishman, ruddy, keg-chested, always smiling. A traveling salesman for Atlas Auto. A big flirt, just like his son. Ever since Jim collapsed with congestive heart failure at the tennis pavilion two years ago, there seems to be a tacit agreement among family and friends to indulge his awful jokes.

"Oh, for Pete's sake, Jim," my mother-in-law groans. "That's *enough.*" She leans in to whisper, "I'd still rather have him around, bad jokes and all." Kathleen suddenly looks at me, squinting and holding up her fingers to frame my head. "I'm telling you, a haircut would do you good."

By the time my in-laws have left, I am intent on getting one of those shaggy styles, something cute and sexy, tousled and Meg Ryanish. I go online, search "Meg Ryan hair," find a publicity photo from her last movie, print it out in full color. Tomorrow I'll make an appointment with LuAnn Bubansky at The Hairport.

"Why would you want to change your hair?" Michael asks, clicking rapidly from channel 1 to 93. "You're fine just the way you are."

My husband doesn't understand that I'm no longer content with fine. I don't want long, boring, parted in the middle, hasn't changed since high school hair. I want sexy, funky, wild, *dangerous* hair. And by the grace of God and LuAnn Bubansky, that's exactly what I'm going to get.

My jeans are too tight. I know I'm not pregnant, and I'm not premenstrual, but before arriving at the only appropriate conclusion, I go through my traditional self-delusional litany: The pants shrank in the wash. They shrank at the dry cleaner. They shrank in my closet. I'm retaining water. My legs are suddenly more muscular, creating the sensation of tightness. I bought these from a rack near the junior section, so they are probably sized more for narrow-hipped middle-school girls, not amply built mothers like me. There's defective stitching along the seams. The pants are mislabeled. The company skimps on fabric so they can sell their pants cheaply.

I shoehorn myself into the jeans and make my way to Hairport, one of the few "beauty parlors" left in town where you can get your nails done for fifteen bucks and hear all the most accurate gossip. The other salons have transformed themselves into "European day spas" where they charge forty dollars on an "aromatherapy pedicure," which never made sense to me: how can it be aromatherapy when your feet are so far away from your nose you can't smell anything? The whole European day spa concept seems a little ridiculous in a town where the "French bistro" is run by people who pronounce crème brûlée "cream brooley" and all the foreign surnames are so anglicized that you'd never know these families had ethnic roots. Mary Lopez calls herself Mary Lopes, pronounced like the verb, one syllable. The Les Jardin family goes by "Lezjarden," accent on the Lez. And did I mention that the Chinese restaurants serve white bread?

LuAnn glances at my photo of Meg Ryan. She pokes at my hair with her fingers, moving in to examine it more closely.

"We're talking perm," she says. "Maybe a few highlights over here to frame your face. You'll look very cute." LuAnn Bubansky describes herself as "happily divorced" and has three gangling teenage sons, all high school basketball stars with apparently realistic NBA aspirations. She drapes a gold vinyl cape over me and pulls out a box of pink perm rods. "You're going to look real cute, sweetheart."

I wave my picture of Meg Ryan, a last-minute confirmation of my original intent. "So, I'll get basically this style, right? I mean, I wouldn't want anything too curly. I'm not looking for curls. Just sort of shaggy, you know?" I force myself to say the word. "Sexy?"

LuAnn shoves a clip in her mouth and proceeds to wind my hair around a rod. "Uh-huh," she mumbles. "Sexy. Shaggy. Not curly. Got it."

An hour later, I look like an Irish water spaniel. I want to vomit. Oh, God. WHAT HAVE I DONE? "It's . . . sort of curly, isn't it?" I ask, trying very hard not to cry.

"Oh, hon, you've got to give it *time.* It takes a good four days for a perm to relax." She pulls on one of my coils, presumably to give me a glimpse of what my hair will look like when it "relaxes." It snaps back with the tension of a metal tape measure.

I check my watch: darn it. Lucy's piano recital started ten minutes ago. I jump into my van and speed all the way to the school, rolling through every stop sign, flying through two red lights. I flip down the vanity mirror and look again. Okay, so it's curlier than I'd expected. But it's kind of cute. I reapply my lipstick, blot my lips with a finger, then dab the excess lipstick onto my cheeks. I check the mirror again. Maybe it's not the shaggy Meg Ryan look I'd hoped for, but neither can it be described as bland.

I race through the parking lot, navigating around hundreds of minivans and SUVs and the occasional Camry and scurry into the building. My heels clatter down the shiny steps to the auditorium. I slide in next to Michael just as Lucy is standing to take her place at the piano. My husband regards me offhandedly—he does not recognize me—then swivels his head for a second look. In that head-swiveling moment I pray that he turns to find me dazzlingly attractive, the wild goddess he has always secretly wanted me to be.

"Interesting look." He evaluates my hair like an insurance agent appraising crash damage.

"You don't like it?"

Michael shifts his eyes back to the stage. "You look like Larry from the Three Stooges. Except female. Just kidding. "

"You hate it."

"No, no. It's cute. *You're* cute. I'm just not used to seeing you with curly hair. Don't worry. I'll get used to it."

Lucy steps onto the stage and Michael reaches for my hand as our daughter centers herself on the piano bench and raises her delicate fingers. I glance at my husband's face and see that his eyes are already brimming. He squeezes my hand harder.

"Remember when she was a baby?" he whispers. "Remember how she tried to play the piano with her feet?"

I want to share Michael's moment of pride and nostalgia but all I can think about is this calamity atop my head, this stiff mass of curls and kink. This is not something I can wash out in the shower. I'm stuck with this monstrosity for the next five months, maybe longer.

Michael does not look directly at me for the rest of the evening. When he talks to me he seems to be addressing my kneecaps. Caitlin says she wants my "old head back." Jake cries when I picked him up from kindergarten. I have made a horrible mistake.

Tonight I set the table with the good place mats, the ones I bought at the Hallmark store for forty-two dollars made of heavy pressboard and laminated to a high gloss. As I set one down at Michael's place at the head of the table, I notice that it's stained, a big oil stain that mars the watercolor skies like a thunderhead. The fat spotted cows are no longer grazing under a clear blue sky but in the gloom of the approaching squall.

I watch Michael pick at his cornflake-crumb chicken and mashed sweet potatoes.

"Something wrong?"

"Not much of an appetite," he mumbles.

"Hard day at work?"

"Not really."

"Is it my hair?" I blurt out. "Just be honest with me."

Michael puts down his fork and the kids stare at their father and wait for his response, hoping, I'm sure, that he will give authoritative voice to their own opinion of my devastated head. He lifts the napkin to his mouth.

"Maybe." He sighs. "You had such beautiful hair, Jules. You're a beautiful woman. Why couldn't you just let it alone?"

"It's a girl thing," I say, falling back on the lamest of alibis.

"It's not a girl thing, it's a mistake." Michael finally makes eye contact with me. "Oh, Julia, I'm sorry. I didn't mean it that way. I'm so sorry."

"That's okay. You're right. It was a mistake." I run my fingers through my hair and hear it crackle. After dinner I take a very long, very hot shower and shampoo with baking soda and vinegar because someone told me it would soften the perm. It fizzes and foams like a science fair volcano, but when I'm done blow-drying my hair is still horrible.

I hear giggles from Jake's room, pull on a bathrobe,

and crack open his door to inspect. Michael and the kids are on the floor in a circle. In the middle is Homer, wearing a cape fashioned out of a red bandana.

"All hail Emperor Shmalla, of the planet Shmalla, in the galaxy of . . ."

"Shmalla!" the kids chime in.

As if on cue, Homer, who has been racing in circles, stops abruptly and sits up on his haunches. "Yes, we are here on the planet Shmalla, where we've been granted an audience with the emperor himself, Most High and Revered Shmoo Shmalla." Michael is speaking into an imaginary microphone.

"Emperor Shmalla is wearing his customary red Cape of Shmallitude. It is believed that this cape, handed down through generations of Shmoo Shmallas, gives his royal highness the power to predict the weather, discover hidden Cheerios, and poop anywhere he wants."

The kids are hysterical and Michael looks pleased. He is the master of the crazy bedtime story, and the planet Shmalla is just one in a rich repertoire that includes Tales of Mr. Doody, the hapless retailer whose key resource is cow dung because he lives on the edge of a dairy farm and it's free for the taking; and G.I. Jimmy, the dimwitted soldier who whines like a baby when his mother forgets to put candy in his CARE package.

"And look who has made her grand entrance! It's the Prime Minister of planet Shmalla, her Royal Curliness, Shminky Shmalla! All hail Prime Minister Shmalla!"

Michael winks at me and scoots over to make room in the circle. He pats the carpet and gestures for me to sit beside him. "Yes, ladies and gentlemen, the prime minister has her own magical powers. She can change the form and texture of her hair in the blink of an eye." I squeeze in between Lucy and Michael, who kisses me on the nose and whispers, "I love you." If only I did possess the power to change my hair.

Before bed I slather myself with maximum control gel, pull my kinky coils back into a tight ponytail, and turn away from the mirror in disgust. My goal is to be asleep before Michael climbs into bed beside me. I suddenly remember that his band is playing at The Rock Barn this Friday night and I had planned to go. I'd even secured a babysitter. Now I'm wondering if I should just stay home with the kids and keep my head out of public view.

Evan Delaney loves my hair, nah, nah, nah na nah!

As Annie and I are striding across campus for a quick lunch we pass Evan on the crooked slate path that bisects the grassy courtyard. Evan is holding his briefcase with one hand, pointing at his head with the other.

"I like it," he calls out. "Your hair. Very pretty."

Already I can feel the blood in my cheeks. "Thanks," I say, bashfully. I move toward him, pulled along by a force not unlike undertow.

"It really is quite fetching." He looks at my hair approvingly, then he steals a glance at the rest of me.

I resist the urge to say: You really think so? You mean, you don't think it was a stupid mistake? You haven't lost your appetite? I'm not a complete idiot for doing this to myself? I don't look like one of the Three Stooges? You don't think I should just leave well enough alone? Are you absolutely positive?

"Thanks," I say.

"So, I'll see you in a few weeks, right?"

"Yes. I'll be there," I say. Annie and I continue on our way, my fingertips twitching as the thrill of Evan's attention ricochets through me.

"Who *was* that?" Annie asks, turning around and craning her neck for another look.

"Who?"

"*Him.* That guy? The good-looking one? The one who likes your hair?"

"Oh. Yeah. That's Evan Delaney. He's a medievalist."

"Uh-huh." Annie is staring at me, smiling.

"What?"

"Nothing."

"Tell me."

"He likes you."

"He does not." I pause. "What do you mean?"

"You know exactly what I mean. And he's a hunk."

"I hadn't noticed."

"Bullshit."

I watch my reflection in a window as we pass Volk Hall and admire the Woman Formerly Known as Bland. What was the word he used? Oh, yes. *Fetching.*

Chapter SIX

May God bestow His beneficence upon the inventor of spandex. These pants make me feel slim and leggy. The pink sleeveless top, on the other hand, exposes too much armpit flubber so I've switched to a gray cotton T-shirt with three-quarter-length sleeves, another garment design concept deserving praise and gratitude. I dig out a pair of black high-heeled sandals bought for a wedding but rarely worn because they give me vertigo. I give myself the unabridged makeup application normally reserved for job interviews, college reunions, and first dates: green tinted concealer for emergent zits, yellow for dark circles, moisturizing foundation followed up with a mineral-based loose powder application. Brow color dabbed on with a tiny stiff brush, burgundy lip liner, matching matte lipstick, quick touch of gloss on the center of the bottom lip for the illusion of fullness like they tell you in the magazines. Granite eyeshadow, one shade for the crease, another for the brow bone, then two coats of ebony non-clumping mascara. A bit of bronzer on the cheeks and a lot of blending and my makeup is finally done. I douse myself with Happy, run a blob of finishing cream through my fetching locks, review the rules with the babysitter, kiss the kids, and hop in the van.

The Rock Barn is empty as usual. Most college kids would rather not watch middle-aged guys play rock and grown-ups are too busy juggling homework, baths, and bedtime to venture out on a Tuesday night. So it's just me in my spandex pants, a craggy bartender named Rooney, the guttermouth drunk in the black tube top, and two secretaries from Joe Patterson's office, both wearing elastic-waist jeans. Michael blows me a kiss as I toddle in on my high heels. Though The Rock Barn is dark as a cave, Michael continues to insist on wearing his prescription sunglasses onstage. Barry Sanders disappears to use the men's room and I remember that his wife had mentioned something about a prostate infection.

There is a blast of humid air as the front door swings open. I assume it's Marcia Simmons, Lucy's Brownies troop leader. Marcia's husband Ned recently hauled his drum kit up from the basement and now threatens to play with The Blue Gilligans, another ensemble of lawyers. At the last Brownie meeting, in which the girls made sock puppets for residents of the Cambridge County Nursing Home, Marcia mentioned that she'd like to watch my husband's band before she granted Ned her "blessing."

It isn't Marcia after all, but a petite young woman in denim shorts, rhinestone-studded platform flip-flops, and a gauzy peasant blouse cropped above her belly button.

She takes a table near mine and I can see that she has a heart-shaped face, a smooth high brow, big eyes, and full, glossy lips. Most striking is her hair, waist length and dark, which swings as she moves to the music. She is too young and attractive to be one of the regulars at The Rock Barn. I wonder who she is.

The girl can't seem to keep her hands off her hair. She pulls it up and off her neck, then lets it drop so it cascades down her back. She winds a section around her finger, then pushes it behind her ears. At some point she puts it in a high ponytail using an elastic band she keeps around her wrist. I fleetingly imagine snipping off that ponytail with a pair of garden shears and sending it to the wig-making company. The fantasy fills me with guilty pleasure.

The girl rests her chin in her hands and fixes her eyes on the stage. I inch my chair a bit farther ahead so I can see who she is staring at. With a dull thud in my chest I realize that she is staring at my husband.

Bass guitarist and law librarian Walter Shope plays the final bars of "Ramblin' Man" before Joe steps up to the microphone. "At this point, ladies and gentlemen"—at this point I have to give him credit for maintaining the fiction of a real audience—"I'd like to introduce our very special guest. All the way from Miami Beach, Florida, give it up for . . . Edith Berry!"

Then the young woman I've been watching rises to her feet, shakes her hair loose, and confidently bounds up to the stage. Michael smiles as she lowers the microphone to lip level. The band plays the first dramatic bars of a song I recognize immediately and with fatalistic surety as

Peggy Lee's "Fever." Edith Berry begins to sing in a low, sultry voice. Now I don't merely want to snip her ponytail off. I want to cut off the entire head. I also feel I should protest the sudden shift in musical genres. Hey, I want to scream, this is a rock and roll band. Somebody pull that girl off the stage!

Edith sits in for a second number, a song she wrote herself. "I smell you on my pillow," she croons, "and it makes me crazy." Michael steps forward to take a solo, and Edith closes her eyes, swaying and nodding and occasionally shouting things like, "Play it, Daddy" and "Yeah, baby."

I want to jump on the stage and grab the microphone out of her hand. He's not your daddy and he's not your baby, I want to say. Take your long hair and your low-rise shorts and your twenty-six-year-old body and go home, *Edith.*

I applaud minimally (two quick claps, palms only) and watch my husband's face as Edith steps down and strides back to her seat. I can't see his eyes through the sunglasses, but based on the angle of his head, it does seem as if he is ogling her with lust and admiration. After the set, Michael jumps off the stage and ambles toward me. His bald spot is pink and shiny.

"How was I up there?" He gives me a sweaty kiss on the mouth. "Did you notice that little thing I did at the end of my solo? I just came up with that. Did it sound okay?"

"You were great. You all sounded great." I motion for him to take off his sunglasses. "Honey, do you mind? I'd like to see your eyes when I'm talking to you."

He complies and wipes his head with a paper napkin. "Hey. Julie. There's someone I want you to meet." He pulls me to a standing position and leads me energetically to—you guessed it—Edith Berry, who gracefully extends a hand and dips her head.

"Much obliged," she says.

Much obliged? I'm immediately irritated by this, and by the fact that Michael is exhibiting far more positive emotion than I've seen from him in weeks.

"Little did I know when I hired Edith that she wasn't just a great paralegal, but a fabulous singer too! And she looks just like Catherine Zeta-Jones, except with longer hair, I think. Don't you?"

Oh, no. Of *course.* This is *Edith* The Paralegal as in, I'll need to call you back, hon, I've got *Edith* in my office and we've got to get through this case file by noon. It hadn't occurred to me that Edith might be something other than a middle-aged married woman who favored capacious denim jumpers and beige knee-highs.

"What a lovely, old-fashioned name," I hear myself say. From the corner of my eye I can see the outermost edge of my permed frizz bobbling as I speak. "Is that a family name?"

"Yes," she says, raising her hair to fan the back of her neck. "My great-grandmother on my dad's side. But most people call me Didi." She nudges Michael with her elbow. "Except for this guy. He's so damn formal."

Under the circumstances, formal would be a good thing and I should be reassured. Shouldn't I?

Remembering my mother's admonitions against jealous needling, I mightily resist the urge to ask Michael about Edith—Didi—Berry. I keep my mouth clamped as we dress for work, say nothing when he calls me at the office to check in, don't make a peep after dinner.

But the need to know burns like a urinary tract infection and by 9:15, as Michael clicks through the channels in search of news, I can no longer hold my tongue. "So . . ." I begin slowly, striving for a casual tone. "This Edith person. She's got a nice voice." Already I am off to a bad start. *Edith person?* Who talks like that, except a desperate, jealous, tragically permed wife?

"Doesn't she?" Michael says, eyes fixed on a badly colorized John Wayne; he is wearing mauve overalls.

"What does her husband do?" I ask, pretending to be fascinated by the label on my spider vein fade cream, for which I paid fifteen dollars even though I suspected then what I know for sure now: it doesn't work.

"Hmmm?" Michael is now intent on a SolarFlex infomercial. His thumb is poised on the channel down button, twitching, eager for the next click.

"Her husband. What does he do? For a living."

Michael looks absently my way. "Oh, Edith's not married." Click. *Bonanza* reruns. Click. Loud talking heads. Click. Cubic Zirconia. Click. C-Span. Click. Hockey. Click. Financial news with that blond woman who always looks like she has spittle gathering at the corners of her mouth.

I can feel my mother sitting like Jiminy Cricket on my shoulder. Don't say it, Julie-bell. Don't say it.

"Engaged?" I ask, flicking mother-bug off my shoulder.

"Huh?"

"Never mind."

• • •

Do you believe in divine intervention? I did not, not until tonight, not until the good Lord led me straight to the Cambridge County Mall, a place I normally try to avoid because it's depressing, a strange hybrid of attrition and growth—Sears closed down two years ago, and JCPenney is on its way out, but there's a new Abercrombie & Fitch, and I've heard that the Body Shop is moving in where the Disney Store used to be. There are always two or three big storefronts with butcher paper and FOR LEASE signs masking the windows, and another handful of shops bearing GOING OUT OF BUSINESS—MUST LIQUIDATE banners. The smaller stores depress me most, the pet shop where rueful overgrown puppies sit in their own poop, the dreary uniform shop, and a place called Stephanie's Treasures, with its homely porcelain dolls, resin dragons, "lucky" bamboo, and license plate frames with phrases like, "We're spending our kids' inheritance!" and "Honk if you're horny!"

So I never should have been here in the first place. But Michael is working late tonight, I am too exhausted to cook, and in an atypical moment of consensus, all three kids wanted to eat at Chicken Charlie's, so off to the mall we go.

As if in direct response to my current crisis of follicular confidence, I see a kiosk called "Marlena's Hair Fantasies" where hundreds of clip-on hair extensions hang from the kiosk's wire frame like so many horses' tails, platinum blond to jet black, in every length and style. Short wavy ones, ultra long ones, curly sprays, spirals, and sleek shoulder-length bobs. These hairpieces have come a long way since my mother had her "fall," a long red mane that she kept in her middle dresser drawer, stretched out like a dead thing amid the stockings and panties. Her fall required masses of thick hair pins to keep in place; Marlena's Fantasies were ingeniously attached to a simple plastic clip.

"Look, Mom! Bethany has one of these! She wears it to school! Her mother even lets her wear it swimming! Can I have one? You can take it out of my allowance! I promise I'll wear it every day! Please?"

I step closer to the booth and try to hide my delight. *This is too good to be true.*

"Can I help you, ladies?" The kiosk is staffed by a high school student who is wearing a Marlena's Hair Fantasy of her own, a streaked curly blond ponytail that blends easily with her natural hair.

"Yes, I believe you can." As I move closer I notice that the girl has one blue cornea and one that's a black and white Playboy bunny logo. She notices me noticing.

"Christmas present from my boyfriend. It's like a contact lens."

The girl slides off her stool and readjusts her wig. Her stomach swells out above her waistband like a beer belly. As if the bunny eye isn't sufficiently provocative, a rather large dream catcher dangles from a sapphire and silver navel ring. When I was in high school, only girls with concave bellies felt entitled to wear crop tops. Now even fat girls seem at ease in low-rise pants and "belly shirts." Maybe it signifies a new generosity in defining the female body ideal. But maybe it's a sign that teenage girls in this part of the country are just fat and clueless; our state isn't exactly a fashion mecca and we have the third highest rate of childhood obesity.

Caitlin waits for me to say something on her behalf, but I am transfixed by a long auburn ponytail clamped above the cash register. It is my old hair, thick and straight with streaks of darker red.

"Can I see that one?" I ask.

"Awesome choice, ma'am. That's the Vanessa. One of our most popular ponies." She unhooks the wig from its spot above the register and points to a tall aluminum stool. "Have a seat. Let's see here. First we put your own, uh, hair back and out of the way." She smoothes my massive shrubbery back with strong fingers and secures it with a rubber band and nineteen bobby pins, then clips on the ponytail and offers me a green plastic mirror. "Ta-da!"

I stare at myself in the mirror. I am instantly transported back in time, before I'd impulsively entrusted my head to LuAnn Bubansky and her satanic pink perm rods. My children stare reverently.

"It's your old head!" Lucy cries out. "Mommy's old head is back!"

I pick out a curly blond one for Caitlin and hand my Visa card to the girl. I don't care if it costs me six hundred dollars. I'm buying it. "I'll take both."

"Cool. That'll be eighty-five total." She reaches out to unhinge the ponytail from my scalp.

"No, that's okay. I'll wear it out, if you don't mind."

Oh, how I love this fake hair! It is thick and full of body, and it sways when I walk. I've taken to twisting a hank around my finger, just like I used to do with my real hair. I've even chewed on it, to further the illusion. Michael will be home in forty minutes. I can't wait for him to see me.

• • •

"Wow." Michael reaches out to stroke Vanessa. He nods his head in amazement. "Wow."

"Like it?"

"Very much. I mean, I liked your other hair too, but this is, well, this is spectacular."

"I know," I say, giggling. "And it was only forty bucks."

"Worth every penny."

Michael succeeds in getting the kids to bed early and leads me from the kitchen, where I'm putting away dishes still hot from the dishwasher, to the bedroom. He dims the lamp by his nightstand and slides under the covers.

"Come here. I want you snuggled up next to me."

"Okay."

"Wait. Take off your clothes. I want to feel you."

I pull off my blouse, then unfasten my bra, watching him watch me. I slip off my pants, then panties, and as I begin to fold everything neatly, as is my wont, Michael says, "Leave it. Get in bed."

He knows I like it when he's bossy, but only in this context. I wouldn't be quite so receptive if he used the same tone around the kitchen: Vacuum the family room. Now.

I climb into bed beside him and he continues the game, commanding me to lie back as he covers my body with soft, wet kisses. Familiarity may breed contempt in some relationships, but in ours it has only produced better sex.

But I'm not stupid. I know that last night's intensity had something to do with Vanessa. And whatever intimacy had been nurtured during that brief interlude seems to have had no residual effect. Michael seems distant again today. He reads the newspaper through breakfast, doesn't call during lunch, gets home after nine, and falls asleep before I brush my teeth.

I am at the bookstore with the kids, who have installed themselves in various corners and crannies of the children's section. Caitlin, true to her habit of picking books significantly beneath her superior reading ability, is paging through a paperback about a superhero who wears a diaper and rescues kids from evil cafeteria matrons. Lucy is on her belly, chin propped on her hands, staring at a picture of a golden retriever. Jake is sprawled across the floor practically drooling over a book about motorcycles. With the kids well ensconced, and after my usual warnings—don't talk to strangers, don't follow anyone into the rest room, don't believe it if someone tells you I was rushed to the hospital, don't agree to help anyone find his lost kitten—I go to the Relationships: Self-Help section to see if there are any books like *Women With Bad Perms and the Men Who Hate Them.*

"Aren't you Michael Flanagan's wife?"

I turn to see Edith Berry, who is clutching a paperback called *Furious Love.* Her fingers are obscuring most of the picture on the cover, but I get the general idea. Busty woman ravished by dashing, half-naked man.

Edith runs her hands through her hair. I run my hands through Vanessa.

"Yes, I'm Julia Flanagan." Fulfilling my dirty deed of the day, I pretend not to recognize her. "And you are . . ."

She puts her hand to her chest. "Oh! Sorry. Edith. Berry. The paralegal? I sing in your husband's band?"

I am immediately struck by her phrasing. "I *sing* in the

band." As opposed to "I sang with the band. Just that one time." I decide to dwell on this distinction.

"Yes," I say. "You sang with the band. At The Rock Barn once. You were wonderful."

"Actually, I'm now an official member of Past the Legal Limit." She puts her fingers around the word "official," as if using quotation marks would make her news any less sickening. "I've been singing with them for a while now." Pause. "I'm surprised Mike never told you."

I recover quickly. "Oh. Gosh. Yes. Of course." I thump my forehead with a fist. "I completely forgot." I'm about to say something about having a "senior moment," then stop myself. No need to remind this nymphet that Michael's wife is old enough to be her mother. I am at the terrifying point in my life where Ethel Mertz doesn't look nearly as old as I remember. Neither does Aunt Bea.

"So," I say, "how do you like it? Singing with the band."

"Oh, I *love* it. The music, being onstage. Hanging with the guys. Your husband's a riot, you know that?"

I run my hand through Vanessa again, but this time I manage to pull it loose. I feel it detach from the back of my head and try to be inconspicuous as I reclamp it to my scalp, but Edith has already noticed.

"Oh, I *love* those things," Edith says. "Marlena's Hair Fantasies. At the mall, right? Here, let me help you."

"That's okay. I've got it." A dull glint reflects off Edith's black leather pants. The smell of something musky is wafting in my direction. Her lipstick seems freshly applied.

"I bought one for my kid sister's thirteenth birthday. She wears it *constantly*. I even think she wears it to *bed*!"

"She must like it a lot." I wish she would stop being so nice. Doesn't this girl understand that she is an abomination to me? I wave vaguely in the direction of the children's section. "The kids. I should get back."

"Sure!" Edith clutches *Furious Love* a little closer to her chest. "Tell Mike I said hey."

Mike?

In the category of living dangerously: Today I look through Michael's wallet. Big deal. If I need cash I take it from my husband's wallet, and when he needs money he picks through my purse, and I did, in fact, need a few dollars. But I had also convinced myself I'd find a little love note from Edith Berry. So after I slip out a ten-dollar bill, I decide to probe more deeply, past the cash and into the little flat slots where all I find is a dry-cleaning stub and school pictures of the kids. I felt like a cat burglar, my heart beating so hard I wonder if I might propel myself into cardiac arrest. If I'd found something incriminating, I'd feel vindicated and completely justified. As it turns out, I just feel guilty.

Chapter SEVEN

I've told Michael that I want us to see a marriage counselor.

"Why do we both have to go?" he says. "I mean, if you think there's a problem, maybe you can go first and just talk things out. By yourself."

"This isn't just about me, Michael," I say, trying not to feel demoralized by his resistance. "It's us. Something's not right. I feel like, I don't know, like you're drifting away from me." I choose not to mention Edith Berry and his failure to tell me that she'd joined the band. Men don't like jealous women, I hear my mother intoning. All needy and clingy and shit.

"Maybe we should save the eighty bucks and spend an hour in bed." He slips his hand between my legs. "Better than therapy."

I remove his hand.

Michael sighs, and in that weary expulsion of carbon

dioxide I imagine him thinking, It's always something, isn't it, Julia? It's like your hair. Or the guest room, that was fine with white walls but you had to try painting a faux finish and now it looks like something out of a shantytown. Or the backyard, which was fine when there was nothing but grass, but you just had to have a *serenity* garden with a fountain, and a cutting garden with long-stemmed perennials, and a kids' vegetable garden but the fountain is full of algae and the only thing growing are prickly weeds that stain your hands yellow when you try to yank them out. The truth is, Michael is patient with and supportive of all my projects, even my ill-fated attempt to refinish the piano (don't ask).

"Okay," he says. "If it'll make you happy, I'll go."

"Don't sound so enthusiastic."

"You want me to jump for joy? I love you, Julia. But, sweetheart, I don't think there's anything wrong with our marriage."

"I do."

Nine days later we are sitting in the spartan office of Dr. Milton Fenestra, who listens patiently behind his cherry veneer desk as I describe the widening chasm between Michael and me. Dr. Fenestra has jolly eyes, silver slicked-back hair, and a green silk ascot. His nose is red as a cherry, like the custodian who got drunk and urinated on the side of the school in front of everyone in the schoolyard. Dr. Fenestra asks us if we are willing to try an "unconventional approach" to improving our relationship.

Michael is circumspect. "What did you have in mind?" he asks. I know my husband. My husband is famously claustrophobic; I know he's starting a slow panic as he considers the possibility that our therapy might involve small, dark, enclosed spaces. If Dr. Fenestra's thinking of some kind of encounter session in a closet, he can forget it.

"What I have in mind, Michael, is square dancing." A wry smile appears at the therapist's fleshy lips. He watches for our reaction.

Under the desk, Michael nudges me with the tip of his shoe, his signal for Oh, Jesus, get me the hell out of here. I ignore him.

"I want you to think of square dancing as a metaphor for marriage," Dr. Fenestra explains, cleaning his ear with the eraser end of his pencil. "It's joyful, but it's also complicated. It's not all do-si-do, you know. There's the weave, and the wave, and the squeeze. There's square the bases, chase your neighbor, reverse explode. And here's the beauty part. In square dancing, you can change partners, but you always return to the one you started with. See what I'm getting at?"

"Not really," Michael says, squirming in his seat.

I am not as irritated as my husband. I am intrigued, at worst I am somewhat disoriented; I'd come to Dr. Fenestra's office expecting—I don't know—*psychology?* I'd expected talk of absent fathers and controlling mothers, maybe even a little pep talk about the natural ebb and flow of long-term marriage, the idea that marriage is a journey with its roadblocks and potholes, et cetera.

I had not expected do-si-do.

Dr. Fenestra hands us a slip of paper. A schedule of square dance classes at the YMCA. "I recommend the

Wednesday night class. Myrna Delorio is a genius." We agree to go Wednesday night, we pay Dr. Fenestra his eighty-five dollars, we walk toward the elevator in silence. Michael folds up the slip of paper and puts it into his back pocket. He shakes his head and gives me an anguished look. "Honey. I just can't do this. Look. We're two smart, insightful people. Can't we figure this out on our own? Seriously. You want us to spend more time together? Why don't we leave the kids with my parents and go to the Caribbean? Once this trial is over. And we're done hosting the Saturday night rock jam at the Greasy Spittoon."

"Since when are you hosting the Saturday night rock jam at the Greasy Spittoon?" This is news to me.

"Um, Joe just booked the gig last week. I was going to tell you, Julia. I've been preoccupied with the trial."

"So this is every Saturday night? Every single Saturday night?"

"For the next three months, yeah. It's a great gig, Julia. We were competing with some of the best bands in town."

The Greasy Spittoon is one of only two topless bars in town. While it's true that the place has a reputation for excellent music, men who patronize the place under the pretext of hearing the band are like the guys who insist they read *Playboy* for the articles.

"So, basically you're telling me that for the next three months I'm going to be spending my Saturday nights alone because my husband is playing in a topless club?"

"I suppose you could put it that way," Michael says, "but you could also say that your husband is having great fun—possibly for the first time in his life—playing music, experiencing the camaraderie of being in a band, finding a safe outlet for the stress and frustration he experiences at work—and maybe you could also come to hear us on Saturday nights, so you're not alone. We can make a date of it."

"I think a date is when two people are actually together, in close proximity. Me being at a table and you onstage, I don't think that qualifies as a date, Michael." And what did he mean, he was having fun possibly for the first time in his life. Didn't he have fun with me? With the kids?

I feel so hopeless and defeated that I can't begin to articulate what I'm feeling, that I don't want to compartmentalize intimacy into a five-day vacation, that I wish he cared less about work and more about me, that I'm still scathed by the Susie Margolis incident and jealous of Edith Berry, that I'm afraid of getting older and losing what little physical appeal I have left, that I hate the way he becomes hypnotized by the TV, that I miss the Julie and Michael who made love until we could hear sparrows herald the dawn.

We do not sign up for Myrna Delorio's Wednesday night square dancing class, or any other class, and we never return to Dr. Fenestra.

No pad.

That's the first thing I notice when I arrive at Sotto Voce clutching my briefcase full of notes on the Mendelsohn mural, but Evan has no pad or notebook or anything to indicate that he intends to work. He has nothing at his place but a glass of ice water. I try to ignore the tendrils of guilt growing at the periphery of my conscience. I have my briefcase, I remind myself. I am here to work.

When I told Michael that I was going to Sotto Voce for a committee meeting it wasn't a total lie. Evan and I *are* committee members, and we *are* meeting on committee business. So this really is a committee meeting, isn't it? In any case, Michael doesn't seem to mind. Past the Legal Limit is playing at the Brownsburg County Public Library, and as long as I find a sitter, he doesn't much care what I do with myself. I suspect he may even be relieved that I'm busy tonight; each of us carries an unspoken accounting system in the head, a ledger where every favor is tallied, every IOU is scrupulously recorded, and every privilege is parsed. If we each have an activity that takes us away from the family, one cancels out the other. Nobody owes anyone anything.

Evan and I are finished talking about the mural by the time the waitress appears to take our order and even though I'm fully certain we won't revisit the topic during the course of our evening together, I leave my pad and pen on the table to bolster the pretext, flimsy though it may be, that we're here on business.

We spend the next two hours traversing wide-ranging conversational terrain. I tell him about the Beach Babes, my fear of flying, my fondness for chocolate-covered graham crackers, my problems with Leslie Keen. I learn that Evan Delaney played rugby in high school, considered becoming a Jesuit priest until he kissed his first girlfriend, loves tangerines and Irish music, rarely drinks, but when he does, favors bourbon over beer. He went to

Northwestern for college, Princeton for his PhD. Between his two degrees, he worked on a sheep farm in Australia and built drinking wells in Rwanda with the Peace Corps. He wasn't popular in high school and considers himself gawky. His only serious hobby is speedway racing, has competed in events in the Netherlands and the Czech Republic, and has broken his arm twice doing something called "ice racing." It isn't until later that he tells me he is a widower; his wife was killed nine years ago by a drunk driver who ran a stoplight as she was riding her bicycle. (I check his face for signs of lingering grief but he describes the story as if all his mourning is well in the past, and now it's a matter-of-fact, albeit tragic, piece of his history.) Like me, Evan never knew his father. And, like me, there are times when he feels unmoored and alone. He chose the academic life because he couldn't imagine being burdened by a conventional job. He had always wanted to study medieval literature, in particular, the poetry of courtly love.

"What *is* courtly love, exactly?" I have a vague notion of knights and ladies in towers, lyres, and paeans.

Evan doesn't say anything at first, just looks at me for a long time in a way that makes me grateful for Sotto Voce's dusky lighting because I know my neck is covered in telltale splotches.

"It was this weird historical anomaly," he says, leaning forward. "Can you imagine a time when it was actually legitimate to actively pursue another man's wife? Among the aristocracy, this kind of behavior wasn't just condoned, it was actually *expected.*"

"Why expected?" I ask, trying to ignore the bird in my

chest that frantically beats its wings against my ribs. This is an academic discussion, I tell myself, and I am a student. In fact, I should probably be taking notes. I cock my head and try to look studious. And I try not to let my eyes linger on Evan Delaney's chest, broad and hard beneath his ribbed sweater.

"In a way, it makes sense. The only real love back then was the love of God, divinely inspired, spiritually fulfilling. Now comes this radical notion that maybe love could exist not just between man and God, but between man and woman. They called it *ideal* love. But it wasn't the kind of love you'd find within marriage. Marriage wasn't about love, it was about mergers and acquisitions. It was a business arrangement. Ideal love could only logically exist outside of marriage." Michael signals the waiter for another bottle of wine. I haven't touched my chicken piccata. I am nauseous with guilt and attraction.

"If I were your courtly lover"—now I feel the earth give way beneath me even though Evan continues in a relatively pedagogic way—"the fact that you're married wouldn't be an impediment to me. Your status as another man's wife would, in fact, be a prerequisite."

"Fascinating," I say, knowing in my heart that we've moved well beyond the bounds of committee business.

"Courtly love," Evan continues, circling the rim of his wineglass with a fingertip, "is a lost art." His eyes seem to linger on my lips, which tingle and swell in response. "If I were your courtly lover, I'd exist to please you. I'd compose epic poems in your honor. I'd joust just for your pleasure. I'd stand outside your bedroom window in the freezing rain only for a fleeting glimpse of your face.

You'd be the first thought in my head when I arise, and the last when I lay my body down for the night. You'd be the center of my universe. And I guarantee, Julia, it would be the singlemost pleasurable experience of your life."

The blood rushes to my head. I suddenly feel very warm and very woozy. I check my watch. "Oh. Gosh. I should go." I grab my pad and pen. "I promised Jake—that's my son, I have three kids, he's my youngest—I promised him I'd read him an extra bedtime story tonight. He'll never forgive me if I don't make it home in time." I am hot and confused. I stand to leave and feel my legs wobble beneath me.

"Are you sure you're okay to drive?" Evan steadies me with a strong hand and my arm burns in the spot he'd gripped.

"I'll be fine," I say, knowing that it isn't the wine that has me in this state, but his hot gaze and the penetrating intensity of his words.

Over the years I have developed an ever-expanding database of my husband's snores. I classify them in the spreadsheet of my miserable sleepless mind according to type, duration, rhythm. There is the Popper and B-52, the asthmatic pug, the ratchet wrench, the freight train, and the draining bathtub.

Tonight it's the Popper, the most maddening of all. At the end of each exhale, his breath is released between slightly parted lips, creating a "pah" sound. Sissssss-pah. Sissssss-pah. Sissss-pah. Sisssss-pah. Unlike the B-52, which is vicious and loud but short-lived, the Popper can last all night. I try to roll him over but he is immovable. In desperation I reach around his head and try sticking a finger in his mouth to part his lips, but he defensively clamps them shut and resumes the sissssss-pah. I've counted his snores like sheep. I've tried to imagine them as waves gently rocking me to sleep. I've pretended that the snoring is a new form of sleep therapy. When I can stand it no longer, I drag myself out of bed, shuffle into Michael's study, and go online. I search the phrase "snoring husband relief." There are 14,660 results, not including the boxed advertisements along the margins. I click through the first ten, then find a site that calls itself "The Official Online Store for Victims of Snoring Partners (VSP)." Here I find everything from two-dollar neon yellow foam earplugs to sixty-dollar white noise machines. I order both, pay the extra for overnight shipping, stick wet toilet paper into my ears, and stagger back to bed.

I try to ignore Michael's snoring and count my blessings instead. I remember all the reasons why I am lucky to be married to this man. I love how he dressed up as Captain Hook for Jake's second birthday party, even though it made all the kids, including Lucy, flee screaming. I love the fact that he spent most of his career defending poor people, that he's the first to dance at weddings, and the last to leave parties because he always volunteers to help clean up. I love the way he wraps birthday presents—horribly, but with sincerity. He kills big bugs on my behalf and is always at the ready with the back of a shoe; I even called him out of a shower once to crush a menacing silverfish and he bounded out, naked and dripping and squashed it with his thumb.

I must have fallen asleep eventually because the next thing I know, Caitlin is tugging my hand and yelling, "Wake up, Mom! We're going to miss the bus!" I've overslept and Michael has already left for work.

"We want a full accounting," says Annie, snapping her fingers in the air. "Don't hold anything back."

A midseason gathering of the Beach Babes minus the beach. We assemble in Frankie Wilson's newly remodeled basement. Husband and kids have been banished for the evening from this subterranean hideaway, with its oak bar, limestone fireplace, and sandy Berber carpeting. A brand-new snooker table sits in one corner, a gleaming air hockey game in another, and a big-screen plasma TV shares a wall with a digital music system and at least three hundred CDs and DVDs. Then I notice the humidor and remember that this elegantly appointed walk-out basement is Jeremy's domain. Tiny like a jockey but strikingly handsome, Jeremy Wilson is a pediatric enterologist with a taste for Cuban cigars and slick gadgets.

Confession: I used to like Jeremy more than I do now. I assumed that his ready investment in Frankie's business ventures was a sign of love and support, but now I have another theory: If Frankie is busy with *Fat Lady* magazine or her disposable frying pan liners or whatever entrepreneurial disaster she's dreamed up, she won't notice how much time he spends at Starbucks with his energetic new receptionist, the one with the big eyes and big breasts and big lips just like Angelina Jolie's. I saw them together three weeks ago and even though they were only talking, something didn't look so kosher. Jeremy was leaning forward in his seat, his hands nearing hers on the table. I never said anything to Frankie because I didn't want to stir things up and besides, it's really none of my business.

My friend has done her best to replicate the decadently caloric self-indulgence of our beach vacations by packing the refrigerator behind the bar with Tequizas, heaping the coffee table with platters of flaky spanakopita, skewered teriyaki chicken, goat cheese, and sundried tomato bruschetta. Dessert is port, chocolate truffles, and a shallow platter of fortune cookies waiting for us on the bar.

"Somebody else go first," I say, sensing what could be the beginning of a panic attack.

Frankie leans into me, wraps an arm around my shoulders, and gives me an encouraging squeeze. "Come on, sweetie. Talk to us. Are you living dangerously?"

"You could call it that." I take a deep breath. "You want to know how far I've fallen?" I chase an olive around my martini glass with the tip of a crystal swizzle stick. "The cashier at Target charged me only $5.50 for overalls when I knew for a fact they were $19.99 and I didn't say a word. I ate all the marshmallow charms in the Lucky Charms cereal and when the kids complained, I told them it must have been a defective box. And as Annie already knows because she CONVINCED me to DO it, I bought the kids a rat and told my husband it was a dwarf Norwegian flat-coated guinea pig, which doesn't even exist."

"Bravo!" cheers Annie, clapping. "Huge improvement."

"Anything else?" Frankie prompts.

"Yes." I close my eyes. This is hard. Say it, Julia. Say it. "I find myself very attracted to someone."

"The UPS guy?" asks Annie.

I can feel heat flood my neck and face. I immediately regret having started this. Saying it will make it real. My friends will be happy for me and that will only aggravate my remorse.

"No, not the UPS guy," I say slowly, surveying my friends' faces and steering my ship of lies onto a new course. "I'm attracted to a saxophone player," I say, forcing what I hope will come off as a mischievous smile. "He plays in a band. And I'm his only groupie."

Annie throws a peanut M&M at my head. "Oh, *you.* I can't believe I almost fell for that."

"And how *does* it feel to sleep with a member of the band?" Frankie asks.

"Groovy." I don't mention that Michael and I haven't had sex in a while.

"Hey. When's he playing again?" Frankie asks.

"I suppose he's okay. I mean, he's having a good time and it makes him happy, that's really all that counts, right?" I sound far more virtuous than I feel. "The band plays again next Friday. One of Michael's partners got them a gig. At the Crappie Festival. All the crappies you can eat, just $6.99 a person. Bring your own beer."

"My kind of party," Frankie says, circling her finger in whoop-dee-doo fashion. "All the crappies you can eat. Imagine that."

The Crappie Festival is one of the major events of the year, though I wish they'd come up with a better name. In the Great Lakes region the very same fish is called white perch. The Latin name isn't bad: *Pomoxis annularis.* But here in Indiana it's strictly *crappie.* "What are we having for dinner, darling?" "We're having a great big platter of fried crappie! Pick up a fork and dig in!" Never mind that locals insist it's pronounced *croppie.* It still looks like crappie to me.

"Sounds fun! You know, I was just thinking, we really need to do more of the county stuff," Annie says. "I haven't taken the kids to a 4H fair in, like, twelve years. And we *totally* missed the rhubarb parade."

It's an ongoing issue, this great town-gown divide. Faculty and corporate types on one side, all clustered within city limits in big houses and tiny barren lots, and the farmers and factory workers outside the city, in tiny houses on hundreds of lush acres. Different area codes, different school districts, different ways of amusing ourselves. They have crappie festivals and we have crappy classic rock bands composed of bald lawyers and one sexy paralegal I'd like to kill.

"Ooh! Let's do it!" Frankie squeals. "It'll give me a chance to wear my DKNY overalls *finally,* they're just sitting in my closet *rotting,* I don't even think I took the *price* tags off. And a straw cowboy hat, little red bandana, get that whole Ellie May thing going."

"Ellie May didn't wear overalls," I say. "She wore short shorts."

"Not an option," Frankie says. "Hey, I say we make it a Beach Babes road trip!"

"I'm in," Annie says. "I just want to hear Michael play again. I think I can do without fried crappies."

I push back into Frankie's plush sofa. "I think I've

contributed more than my share tonight." I am thinking of everything I didn't say. "Somebody else go."

"Okay," says Annie, reaching for a spanakopita. "I told Kelly London that my father's family descended from Alexander Hamilton."

"Did he?" I ask.

"Are you kidding? My father's family came off the boat in 1937. That's why my dad's named Ellis. As in the island."

Kelly London is one of those genealogy freaks, always blabbing about how she traced her family back to King Henry IV, and how her ancestors came off the *Mayflower* in 1620 and how she's related to William Bradford, leader of the Plymouth Community, and how her foremothers taught Indian squaws how to make sweet potato pie.

Kelly London has never asked me about my father, but if she did, I would want to tell her that he died in combat before I was born. I'd want to construct an entirely new genealogy for myself, a family history so spectacular it would make Kelly London's eyes explode in their sockets. As I build my lie taller and taller in my head I actually feel myself becoming that person, a woman whose family history filled her with pride and prestige, a woman whose father died a hero, not a woman like me, who doesn't even know her father's name, who carries family shame like a bag of bricks across her back.

"But don't you feel guilty?" I ask Annie.

"Guilt isn't in my vocabulary, sweetie, and I suggest you strike it from yours as well." She props her feet up on the ottoman and wiggles her long toes. "Isn't this a great pedicure?"

We finish off the Tequizas and move on to Diet Coke, and now it is Frankie's turn to check in. "I don't have any dirty deeds to confess, but I do have an exciting announcement, and no, I'm not pregnant." Frankie retrieves the platter of fortune cookies from the bar and passes it around. "It's an idea for a new product."

"Yet another innovation from the brain trust of Frankie Wilson, entrepreneur extraordinaire." Annie views Frankie's business ventures with affection and amusement. "What is it this time?"

"You're holding it." She's pointing at the fortune cookie. "It looks like an ordinary fortune cookie, but wait 'til you see what's inside. Go ahead. Open it."

We crack our cookies apart and pull out the paper strips inside. Annie reads hers first. " 'Your unresolved family of origin issues will come to a head this holiday season.' "

Frankie opens hers next. "Oh! I love this one! 'A thorny someone in your life is actually bipolar. Be compassionate and tread lightly.' "

She claps her hands. "Get it? Therapy fortune cookies! Coming to a Chinese restaurant near you. Don't you love it?"

"Are they really coming to a Chinese restaurant near me?" Annie asks.

"Well, no, not yet, exactly. The problem is, the Chinese restaurants already have their suppliers. There's a lot of loyalty there, you know. So I'm having a little trouble breaking in. Plus they don't exactly understand the concept. You know, it's not easy explaining therapy to a non-English speaker."

"I think it's a great idea," I say. "Forget the Chinese restaurants. How about something more offbeat and, I don't know, experimental. Like that burrito place downtown, the one with all the kitschy Elvis stuff." I snap my cookie in half and pull out my fortune. "Let's see here. 'You are sexually attracted to a tall, dark stranger but he is only a projection of your shadow self. Beware.' "

Chapter EIGHT

Leslie Keen is off on one of her Sex on the Seas seminars, in which she and a boatload of university retirees take a cruise to Cancun while discussing "Foreplay in the 21st Century" and playing shuffleboard. Meanwhile I'm evaluating Kiren Parnell's proposal for an exhibit on burlesque queens of the forties and fifties. Though these gals were undoubtedly the inspiration for many a wet dream, they are chaste by today's standards, June Cleavers in fishnet and pasties, with their perfectly coiffed hair and overdone eyebrows. Princess Tom-Tom, with her titanic feathered headdress, painted tom-tom, and one-piece bathing suit. Bubbles Coquette, "America's most exciting bosom," is wearing what looks like a Mardi Gras mask with giant ram's horns. Franki Valone is billed as an "exotic danseuse"; her specialty is the "dance of the sacred parrot." Greta Goodly, "the Farmer's Daughter," has six big brass cowbells attached to her panties. Most of these women would be in their late seventies or eighties by now. I wonder if any of them are still alive and whether their bodies have held up. I feel sad. I need fresh air. I slide the photos and pad into a big manila folder and take my work outside.

"Julia!"

I turn, but see no one. I hear it again. "Julia!"

I look up to see Evan Delaney standing at his crank-case window, grinning at me. He is shielding his eyes from the sun with one hand, holding a black mug with the other.

"Taking a break?"

I nod. Even at this distance, I can see the divot in his chin.

"Come up and have a cup of Turkish coffee with me," he calls out, waving his mug. "I just made a fresh pot."

"I can't." I wave my folder in the air. "I've got a ton of work. I'm already running behind."

"Ten minutes. Please. Just enough to revive you." He smiles again. "I insist." Then, plaintively, "I've been grading papers and I'm ready to climb the walls. I need the distraction. Please, Julia."

I don't really need the revivifying effects of coffee but how could I resist the "Please, Julia"? I climb the three flights to his office, brace myself at the top landing, and wait for my breathing to assume a normal rhythm. I don't want Evan to see me panting like a fat plumber.

He meets me at the door with a steaming mug. "There you go."

Evan is wearing jeans and a black T-shirt advertising the East Newark Motorcycle Club. He smells of pipe tobacco and spice and something else, something natural and warm and entirely male. I look out through the windows, down to the spot where I'd stood only moments ago, on the stone path from which I should never have strayed.

"Nice view," I say. I work very hard not to notice too much about that office. I don't want to absorb anything. I want to leave there as clean and smooth as when I'd walked in.

Evan Delaney's office looks designed for quiet contemplation. Two chairs near the window, two bookcases filled to capacity, a healthy ficus, a happy spider plant that hangs from the ceiling and trails to the floor. There are two framed prints; one a lush woodland scene in greens and golds, the other a black and white portrait of John Coltrane. He hands me a speckled gray mug with a sculpted handle. On closer inspection I see that the handle is in the form of a nymph, arms outstretched above her head, back arched, naked. I slip my finger around her elongated waist.

"A gift from May Jones-Clayton at Oxford." Then, as if in response to my jealous musing, he adds, "She gave one to all the discussants. Rather nice, isn't it?"

"Very." I settle into a threadbare wingchair and take a sip. I've never had Turkish coffee before. It smells inviting. It tastes like dirt. I try not to grimace.

He gestures toward my Vanessa and squints. "What's that about?"

"Oh, this?" I reach up to touch the ponytail. "Nothing. A clip-on thing. Just until my, you know, perm grows out."

"I see." Evan sips his coffee and keeps his eyes on me. His stare feels like a laser beam. "Uh, I'm assuming your husband didn't approve of the curls?"

"He hates it." I should feel guilty for sharing this. I don't.

"Oh."

I notice for the first time a chipped front tooth and I am mesmerized by that tooth. I imagine feeling its contours with my tongue. I bite the inside of my cheek to stop these thoughts. Jesus, God. What is happening to me? I don't want to look at him, his mouth, his chipped tooth, his strong hand gripping the mug, the way a few curly black hairs peek from the top of his T-shirt. I force myself to fix my eyes on the painting over his desk.

Evan follows my gaze. "Betrayal of Arthur," he says. "I bought it at a flea market in London." He points to a couple embracing on the forest's mossy floor. "Do you know who they are?"

"Tell me," I say.

"Well, that one's Lancelot, most noble and courageous of the Knights of the Round Table. The naked woman in his arms, that's Guinevere, beloved wife of Arthur, the most honored woman in Camelot."

"They look like they're having, uh, fun."

"Yes." Evan points to a small figure at the bottom of the canvas, partly hidden behind verdant branches, a quiver of arrows slung over his back. "How about this fellow over here? Do you know who he is?"

"I'm assuming that's Arthur?"

"Yes. He is lying in wait."

"Why?"

"Well, according to legend, Arthur suspects, rightly, that his wife and favorite knight are lovers." (This word, "lovers," from this mouth is enough to trigger a full-body flush.) I arrange my face into a facsimile of composure. "So he tells everyone he's going hunting. And he is, though not for game. He's hunting for the truth. And as you can see by this painting, he is about to find it."

I stare at the picture, and for a moment I see my husband there at the bottom of the canvas, hiding behind a bush, balding head and khaki Dockers.

"I really should get back to work," I say.

"Of course." Evan jumps to his feet.

"Thanks for the coffee."

"The pleasure," he says as he walks me to the door, "was all mine." As I reach for the doorknob a photograph slips from my folder and falls to the floor. Evan bends down to retrieve it. He turns it over. "Ah. Lorelie, the lovely and charismatic girl in the clamshell," he reads aloud.

We stand there for a moment, awkwardly, while Lorelie, with her soft curves and conical pasty'd breasts, looks back at us. I take the postcard from his hands and stick it into my book.

As I reach for the doorknob, Evan steps back to pull something off his desk. "Ah! I almost forgot." He hands me a folded sheet of paper. He shoves his hands in his pockets and encourages me with a tilt of his square, stubbly chin. "Go ahead. Take it."

"What is it?"

"It's an idea for an exhibit. At the Bentley. You can read it later." He pushes a stray curly lock out of my eyes, a gesture so dear and loving I want to scream. "I don't think the Bentley's done anything on courtly love, am I right? I thought it might be, uh, interesting. To work with you. On this. I mean, I was thinking, my chair wants to see more interdisciplinary work. This seems perfect. Don't you think?"

"I do."

"Really?"

"Yes. Really."

"It just came to me. I was preparing for class, reading this poem which I've probably read a hundred times before, it's one of my favorites, and I thought of you. And then I thought of the Bentley, and well, that's when it came to me."

I try not to dwell on the fact that one of his favorite poems made him think of me. He thinks of me when he's working. He thinks of *me.* Stop it, Julia. This is a business conversation. Evan is proposing an exhibit idea to the assistant director of the Bentley. I'll mention it to Leslie and if she likes it, we will move forward. It's all very straightforward. With any luck she'll hate the idea and I won't have to see Evan Delaney again.

I find myself wondering whether he likes to sleep late, eat breakfast, read the paper in the morning, if he drives with both hands on the wheel or just one. And then, when I allow myself, the other questions: What does his mouth taste like? What does he wear to sleep? A T-shirt and underwear, just bottoms, or nothing at all? Does he have sex with his eyes open or closed? And when I'm feeling especially daring, I wonder how he looks when he comes.

Eyes closed or open? Any noise or words? Does he fall asleep right away or rouse himself for more?

"Oh, JULES, it's FABulous." Leslie is wearing a pink Chanel suit, opalescent hose, and pink pumps. I can never decide if my boss looks fashionable or if she looks like an after-dinner mint. "And PERfect timing! There's a new grant out of the dean's office. Interdisciplinary Education in Art. IDEA grant, very clever. Partly funded by the Bean Family Foundation. Wait a second. I have it right here." Leslie spins around in her chair and clicks the mouse. "Wait. Wait. No, that's not it. Fuck it. Wait! Here." She clicks a few more times and begins reading aloud. "IDEA grant interdisciplinary blah blah excellence in educational approaches to blah blah promoting the academic unification of distinct blah blah blah yada yada yada the usual crap." She turns back to me. "It's ours if we want it. The whole medieval thing's very fundable right now. And all the other proposals suck."

"How do you know?"

"Let's just say I have my sources in the dean's office. The guy can't give head to save his life. But he makes a great Spanish omelette." She turns back to the computer, a few more clicks. "Shit. FUCK. It's due Friday. Can you get me something by Friday? Nothing fancy. I'll write the grant. I can do it in my sleep, for Christ's sake. I just need *something* to go on. Please, Jules? I'll be your best friend for life."

I'm not sure what to expect when I unfold the paper Evan gave me. What if it isn't a medieval poem but a love letter, a passionate declaration, or something explicitly sexual? But when I finally allow myself a glimpse I see that it is in German.

I find Evan's office number in the campus directory. "There's a problem," I say, fully aware that this new project gives me license to call him anytime I crave his voice, which I don't plan to do but the option is tantalizing. "This poem, it's in German."

"It is? Oh. Sorry. I meant to give you the translation. I've got it right here on my desk. Why don't you stop by? Or I can drop it off."

"No, that's okay," I say, rubbing my wedding band like a talisman. I don't want to see him. I already feel myself slipping and I can't let it happen, not me, not ever. "Just put it in campus mail. No rush."

I look again at the poem, letting my eyes scan the hard consonants and clipped syllables in search of a familiar word. I've always been fairly good with languages. I decide to try decoding it myself, now. The prospect of finding some provocative message in Evan's note is too thrilling to bear. My heart thumps as I climb the dark stairwell to the Bentley library, sequester myself in a carrel in the back, and begin picking apart the paragraph with a German-English dictionary I've found in the reference section.

Is aber daz dir wol gelinget, so daz ein guot wip din genade hat, hei waz dir danne froiden bringet, so si sunder wer vor dir gestat, halsen, triuten, bi gelegen.

In forty minutes I have only managed to get through the first few words and there is no love message hidden here. In fact, the passage makes no sense. "However with it hope for success, with it one guot (?) recover or recuperate from thence with your . . ." This cannot be modern German.

I am ready to abandon the project. Then I remember Mrs. Hoffman who owns the German bakery. I recall that she offhandedly referred to her "other life" when she taught Germanic languages and linguistics at the University at Gottingen. She and Albert were fired in 1935. They fled first to Cuba, then the United States in 1956. "We didn't care so much about losing our jobs," she told me. "We were happy to escape with our lives. Professor, baker, I care? As long as we were alive, and we were together."

Albert Hoffman died of a heart attack last year and Nina took over the shop, the only real bakery left in this town, all the rest having been extinguished by chain supermarkets and their fake bakery departments where nothing is ever mixed from scratch, just thawed and heated or simply transferred from the back of a truck. I loved everything about Hoffman's, the heavily shellacked, slopey hardwood floors, the prim white cardboard boxes and the thin cotton string used to secure them, the air, thick and spicy and intoxicating, the display cases filled with honeyed loaves of hutzelbrot and hazelbrot, the nutty rum-glazed pfeffernuesse cookies and raspberry-filled linzer tortes.

"Let's see what we have here." Mrs. Hoffman adjusts the reading glasses she wears on a beaded chain around her neck. "Ah yes. Old German. Probably written sometime between 800 and 1500." She begins to read. "Should it happen that you are successful and a sweet woman grants your request . . ." She looks at me.

"Go on, go on," I implore.

Mrs. Hoffman's pale freckled fingers flutter at the nape of her neck. "And a sweet woman grants your request, oh, what joys await you when"—she pauses for a breath—"when she stands defenseless before you. Embracing, fondling, lying with her." Mrs. Hoffman folds the page and returns it to me. "*Interessant.*"

"Yes. Isn't it? Very interesting." My skull is reeling with the idea that this poem made Evan think of me. "Really, really interesting. I work at the Bentley Institute, you know."

She peers at me. "Ah. I see," she says, austerely.

"We have pages and pages of letters like this. Yes. Pages and pages." I can hear myself babbling. "Yes, indeed. We sure do. From all over the world. Germany, India, Spain, China. You don't speak Mandarin, by any chance? Do you? Hah-ha. Just kidding."

Mrs. Hoffman is still leveling her eyes at me. "How is your husband, Mrs. Flanagan? Such a nice man."

"Michael? He's fine. He's just fine. Thank you for asking, Mrs. Hoffman. That's very kind of you to ask. And yes, he is a very nice man."

"Take care of him, Mrs. Flanagan."

I can't eat dinner tonight and I cannot sleep. I have the chills, then hot flashes, followed by piercing cramps. I remember Evan telling me that Ovid described love as a sickness with observable symptoms. I lie in bed and listen to Michael's B-52 and wonder what my friends would say if they knew about Evan Delaney. Would they think that this little experiment in living dangerously had gone too far? Or not far enough?

• • •

The thirty-second annual Crappie Festival is exactly the way I'd envisioned it. Hot, buggy, packed with people and stinking of fish. We'd driven in Frankie's white Escalade that sticks out like a pair of Blahniks among the Dodge and Ford long-bed pickups and now we're trudging across the gravel parking lot, Frankie leading the pack in her farmer's daughter getup.

Michael had arrived early to set up and wouldn't go on for another hour. The gazebo is empty except for the instruments and amplifiers. I see my husband's old saxophone propped against a beam. There's also a microphone stand in the center of the stage. I send up a quick prayer. Please, Lord, don't let it be Edith Berry. Let it be that big fat guy who owns the tattoo parlor, the one who looks like Orson Welles and sings like Steve Tyler. Or if it has to be a woman, how about Helen Zimp, who sang with the band at the last open mike gig; *she's* got a great voice and I happen to know that she's in a happy, long-term lesbian relationship.

"I see him!" Frankie calls out. "I see Michael! Over there!"

"Where?" I'm roasting in my long-sleeved rayon shirt and my thighs are beginning to chafe.

"Over there. With the—" Frankie stops herself. Then, reluctantly, "With the girl in the bra. A girl that looks like Catherine Zeta-Jones."

Michael and Edith are sitting on a picnic bench, elbow to elbow, reading something on a clipboard. They're probably just looking over their list of songs, maybe making a few last-minute adjustments.

"That's not a bra, Frankie," I say. "It's a halter top."

"Sure looks like a bra to me," Frankie mumbles as we get closer.

"That's Edith," I say. "She sings with Michael's band."

"Is that *all* she does with Michael's band?" Frankie sniggers.

"Enough," says Annie.

I must admit, it *does* look like Edith is wearing a bra or maybe a bathing-suit top. I'd wanted to see Michael before the show and wish him luck, but upon reconsideration it's probably best not to talk to him now. I know how he gets before he performs. He says he goes into what he calls "The Zone" before every performance, some kind of Zen-like state of intense focus. I've learned by now that The Zone doesn't have room for The Wife so I suggest we check out the quilt booth.

The band has assembled itself onstage and at precisely twelve o'clock Amos Brewster Jr., president of the Rotary Club, takes the stage. It is disorienting to see Amos Brewster in a bright orange T-shirt and long, baggy shorts that expose his fat, veiny legs. Amos Brewster is a loan officer at the First Federal bank and until today I have never seen him in anything but dull gray suits.

"Well, I've got to admit, I wanted the bluegrass band we had last year, but I'm not on the music committee so I guess I don't get a vote."

I want to force myself to laugh but it's too hot. Amos mops the sweat from his forehead with a white handkerchief and holds up his hands.

"Just kidding. Actually, Joe Patterson's a good buddy of mine, and when he told me he had himself a rock band, I said, Joe, you gotta play the Crappie Festival, because we'll give you a mighty warm reception and all the fried crappie you can eat. Am I right, ladies and gentlemen? So join me, please, in welcoming Past the Legal Limit!"

A faint cheer dribbles through the crowd. Amos wipes his thick neck and steps gingerly down the plank steps. The band opens with "Long Train Runnin' " and then Edith appears from the back of the stage and grabs the microphone off the stand. She is lithe as a gymnast, is wearing a short red skirt and platform sandals, and, of course, the halter/bra thing that just barely covers her areolas, and she's wiggling her rear end and shimmying her boobs and singing and sweating and draping her arms around the various band members and at one point drops to her knees and sings real close to the mouth of Michael's sax while he thrusts his hips in a kind of mock display of fellatio and I think I'm going to have a heart attack. Now I know why Michael hasn't been interested in sex. He's already having it, here onstage, where there is passion and throbbing energy and sweat and crescendos and climaxes, one after the other. Here is where he finds the connection, the intimacy, the power and release. Not with me, not in our bed.

"Sexy girl," Frankie mutters. "Should we shoot her or strangle her?"

Frankie doesn't have much patience for young flirty things, not since her first husband had a three-night stand with a Steak 'n Shake waitress while Frankie was visiting her ailing father in Salt Lake City. Frankie came home unexpectedly early and found them both naked in the kitchen foraging in the fridge for a post-sex snack.

"It's okay, Frankie," I say, trying not to cry. "She's a singer. They're performing."

"Sure they are," says Frankie.

Edith is holding a bottle of Corona in one hand, a lit cigarette in the other. Somewhere in the middle of "Brown Sugar," she leans forward, pulls the cigarette out of her mouth, and holds it to Michael's lips while he takes a drag.

I have never seen my husband smoke.

I feel a clawing inside my chest, the force of rage and confusion fighting to rip through me. I will not cry. I will not cry. I will not cry. Not now. Not here. I insist on going home before the show ends and we're halfway to Frankie's Escalade when I hear gravel crunching behind me. It's Michael, panting and looking concerned. "Hey. Hon. Are you okay? Why are you leaving? We still have another set."

"I'm feeling a little . . ."

"She's feeling a little *overwhelmed,*" Frankie says, glaring at him.

Michael looks confused. "What do you mean?"

"When did you start smoking?" I said, trying to sound casual but wanting to tear out what little hair my husband has left.

"Is that it? You saw me take a puff of a cigarette? Oh, honey, sweetie, it's nothing, it's just part of the act. I don't even inhale."

"Don't worry about it," I say, backing away. "It's nothing. I'm just a little, you know, the heat. I'll see you back at the house, okay?"

"Can I bring you back anything?" I can't decide if the offer is sincere or guilt-ridden. "Ice cream? Aspirin? Anything?"

"I'm fine. Have a nice show. Break a leg, okay?" I realize that my friends have flanked me like a couple of bodyguards.

"Hey, don't forget I won't be home 'til late tonight," he calls out. "We still have that gig at the American Legion hall."

"Yeah, right," I say, weakly. I go home to feed, bathe, and cuddle the kids and then, thanks to a sleeping pill and hot bath, I am out within thirty minutes. The next morning I decide not to mention anything to Michael. I tell him that he was spectacular at the Crappie Festival and I go to work knowing that I will see Evan Delaney and all will be right with the world.

Chapter NINE

One week has passed since the Crappie Festival and I feel more turmoil than ever but not because of my husband or Edith Berry or gnawing memories of Susie Margolis, which are all bad enough but not the worst of it. The worst is that my head throbs with fantasies of Evan Delaney and the guilt is unbearable. If I keep this to myself any longer I swear to God it's all going to come shooting out of the top of my head like a Roman candle. I must talk to Annie, dear Annie, sturdy and stable Annie, pillar of church and community, confidante, counsel of, and comforter.

We meet at the Freedom Café, a vegetarian restaurant that first opened its doors thirty years ago by hippies who had moved here for college and never left. The restaurant bears few of its early trademarks: Even the original vegetarian menu has been expanded to include fish, free-range chicken, and buffalo burgers. The waiters are no longer touchy-feely weavers and sculptors. They are aspiring actors who comport themselves like pampered house cats, bored and aloof and frequently hostile. When Annie asks for the standard basket of rolls, our skeletal waitress says nothing but arches a single eyebrow and steps away. Eventually she reappears with the bread and drops it on the table with a loud sigh. Annie lifts the napkin and notices that there is no butter, but we're both too scared of the waitress to say anything.

"So, what's going on, my friend?" Annie splits open a warm roll and inhales the steam.

This is like jumping off a diving board. It would have been so easy to turn around, but I'd gotten myself to this point and had to force myself to step forward and plunge in.

"Remember when I said I was attracted to someone?"

"You weren't talking about your husband, were you?"

"No. I wasn't." My face is burning. "Oh, God, Annie, this is so stupid. It's embarrassing. I'm such an idiot."

Annie puts her hands over mine. "You're not an idiot. You're a wonderful person and you're trying very hard to be a good wife. Whatever you're feeling, Julia, it's allowed. Can you please believe me when I say that?"

I nod feebly. Then I tell her about Evan. She asks me if we'd kissed and I say no, of course not. She asks if we'd touched and I say no, not intentionally. She asks me what I like about him, and I am filled with warmth and light as I tell her that he is kind and attentive, handsome and interesting. But what I like most about Evan Delaney, I say, is that he actually wants to *be* with me. I am attracted to him, and I am attracted to his attraction to me.

"He likes my perm," I say, "and my orange sweater." I can feel my head flooding with tears.

"That's okay, that's okay," Annie says. "You're married. You're not dead. Who wouldn't enjoy that kind of attention from a great-looking guy? But look. Julia. The important thing is, you're not acting on it. You're just basking in it. What's so wrong about that?"

"Because I *want* to act on it." I tell her about the poem, the one that made him think of me.

"So maybe he's flirting with you. It keeps life interesting. You're not allowed to flirt back? So you want him. Big deal."

"It *is* a big deal, Annie. I'm a married woman."

"Well, how about your marriage, Julia? Are you guys okay? You don't think there's anything going on with that singer girl, do you, whatever her name is, the one with the bra."

"Edith Berry. No. Michael's not like that. And it wasn't a bra, it was a halter top."

"You sure he's not messing around?"

"Yes, I'm sure."

But, honestly, how could I be? After the Susie Margolis Incident, anything is possible. Maybe having an affair is like crack cocaine. You've got to have it again. I've read the magazine articles, I've heard the horror stories passed around at The Hairport, wonderful husbands dropping bombshells, destroying families, remarrying, having babies with younger wives. Look what happened to Alexis Merriweather. Alexis and Paul, married nineteen years, the *perfect* couple, and I don't just mean because they looked good together, which they did, but because they were friends. They actually did things as a team, like build a canoe in their garage, take a Chinese cooking class, go on a cross-country bed-and-breakfast tour while the kids were in summer camp. Michael and I couldn't even manage laying self-stick tile in the basement bathroom without bickering. Then one day I see Alexis in Borders reading a book with a title like *Leave Him Without a Pot to Piss In: A Smart Woman's Guide to Divorce.* I heard through The Hairport grapevine that Paul e-mailed Alexis one day (yes, *e-mailed*) to say that he was moving out and nothing could stop him; he'd been having an affair with their dog groomer and had never been happier. It reminded me of that poor woman in New York who was killed when an air conditioner fell on her head. Alexis never saw it coming.

"At least I don't think he's fooling around. But he does have this new life with the band, this exciting new life." I feel the pressure of tears building behind my eyes. "I guess I just feel left out."

Annie smiles and raises a finger in the air. "Wait a second. Wait a second. I'm getting an idea here."

"What?"

"Why can't *you* be part of Michael's new life?"

"What do you mean?"

"I mean, you could sing with Michael's band. I've heard you sing, Julia. You have a *beautiful* voice. You could show up on open mike night or whatever they call it and blow them all away. Your husband will see this sexy creature up on that stage and he won't be able to take his hands off you."

"You really think so?" I hadn't sung publicly since

ninth grade, when I was in a girl band called Raspberry Sorbet. I played electric guitar (passably) and sang (nicely) "Bennie and the Jets" and "Billy, Don't Be a Hero." With my best friend Jenny Thurmon on drums and Carrie McQueen on bass, we won second place in Thomas Edison Middle School's battle of the bands, and then played in a variety show to benefit the animal shelter. The band broke up when Carrie got a boyfriend, I never forgot how it felt to be onstage. I was in a *band.* People *applauded* me. I was a *star.*

In the category of living dangerously: I peeked at Michael's e-mail box. Okay, I didn't exactly peek. I hacked into his system and then sorted his messages by sender: VeryBerry1979. I know that some people might be appalled at my spying but after that oral sex routine at the Crappie Festival, I should be checking his e-mail every day as far as I'm concerned. No guilt whatsoever.

There were seventeen messages from Edith. All were related to band activity but as I read them more closely I could detect an increasingly intimate tone and developing relationship.

E-mail #4: You sounded great last night!

E-mail #7: How's your cold?

E-mail #14: Does Frank seem depressed to you?

My eyes rested bleakly on the last message from Edith: Want to grab lunch today?

I was about to check my husband's Sent box to see how he responded to these queries but I hear the garage door rumble open and quickly log off.

• • •

Lucy wants a Calico Girls birthday party. I do not. I have already spent more money than I am willing to admit on Calico Girls and all their Calico crap. Lucy has eight Calico Girl dolls such as Donna, the rancher Calico Girl, and Alisa, the factory worker Calico Girl. Her closet is packed with giant blue Rubbermaid bins full of Calico Girl accessories, most of which she played with twice and abandoned. Now she's at my elbow, haranguing me about a Kelani Calico Girl Hawaiian luau party.

"Look at all this cool stuff," she says, pointing to the catalog. "You get grass skirts and flower necklaces, plates and cups and those pink straws shaped like pineapples. And look at this, Mom, a real plastic Hawaiian tablecloth, and a tape that teaches you how to dance the hula."

I take a closer look at the catalog. The price of Kelani's Hawaiian Calico Girl party? Just $175 plus shipping and handling. "Oh, honey. I don't think so." My daughter doesn't handle disappointment well. She is already starting to hyperventilate. "This is an awful lot of money for a birthday party. Hey. You know what? I bet I could buy every single thing on this list at that store in the mall, what's it called? The Party Place?"

Lucy's lower lip is already quivering. "But I want a *Calico Girl* birthday party."

"But it'll be exactly the same stuff, honey. The same grass skirts, the same flower necklaces. Just not so expensive. I bet I can get all the same pretty luau things for forty bucks, maybe less, at the party supplies store."

"But it *won't* be the same. You'll *never* find a tape of hula music."

"I bet I can. I bet they have it at the library."

"No they *don't.* They don't have *anything* good at the library. This is going to be a *horrible* party. This is going to be the *worst* party *ever*! I HATE YOU!"

Here comes the teaching moment. I hate the teaching moments. "You know what, Lucy?" I close the catalog and push it away. "I'm sorry but you won't be getting a Hawaiian party. Not a Calico Girl Hawaiian party, or even a party supplies store Hawaiian party."

"WHAT?"

"You heard me, Lucy Marie Flanagan. You're acting like a brat and brats don't get special parties. Look. If you want to have a few friends over on your birthday"—at this point my daughter is screaming so hard the veins in her little face are bulging—"we can rent a video and get a pizza and birthday cake. You can even have a sleepover if you want. But no Hawaiian party. I'm sorry."

Two weeks later Michael is greeting Lucy's guests in a grass skirt and pink lei. But this is the only concession we've made to the Hawaiian theme.

Eventually the last guest arrives and Michael directs her downstairs to the basement. Soon afterward Lucy races upstairs and glares at me, little hands on little hips. "*Why* did you invite Mackenzie Taylor?"

"Because you asked me to invite her, sweetheart."

"No I *didn't.* I told you to invite Taylor *Mackenzie,* not Mackenzie *Taylor.* You invited the wrong girl!"

I try to make a joke of it. "Mackenzie Taylor, Taylor Mackenzie, what's the difference?"

"There's a *big* difference, *Mom.* I *hate* Mackenzie Taylor. She's the meanest girl in my whole school!"

"Oops."

I watch my daughter stamp back downstairs and decide that I have completely failed as a mother. I invited the wrong Mackenzie because I've been distracted and inattentive. Worse than inviting the wrong Mackenzie, I've raised a child who demands Calico Girl parties and screams that she hates me when things don't go her way. My other daughter refuses to brush her hair and my son is a couch potato. Why did I have children in the first place? Why didn't I just buy a spider monkey like I'd wanted to? Why did I even get married? I could be single, no whining children, no snoring husband, just me and a real pet, a dog even. And Evan.

Evan Delaney is out of town all week, affording me one hundred sixty-eight hours with no phone calls or e-mails about the Courtly Love exhibit, no possibility of running into him in parking lots or on the path to Volk Hall, or hearing him summon me from his crankcase window with offers of Turkish coffee. I am a free woman with a new focus: dedicating myself to my upcoming stage debut. I could do a tough rocker chick song like "Hit Me With Your Best Shot," or something folksy like "American Pie." Then again, I'd love to do a Doobie Brothers number, like "China Grove." How would I choose? And what would I wear? It has to be cool. Understated, but flattering. Black, obviously. Black and tight and sexy. Skirt or pants? Boots or stilettos? Should I sparkle, shine, or go matte? I could wear that black tank top with silver bugle beads. Maybe the shiny black rayon top, the one I bought last year for New Year's Eve. Or I could go alternative with one of those vintage T-shirts like the Uncle Bob's All-Night Fish Fry top I found at the Salvation Army store. I'd wear Vanessa. Definitely. Or maybe I will buy myself another ponytail. Or a wig. A black wig. Or a blond one. A long blond wig. Yes! Oh, God, I can't wait to see the look on Michael's face when I join him onstage.

I have my song, I have my outfit, I have my wig, and I have practiced in my basement for three days. My voice is fine. No, better than fine, it's darn good. And yet. Something isn't quite right. I feel tight and hunched, hesitant, inhibited. I want to command the stage. But how? I haven't performed in twenty-seven years. My arms just hang there like a couple of logs. My legs are rooted to the spot. I know I should be shaking my hips or prancing about, but I can't seem to remember how to move my body.

The big cork board nailed to the back wall at Abundant Organics is plastered with flyers: apartment rental, used bikes, massage therapy, lost cats, La Leche groups, French lessons, solstice celebrations, house painting, computer repair, women's self-defense, herbal healing, babysitting coops, cooking classes, knitting lessons, and this, right in the middle of the board, like a message from God: PERFORMANCE COACHING. "Whether you sing for fun or profit, Candace Westfall will help you find your inner superstar! Improve your staging and vocals. Be sexier on stage. A dynamic new you, guaranteed!"

There is a fringe of pull-off phone numbers at the bottom of the flyer. A couple of these have already been torn away but I suspect that Candace herself did this as an inducement to others. I rip off a tab and slide it into my wallet behind my Visa. Then I take another in case I lose the first. Already I feel different, anxious and eager.

As I pass Michael's office I spot his Honda wedged in between two SUVs on Strathmore Road. Remembering a tip I'd read in *Cosmo,* I double park, whip out my lipstick, and scribble "I LUV U" on the windshield. As I'm slipping back into my van I see Michael—and *Edith*—crossing Strathmore. Edith is laughing and brushing the hair out of her eyes. She punches my husband playfully on the arm and he punches her back. They don't see me. I wish I hadn't seen them.

I am online now, Googling these five words: "women suspect husbands having affair." I click on the fifth option among 9,005 results: The Infidelity Forum: where women find solidarity as they share thoughts and feelings about their cheating husbands.

I scroll through the discussion boards until I locate what I'm looking for: telltale signs that indicate an affair. The list is depressingly long. I'm almost afraid to read but I force myself. I apparently missed the signs the first time. I will not let that happen again.

1. Lovemaking has come to a halt. (Not quite but close.)
2. He doesn't say I love you anymore. (He says it now when he's half-conscious, drifting into sleep. Does that count?)
3. He picks on you for little things. (Not really.)
4. Goes in to work earlier and stays later. (Yes.)

5. Starts working out. (No.)
6. Used to hate a particular music—rap, classical, opera—and now loves it. (He's suddenly playing in a band. Hmmm.)
7. Takes two hours on errands that should take half the time or less. (As a matter of fact, when Michael said he was going out to buy new tires, he came home three and a half hours later. And he looked too happy.)
8. Wears cologne when he never did before, or switches to a new brand. (No.)
9. Other woman leaves text messages on cell phone like 696969. (I've never checked Michael's cell phone.)
10. Says he wants new underwear or buys it for himself. (No.)
11. Keeps cell phone at his side at all times, even when sleeping. (No. Michael hates his cell phone. Half the time he forgets to charge it.)
12. Showers as soon as he gets home. (Sometimes.)
13. Caller ID always indicates no new numbers because they're being constantly erased. (I don't think so.)
14. Buys and uses a calling card so you cannot trace his calls. (I don't know.)

Later, same night: I hear Michael rattling around in the garage. Some husbands are garage guys, puttering around with power tools and little projects. Michael is not a garage guy, so when I hear him banging around in there, I figure either he's looking for an old triple-A Trip Tick or a tiny screwdriver to fix his eyeglasses. "We got any of that bug tar remover?" he calls out.

"Check the clear bin with the Turtle Wax."

"I already did," he yells. He's back in the house, pulling open junk drawers.

"What's the problem?"

"Someone wrote something all over my windshield. Can't get it off. For God's sake, who would do something like that?"

In the category of living dangerously: I took the kids to see *Grease* at the university theater. We moved to better seats during intermission, which had actually been Caitlin's idea; she'd spotted the seats before the house lights went down and when they were still empty at intermission she begged me to move down. When I was a child, my mother switched us to the better seats at a Pacers game, right behind the bench. Twenty minutes later, a man loudly insisted that we move before he called "the authorities." His teenage son tittered as we slinked out of the seats (actually, only I was slinking, my mother behaved like the aggrieved one, even as the man waved his tickets in her face).

I didn't want to change my seats today. But Caitlin kept begging and I relented and once I felt I could be sure no one would kick us out of the seats, I began to relax and enjoy myself. We were close enough to see the little microphones taped to the actors' cheeks. They all looked so young and happy and alive.

I thought about those performers as I made my way to Candace Westfall's house, a low brick ranch in the

TimberLand subdivision that, incidentally, has no trees in the same way that the Roaming Deer subdivision on the north side of town wiped out all the roaming deer by the time the graders came in to level the land.

With its immaculately swept but barren front steps and dull white shutters the house has a geriatric sensibility that worries me; I'm looking for youthful vigor in this whole endeavor. Candace Westfall had better not be an old lady.

I press on the doorbell, releasing a cascade of chimes. The door swings open and there she is, smiling as if she's known me her whole life. Candace is a short, curvaceous woman in her early thirties with glossy dark hair and a Kewpie doll's face. She's wearing black flowing pants and a stretchy crimson top with a ruffled collar and deep neckline, which instantly draws the eye to her ample cleavage. When I reach out to shake her hand, she startles me by pulling me close for a hug.

"None of this handshaking nonsense," she says. "I'm a hugger."

Candace glances at the tape player I'm holding: Jake's tape player, actually, the kind designed for toddlers in primary colors with giant buttons and a bright red microphone attached by a springy red rubber cord. "I see you've come with your own sound system."

"Oh, this? It's my kid's. Obviously." I am feeling crazy, ready to bolt. What am I doing here, a woman with three young children and an overworked husband at home?

Candace leads me to the living room, a space that could only belong to a single, childless woman, a delicate, comforting room with faded but beautiful Oriental rugs, a small varnished bamboo table bearing a floral porcelain tea set, fragrant candles along the windowsills, and everywhere framed photos of Candace and her female friends. At the foot of a white-capped mountain, on a corner in Times Square, below the Golden Gate Bridge. In every picture Candace Westfall looks absolutely thrilled.

I sit in a canvas folding butterfly chair. Candace takes the wood ladder-back rocker across from me. She asks about my work, my kids, and my brief history as a middle-school rock star. She listens carefully, nods and murmurs warmly, jots down a few notes in a spiral-bound stenographer's pad.

"Why do you want to perform, Julia?" Candace tilts her head, searching my eyes for clues to this fortyish wife's sudden yearning to sing onstage. "Here we are all these years after the Raspberry Sorbet. Now you want to put yourself out there again. What are you hoping to get out of this? Why now? Are you thinking of a career change?"

"Oh, no, of course not, no." I shake my head. "Nothing like that."

"Well, are you doing this for yourself or for someone else?"

"Both, actually." I am surprised by the intimacy and invasiveness of the question. "My husband. Michael. He's in a band. And I haven't seen a lot of him since he started playing. So my friend, Annie, she's a social worker, and she thinks I have a nice voice, she suggested I sing. With Michael's band."

Candace makes a little face. I guess that was the wrong answer. "And what does Michael say about that?"

"Actually, I haven't told my husband yet. I want to surprise him."

"You sure you want to do that?"

"Very sure. The Rock Barn does an open jam every other Wednesday night. Michael's band hosts it. Anybody can get up onstage and perform with the band. You don't need a special invitation. I thought it would be fun."

"Is that what you're hoping for? To have a little fun? Or did you want something more?"

Is this woman a vocal coach or a psychic? "Just fun." I am lying and she knows it. "Something to do on a Wednesday night. Change of pace."

"Alrighty, then." She's not going to push the issue. She sits back and folds her hands in her lap. "Show me what you got, girl."

I punch the giant red play button and launch into "Hit Me With Your Best Shot." I try to affect a rock bitch quality, move my behind a bit, play some air guitar. At "Fire away!" I cock my finger like a gun, which had seemed like a nice touch when I tried it in the privacy of my basement but now I just feel like Queen of the Dorks.

Candace watches me closely, and when the song finally ends she invites me to sit down again. She smiles patiently. "Why this song, Julia? What does it mean to you?"

I hadn't thought of that. Hit me with your best shot. It means what it means. I don't know. "Ummm, it's, you know, a rock song. Tough woman takes on the world. I guess."

"Is that *you*? Is that *your* story? Tough woman taking on the world? Is this the big event in your life right now?" Candace asks in a warm and imploring voice. "Think about it, Julia. *Hit me with your best shot.* Is that what Julia Flanagan wants to say to the world?"

I don't know what to say.

"I need for you to listen to me very closely, Julia." Candace angles her head and looks into my eyes. "A good performance isn't about shaking your ass onstage. It's not about what you do with your hands, or wearing a wig. It's not about having the perfect outfit, or even the perfect voice. It's about telling your story. You pick your song—*your* song—and you plant your feet and you sing out. You put yourself out there, honest and bare. You connect with your music, you connect with your audience. Does that make any sense?"

"Sure it makes sense," I say, quietly. I feel chastened and a little sheepish. But I am not ready to give up.

"Do you want to try it again?" Candace asks, gesturing toward my tape player.

"No, not now," I say. "I think I need to find another song."

In the category of living dangerously: I lied to a waiter today. He seemed disappointed that I'd ordered only a glass of water instead of something alcoholic, I told him that I was in recovery and hoped he'd respect my effort to get clean and sober. I am *sick to death* of waiters trying to shove their drink of the week down my throat. These stupid chain restaurants with their Margarita Grandiosas. Do they get a commission for every margarita they sell? Do they get penalized if they forget to mention the margarita? If I don't order a drink, does that mark me as a geek, a cheapskate, a loser, a bad tipper? Sure, I could have told him the truth, could have said that I'm just not in the mood to drink, especially since I have to drive home and be a mother to my three children and if you don't mind I'd like to be *sober* when I greet them at the door. But I felt so righteous when I told him I was in recovery, and the look on his face—mortified embarrassment—was so priceless that I'd do it again if I could. Sometimes it feels good to lie, I am discovering. Sometimes it's really your only option.

In spite of my mother's best efforts, I was never the sort of take-charge girl she hoped I'd be. I wasn't a self-starter, but I was a heck of a follower; not a maverick, but a dependable team player; not an iconoclast but a true believer in all the fundamental things: God, love, marriage, family, hard work. I don't mean to sound like a dolt. It's just that I've preferred to let others make the waves while I stand closer to shore, watching.

So it would surely have floored my mother when I pick up the phone to call Evan Delaney. I was marinating in my suspicions about Michael and Edith. I needed to do this.

"I'm bored and it's a beautiful day," I say. "Care to join me for a walk? We could talk about the exhibit."

There is a moment of stupefied silence and then Evan says: "I'd love to."

He will meet me at the Bentley in fifteen minutes, which gives me just enough time to wipe off the smudged mascara around my eyes and reapply my lipstick, "Saucy Wench," a shade of red the color of taco sauce purchased on impulse during a premenstrual moment, which is when I'm most apt to buy things I wouldn't otherwise wear. I check myself in the ladies' room mirror twice, and then again, return to my office and wait. I arrange myself to my best advantage; collar pulled up along the jawline, hair tucked behind my ears, shoulders back, legs purposefully crossed like a morning talk-show host to expose a shapely calf. I am grateful for having chosen the slimming black knit skirt, the black ribbed top and black microfiber tights, a look that shrinks my total perceived poundage by four at least.

I hope Evan can find his way to my office. Bentley fired its receptionist during the budget cuts of the nineties, and now there is no front desk at the top of the wooden stairs, just a telephone on the floor, a half-dead diffenbachia, and a faded gray cardboard sign: "Welcome to the Bentley Institute. Use the phone to dial your party's extension."

It isn't what most people expect of the world's foremost sex research institute. The room is empty except for a couple of old display cases along the wall featuring some of the Bentley's less controversial, and consequently less valuable, artifacts. A copy of a love letter from a World War I army private to his sweetheart in Ohio, no sexual references. A collection of Japanese snuff boxes engraved with geishas. An etiquette handbook about dating, circa 1950. A selection of early birth control devices, including the patent for the first IUD. This is supposed to be the grand portal to the top sex institute in the world and it looks and smells more like the office of a dentist who plugs away long past retirement age, a place that is static and old and antiseptic, a place of small amber bottles, mortars and pestles, of mercury and alginate molds. As Leslie Keen has told many an overeager graduate student, "We don't celebrate sex here. We study it. So if you're looking for sexy, you've come to the wrong place."

This is a useful fiction if one's goal is to discourage the prurient, but it is, ultimately, a fiction, and not only because the Bentley has the largest collection of dirty magazines and movies in the world, but because this place has been implicated in one sexual controversy or another since the days of old Eliza Bentley herself, who was rumored to have enjoyed a succession of young lovers, male and female, handpicked every year from the new crop of graduate students. In the late 1960s, the Bentley hosted private "key parties" where selected staff and benefactors would view erotic films, get soused, toss their house keys into a shapely brass urn, and wind up bedding someone else's spouse. (I never really understood the practical mechanics of this ritual! How do you know which key is whose? What if you pull your own key from the bunch? And what if you're paired with someone so utterly repugnant you'd sooner take a bullet in your head than touch his sagging body?) Seven years ago, Leslie's predecessor, Jorge Batunga, was fired after a group of prospective students and their parents, touring the campus, found Batunga humping his male secretary in the dense woods behind Volk Hall. And only last year, Leslie was embroiled in a mess of her own after she'd told a reporter, believing she was speaking off the record, that she preferred black men because "everything you hear about their size, as it happens, is absolutely true."

I hear muted footsteps in the corridor and realize that

with a single impulsive phone call, I have summoned this delicious man to my office. Evan Delaney, who only moments ago was sitting comfortably in his office across the quad, has now exerted himself because of *me.* I pretend to concentrate on the safety instructions for my coffeemaker—do not operate in the bathtub—as he steps through the door.

"I guess this is the place." Evan smiles and gives me a sort of half wave as he ambles into the room. He surveys my office. "Nice." His wide-wale corduroy pants are the color of tobacco; they make a soft whooshing sound as he walks toward me. He lowers his large frame into my leatherette swivel chair and rolls closer to me. "What are you working on?" The room feels smaller now, and warmer, and the air electrically charged, like a hot dryer of clothes when I've forgotten the dryer sheet.

"Oh, this?" I feel as if I could bust wide open. My voice is pinched and high. My hands are as cold as those blue ice packs I tuck into the kids' lunchbox. "Nothing much. Writing up catalog blurbs."

"May I?" He reaches out to examine the pair of figurines on my desk, an extremely well-endowed man and smiling woman, carved as separate pieces but designed so they can be arranged, like a three-dimensional puzzle, in several different positions: missionary, doggie style, 69. Fashioned from ivory tusk and delicately detailed, the figurines date back to the Qing Dynasty.

I watch Evan's eyes widen as he slowly grasps the full import of this little puzzle.

"Hmmmm."

"So, first I do the write-up, then we take the pictures.

I'm almost finished, thank God." I expect him to rearrange the pieces all three ways, and he seems to know that this is an option, but he leaves them in their original position, with the man curved over his lover's back like a wrestler.

As Evan returns the figures gently to my desk, I sigh and say, "Two hundred eleven items, fifty words per item, ten thousand five hundred fifty words total."

"You make it sound like a chore, like you might as well be cataloging, I don't know, automotive parts."

The comment feels like the sting of a sweat bee, not awful but bad enough. Evan Delaney has discovered my darkest secret: I am a bore. Put me in a room full of erotic art and I'm the one calculating the exhibit's total square footage. I may work for the Bentley Institute of Sex Research but could just as easily be sorting through anodized nails at Sherman's Hardware. My husband hasn't shown any interest in me since I brought home Vanessa, and now I know why. I will never be anything more than this, a paper pusher who happens to work at the world's most famous sex institute. Or to put it another way: *If you're looking for sexy you've come to the wrong place.*

Evan is flipping through a draft of the paper I'm coauthoring with Leslie [a.k.a. I'm researching and writing all of it and she's sticking her name (16 point type) above mine (12 point type) on the cover sheet].

"What's this about?"

"That's my next project. You know the Kama Sutra?"

"Sure. I mean, I know *of* it. I've heard of it. But I don't *know it* know it. I mean, I'm sure I know some of what's in it, know how to do it, Jesus, you know what I mean."

Evan's face is crimson and I'm sure mine is too, but there is something so darling and sexy about him, I want to just scream.

I have to look away from that face. I page absently through the manuscript. "A lot of people think the Kama Sutra was the only game in town, but actually, uh, there were lots of similar handbooks floating around long before the Kama Sutra."

"Such as?"

"Such as the Handbooks of Sex by the Chinese Emperor Huang-ti. The Koki Shastra, the Ananga Ranga, the Kamaled-hiplava. You'd be amazed, really. We didn't invent sex."

"We?"

"Not *we.*" I'm blushing again. "I mean, modern man. Woman. Hippies. Dr. Ruth. *The Joy of Sex.* Whatever."

Evan gestures toward a volume on my desk, an early translation of the Kama Sutra. I lift it off the top of the stack and run my finger over the gold embossed title. I hand the book to Evan.

He opens to a random section, reads a bit, and laughs. "Whoa. Wow. This is incredible stuff. Listen to this. These are the ten degrees of love. Love of the eye—I assume that's when you can't keep your eyes off her—" He looks at me and I must avert my eyes before my head busts open. "Attachment of the mind, constant reflection, destruction of sleep, emaciation of body . . ."

"Turning away from objects of enjoyment," I say, slowly and quietly continuing the list from memory, "Constant reflection. Madness. Fainting. Death."

"I'm impressed." Evan smiles and continues thumbing

through the book. "Ah. Okay. This is interesting. A man must sometimes resort to another man's wife. And, apparently, some women are easier than others. There's a whole list of easy women here."

"Yes, I'm familiar with that list as well." I start to go for my purse. Why weren't we outside walking as planned? Why were we sitting here in my office reading the Kama Sutra?

"Okay then." Evan covers the page with his big hand. "Pop quiz."

I sigh. "Do I have to?"

"Please, Julia. Humor me."

"Fine." I sit down again. "Women who are easily won over include the following: A woman who stands in her doorway. A woman who looks at you sideways. A woman whose husband has taken another wife without justification." I look at my watch. "What else. Oh, yeah. A dwarfish woman. A sick woman. A poor woman. Blah, blah, blah. Do I pass the test, Professor?"

Evan glances down at the page. "You left out some of the big ones." He slides his finger down the page. "Hmmm. A woman who has been slighted by her husband."

I fix my eyes on a spot near my feet. "Yes, that too. Can we go now?"

Evan is still reading.

"You can buy your own copy at Borders," I say. "Seven bucks."

"No. Wait. This, this is *intriguing.*" He is studying the page. "What do they mean by 'the art of scratching'?"

"Scratching, biting. They considered it a mark of affection. Like a souvenir. Usually made on the cheeks, neck, back. And, uh, more intimate places." I know I shouldn't, but I can't help but indulge the seventh-grade show-off in me. "There are eight different imprints. The knife, the half moon, the tiger's claw, the lotus leaf . . ."

"Show me." Evan pushes up his sleeve, exposing his powerful forearm. "Mark me."

I hesitate, smile idiotically. "Uh."

"Come on, Julia. I want to see what it looks like."

I take him by the wrist and slowly turn his arm so that the tender skin is facing me. I press firmly with the thumbnail of my left hand, first one way and then the other, to form an oval. "There."

Evan studies his arm, traces the mark with his finger, and grins at me. He is ready to go for our walk now, but I've changed my mind. I tell him I have too much work, can't possibly spare the time, shouldn't have bothered him. He says he understands. He is only inches from my face now. His eyes are lingering on my lips. I feel the heat rising in my cheeks as he moves slowly toward me. I could have backed away or turned my face but I feel myself tilt my chin and accept his lips. His hands are cradling my face and he is kissing me and his mouth is so soft and his breath smells like spicy orange tea, and without even realizing it I raise my hand to the back of his head to hold him tight as I kiss him back. I slip my tongue into his mouth, tentatively at first, and then more boldly, and if I can be completely honest here, I am spurred on by one image now, the image of Edith Berry slipping a cigarette between my husband's lips. This image alone blots out all misgivings and pushes me along like a great wave. Evan makes a low sound, full of pleasure. When the kiss is finally over I am nearly gasping for air. I've been holding my breath the whole time, and I'm dizzy and hot. I've done it. I've kissed a man who isn't my husband.

"You're a great kisser," he says, grinning.

"Likewise," I say.

"You taste good," he says.

"Thank you."

"So I guess I'll be going now," he says.

"I guess so. I need to, you know, get some work done," I say, wanting very much to kiss him again. I'd rehearsed this moment a thousand times in my head and now I am amazed to see that nothing I'd anticipated matches the truth. I thought I'd resist. I didn't. I thought I'd feel regret. I don't. I thought I'd promise myself that this will never, *ever* happen again. I make no such promises. I sit alone in my office feeling light-headed. I call my husband but there is no answer.

Chapter TEN

When I contemplate dinner with my in-laws, I remind myself that it can't possibly be as bad as a barium X-ray, which itself is considerably more painful than childbirth, even Lucy's birth, twenty-seven hours of back labor, her big head asserting itself against my spine as I begged my obstetrician for a caesarian. The barium X-ray, designed to diagnose my chronic abdominal pain, was worse: cold air pumped into my tender colon as a technician in a distant radiation-proof glass room used remote controls to rotate me midair like a pig on a spit. Now whenever I have a dreaded event on my schedule, I console myself with the knowledge that it can't possibly be worse than a barium X-ray. I'd like you to try this sometime.

"We're here!" Kathleen cries as she steps over the threshold. "And we come bearing gifts!"

Kathleen Flanagan is the best-dressed woman I know. She would want you to believe that she is also the luckiest bargain hunter in America. She will tell you that she paid two dollars for her fringed pink suede belt at Marshall's, five dollars for the boots at T.J. Maxx, nineteen dollars for the coat on clearance at Nordstrom.

She would be lying, of course. My mother-in-law has plenty of money—her father held the patent on three medical devices and she was the sole heir to his estate—but Kathleen doesn't want you to know that she has plenty of money. She isn't shy about using her senior citizen discount card, catches the early bird specials at restaurants, and insists that everything she owns, from her new Coach bag to the Gucci stilettos, costs no more than six dollars. The topaz ring? An amazing $4.95. The velvet Kate Spade bag? Two dollars at a yard sale! I can't think of the last time I paid two dollars for anything. I can't even buy a magazine for two dollars. A pair of shoes?

"Can you believe my luck?" she says, gesturing toward the giant Louis Vuitton tote, which probably cost as much as the down payment on our first house. "Twenty-seven dollars on eBay." She reaches into the bag and pulls out three gaily gift-wrapped boxes. "Where are the kids? Nonnie has goodies!"

I summon the children, who have learned over the years not to expect much when Nonnie comes bearing gifts. While she clearly spares no expense on herself, Kathleen is almost sadistically frugal when she spends on others. For Lucy, she has bought (or perhaps picked out of a Dumpster) a sweatshirt bearing a character from a Disney movie that came and went long before my daughter was born. On closer inspection I see that the character isn't even from a Disney movie, but one of those Disney impostors, where the animation isn't quite right, the colors are dull, and the characters aren't charismatic enough to penetrate popular culture.

"Isn't this *adorable*?" Kathleen croons, holding the sweatshirt up against her chest. "When I saw it, I just knew I had to buy it for my darling grandbaby!"

Caitlin gets a windup fuzzy chicken that breaks when she overwinds it, and lucky Jake scores three pairs of sweat socks with Harley-Davidson emblems. To her credit, she remembered that her grandson is interested in motorcycles. Unfortunately, the tag indicates that these are ladies socks, size 9–11. My guess is she got them at a flea market for a buck. My kids stare bleakly at their bounty.

"What do we sa-aay?" I prompt.

"Thanks, Nonnie," comes the inculcated reply.

"You are so welcome!" she says. "You know how much Nonnie loves her grandbabies!"

I really shouldn't complain. As Michael is quick to remind me, at least his parents give a damn about the kids. My mother materializes once a year usually on her way to somewhere else and insists on being called Trina, "Never Grandma or Nana or Mamaw. Lord knows, I don't need to be reminded that I'm getting old." Given my mother's unwillingness to wear the mantle of grandmotherhood, I try to be grateful for my in-laws.

"Hey, did you hear the one about the Polish lesbian?" Jim asks.

"No, Dad, I didn't hear the one about the Polish lesbian."

"She liked men. Get it? She liked *men?*"

I look around to see whether any of the kids had been listening in. But they are all back in the family room watching a TV show about snakes, Nonnie's gifts abandoned in a sorry little heap on the coffee table.

"Oh, Julia, you're too serious," my father-in-law bellows. "You need to lighten up, young lady." (So I've been told, I'm thinking. And you have no idea how far I've come.)

Michael shakes his head and throws a sympathetic look my way. "Give her a break, Dad."

When I first met Michael's parents, I was, frankly, charmed. Whereas my last boyfriend's parents were as quiet as monks, these two yammered all the time. I loved Jim's earthy wit and Kathleen's sense of style, and the way she conferred with me as if I were her co-conspirator. "Julia," she'd say, hauling out giant binders of fabric swatches. "I need your expert opinion. Which of these do you like better? The floral or the stripe? Not that I can afford to reupholster now." We'd sit on the couch and sift through the books while Michael and his father watched the game, and I felt honored and special because she seemed to want my opinion.

I hadn't realized that Michael's parents were like Rock 'Em, Sock 'Em robots, bickering endlessly about one trifling thing or another. Nothing got settled, no one apologized for anything, and sometimes neighbors called the police because they yelled so loud. Michael told me that his parents once argued from *Love American Style* to *Johnny Carson* just because Kathleen said she'd been a size four when she got married but Jim insisted she'd been a seven. Jim didn't like the way Kathleen had loaded the dishwasher and insisted she watch him reload it, the "right and proper way." They fought about that for the rest of the night, then

Kathleen barreled out the door, got herself a suite at the Best Western, and didn't come back until the next morning, around the same time her sons were finishing up their breakfast of root beer and Snickers. Of Kathleen and Jim's three boys, one grew up to be a bickering husband, now a sour divorcé; another refuses to marry; and the youngest would rather watch TV than argue. That last one would be my husband, in case you're wondering.

I'm clearing the dishes when the phone rings. Lucy gets to it first and I overhear her say, "My mom's in the kitchen. Who's this?"

I'm no clairvoyant but I know with utter certainty that my daughter is talking to Evan Delaney. It has been only a few days since we kissed in my office and with the exception of a few benign e-mails, we've had no contact. I take the phone and send Lucy into the living room to be with the rest of the family. In the time it takes to bring the receiver to my ear I imagine Michael picking up the upstairs phone, overhearing some intimate exchange, charging back down the stairs, ripping the phone from my hands, and demanding a divorce. None of that happens, of course. Michael is safely locked in fierce debate with his father—whether or not Villanova deserved to win the NCAA championship in 1985—and well out of earshot.

"I want to see you," Evan says.

"I can't. Not now. It's not a good time," I whisper. "I have company."

"Just for a few minutes. I'll meet you anywhere. I'm losing my mind, Julia. I have to see you."

My hands are shaking, my face burning. "The playground in Brewster Park on the north side. Ten minutes."

Oh, shit. I've taken the next step. I've arranged a clandestine rendezvous.

I tell Michael that we're out of dishwasher detergent, which happens to be true. "I'm going to run to the store," I say. "I'll be back in a few minutes."

Michael jumps to his feet. "Hey. I'll go. I'll take my dad. He loves going shopping." This is true. Jim Flanagan has an unusual affection for supermarkets and never passes up the opportunity to go food shopping. He takes particular pleasure in noting all the items that are more expensive here than at his own neighborhood grocery store. "A dollar eighty-nine for a can of baked beans? That's just criminal."

"No, that's okay. I'll go," I insist. I notice the bewildered look on my husband's face. It's time to play the gender card. "I have to, you know, buy a couple of other things." I waved my hands vaguely around my crotch. "You know."

"Oh. Sure, hon. You go ahead. We'll be fine."

For all his sophistication, Michael has only the most rudimentary understanding of female anatomy and ailments and has no desire to augment his knowledge base. It takes me nine minutes to get to the oval parking lot at the Brewster Park playground. There is only one other vehicle there, Evan's black Jeep. He reaches across the seat to throw open the passenger side door. I climb in and sit there with my hands folded in my lap. This is a big mistake. I should be back home with my husband, my children, my in-laws.

"So. Here we are," I say. "Hey. Nice ride. I've always wanted a Jeep. So rugged, so, you know, so outdoorsy. Actually, I almost bought a Jeep in college. It was green and it was a little banged up but they were asking only—"

"You are the most compelling woman I have ever known," Evan says.

"Compelling?" I can barely hear him over the dull roar in my head. I want to kiss him again.

"Captivating. Beautiful. Wickedly sexy." He picks up my hand and brings it to his lips. His mouth feels so soft and warm against my fingers. "I've missed you, Julia. Missed you so much it aches."

"Listen," I say. "I think we need to cool it. Seriously. I'm a happily married woman."

"Happily?"

"Yes, happily, Evan. Maybe it's not fireworks all the time, but it's solid and predictable and—"

"Are you talking about your marriage or a bowel movement?" Evan drops his head and rubs his eyes. "That was crass. I'm sorry."

"Don't be. You're not wrong. But it's still my marriage, for better or worse. And we're working on it. But it's hard for me to concentrate on Michael when I've got you in my life, your kindness, your kisses . . . frankly, Evan, your body is a distraction in itself."

"My body is a distraction?"

"Yes. It is."

He begins to reach for my hand again, then stops himself. "Okay. Fine. I'll step back. You work on your marriage. But if something changes . . ."

"I'll let you know."

"I'll just take my cues from you, then," he says.

"I don't expect there will be any more cues."

"Whatever you say."

Chapter ELEVEN

After three grueling and exhilarating sessions with Candace Westfall, I am ready to make my debut at The Rock Barn, a fact I've somehow managed to conceal from my husband and children, even after I sent a mass e-mailing to nearly everyone in my address book. Publicizing my debut was Candace Westfall's idea. "Show yourself to the world," she exhorted. "Let them see the real Julia Flanagan."

She asked me to wear clothes that make me feel beautiful but also physically at ease, which ruled out stilettos, tank tops, and tight anything. After trying on every possible clothing combination in my closet I finally came up with black boot-cut jeans and my favorite shirt, a lightweight silk knit the color of a Noxzema jar. Candace forbade me from wearing Vanessa. "We want to see the real Julia up there."

In the meantime I am supposed to be gathering material for an exhibit on the cultural history of the human penis.

All I have so far is a fascinum (a replica of an erect penis worn by ancient Roman boys to remind them of their potency), and the beginnings of a small subset involving cigars (Freud, Groucho Marx, Bill Clinton). I've decided to ask one of the graduate students to take over. I need to focus on my debut.

Thanks to my shameless self-promotion, The Rock Barn is bustling. All my friends are here—and on a school night. The Beach Babes have a table right by the stage. The staff at Bentley's are also here (minus Leslie, who would never abide someone else in the spotlight, not even as a favor). I see Jake's teacher with her fiancé, Karen and Brad making out in the back, my dentist, my cleaning lady, my aerobics teacher, and of course Candace Westfall, looking contemplative sitting alone on the upper deck, a glass of wine in her hand.

I am standing at the bar sipping cool water and trying to breathe the way Candace taught me, deeply and deliberately, in and out through my mouth. I've already been to the bathroom twice with stomach cramps. I try more deep breathing, then stop breathing altogether and suddenly feel vertiginous. I had been fine—excited, even—until I realized everything that could go wrong. What if I forget the words? What if my voice cracks? What if I pass out? What if I start in the wrong key, or hit a bad note, or trip when I'm climbing the rickety plywood steps to the stage? What if I get nauseous and start gagging or actually throw up? What if I asphyxiate on my own vomit?

As it turns out, none of these catastrophes come to pass. What happens is worse.

It is nearly 10:00 P.M. and almost my turn to go. With heart palpitations and cold sweats, I have endured five acts before me. A seventy-year-old toothless bluegrass banjo player. A middle-aged housewife who looks like a tax accountant and sounds exactly like Aretha Franklin. A heavily pierced young man who plays classical guitar and sings through his nose. A slovenly drummer who does a fifteen-minute tribute to Buddy Rich. A blues singer named Mamie Jean O'Henry, passionate and tone deaf. Missing from the lineup is Edith Berry who is home, thank you, Jesus, with a stomach virus.

At last Joe Patterson picks up the roster and winks at me. "And now, ladies and gentlemen, we have a very special guest making her debut at The Rock Barn tonight. Let's give it up for Ju-lie Flanagan!"

A wild cheer goes up from the Beach Babes table and I start toward the stage with unexpected confidence. Then I see Michael's face and realize that I have miscalculated. He unhooks his saxophone and props it against the amplifier. "I'll sit this one out," he tells Frank. He turns and whispers, "Good luck, Jules."

I don't understand why he walked off the stage but I can't think about that now. I've got a song to sing. I turn to Curtis and whisper, " 'The Thrill is Gone.' Key of D minor?"

"You got it, sweetheart," he says, winking. He plays the first bar, then the next and then another as I close my eyes and just breathe. After the twelfth bar, I step forward to the microphone and begin the song. *My* song. Just as Candace Westfall had wanted, I feel every word of that song in the deepest part of me. Then I see Evan Delaney, leaning against the bar. He raises his beer bottle and smiles. And though I can't hear him over the cheers and applause, I can read his lips: "Beautiful."

I step off the stage and absorb the compliments from everyone who has come to hear me. Michael passes me on his way back to the stage and nods vaguely in my direction. I can't believe this. My own husband is ignoring me?

On the way home I remember the excitement of hearing my own voice, strong and clear, and just as vividly I remember how Michael's departure from the stage sliced through me like an X-Acto knife. I have never been so fiercely angry with my husband. But if I can be totally candid here, I also feel a spark of pleasure because Michael's absence means that there is more room now, in my heart and in my fantasies, for the man who did stay to hear me sing.

Instead of going straight home as planned, I make a U-turn in the middle of Broad Street and head for Brewster Park.

As if by tacit agreement, Evan Delaney is already there. The playground is empty and dark except for a shaft of silvery moonlight illuminating the playground, where Evan sits on a low swing, dragging his shoes in the gravel beneath him.

"Be with me," he says.

I move toward the swing beside his but he takes my arm and leads me toward him. "No. Here." He guides me so that I am facing and straddling him. "That's better." Evan eases up my skirt and as we sway silently I feel his fingers between my legs, gently pulling the panties aside, and slowly sliding inside me. It feels outrageously good.

My breathing quickens with his rhythm and now he is staring into my eyes, watching me. It doesn't take long to climax once, then again, as I bury my face in Evan's neck. He turns to kiss my head, my face, my lips. "I adore you, Julia Flanagan," he whispers.

He reaches down again and unzips his jeans, and now we are locked together, swinging slowly as Evan moves his hips almost imperceptibly. He wraps his arms around me tightly, kisses my mouth, whispers my name, and looks into my eyes with such tenderness and pain it makes me want to cry.

I'd pretended to be asleep when Michael finally came home, which was cowardly but easier than confrontation. My husband slipped into bed and pulled me close and I curled in the opposite direction, unwilling to accept this gesture of reconciliation. Now all I can do is lie here and listen to him snore and wait for the sleeping pills to take effect. I wonder what Michael's sinus cavity looks like, the whole thing, with all its crypts and passageways, and I wonder which wretched part of this cavity could possibly make tonight's insufferable clicking noise. Is it a flap of skin? A clogged airway? A bug?

Michael is in his study nuzzling Homer's head with the tip of his nose and whispering in baby talk. "Shmoozy, shmoozy, who's the cutest Homeroozy?"

"Don't you think we should talk about what happened last night?" I say, quietly. And by that I mean, don't you think we should talk about the fact that my husband refused to share the stage with me, *not* don't you think we should talk about the fact that I had sex on a swing with Evan Delaney. I have consummated an affair that probably started the night I dreamed of making love to Evan in the basement of the Bentley. It's an affair I nurtured in every waking fantasy, in every cute or coy e-mail, in my willingness to meet him at Soto Voce when I knew it was wrong. My cheating heart took its shape as soon as I decided that my husband was more interested in his band than in me, and grew stronger as I tormented myself with memories of Susie Margolis and nightmares of Edith Berry. And now, girded by a justification I single-handedly built to propel me, justification made of bitterness and strong as steel, I am not thinking about my affair with Evan Delaney. I am thinking only that my husband has disappointed me yet again. I intend to find out why he left the stage.

I survey Michael's tidy study. Until he joined Past the Legal Limit, a small shelf was all he needed to hold his entire music collection, a motley assortment of tapes and CDs he never listened to. The study was then an extension of his office downtown, oak bookshelves with heavy volumes of state statutes, litigation forms, court rules, taxation guidelines. Today his bookcase buckles under the weight of a sleek new stereo system and hundreds of compact discs acquired five, sometimes ten at a time. His diplomas have been removed from the walls to make space for a Rolling Stones World Tour poster. Michael, who never bought himself anything but shaving cream and condoms, is finally finding pleasure in his life and I cannot begrudge him this.

He gently lowers Homer in his exercise pen. "I don't

get this," he says, picking up a bag of timothy hay. "The woman at the pet store told me guinea pigs love this stuff. Homey won't touch it."

"Maybe he's just, you know, a picky eater." Or maybe he doesn't eat timothy hay because he's a *rat,* I do not say.

"Maybe." Michael opens a CD case and begins to gently rub a Rolling Stones CD with a flannel square soaked in some sort of solvent. "So what's up, Julie?"

"What's up? Are you serious?" I force myself to slow down. I inhale. I exhale. "Let me start again. What happened last night, Michael, well . . . it made me feel very sad. I wanted to surprise you. I thought you'd be happy."

He makes a face that is at once agonized and bewildered. "Why would *I* be *happy*?"

"Because I was part of your, you know, your thing. Your band."

"I should be happy because you were part of my band? No offense, but why would I want my wife in the band? I mean, how would you feel if I showed up at one of your staff meetings? Or if I decided to join you and the girls on your, whatever you call it, your Beach Babes night out?" Michael shakes his head and sighs. "Sweetie, I love you with all my heart but sometimes I really don't get you."

"Wait a second." I squeeze my eyes to dam up the tears. "I never wanted to join your band." What I don't tell him, of course, is that I'd secretly hoped that after they heard me, they'd beg me to join. "It's just that since you started playing in the band, I feel like we haven't spent a lot of time together. And, well, I could see you were having all this fun and I guess I wanted to be part of that. Is that such a bad idea?"

"Actually, honey," Michael says, sighing, "I think it is. Look. Jules. You're a beautiful, talented, sexy woman. And you have a great voice. But you're my wife. I don't want you to be my bandmate. That would just be too weird, you know?"

"I suppose," I say, blinking back more tears. "I guess you're right. And I'm sorry."

"Come here, you." Michael reaches out to pull me into his arms but I step out of his reach. "Please, Julie." He drops his shoulders and looks at me with a sad, defeated expression. "I love you so much. And I feel like we're just moving farther and farther apart. I miss you, Jules. I miss your happy smile. You don't smile anymore, you realize that? I miss snuggling in bed with you—it seems like you're always on the outermost edge of the mattress, or am I imagining it?"

I don't say anything. He's not imagining it.

"If it's something I've said or done, Julie, I'm sorry. I love you. I'd never do anything to hurt you."

All I can manage is a feeble, "Thanks."

Evan is the first thing I think of in the morning and the last when I slide into sleep. I pray that every phone call is his and when my inbox registers new mail I silently whisper his name and pray for a message from him, then curse when I don't see one. I reload and reload and reload the page. I reread old e-mails, the ones he sent to me and the ones I sent back, just to feel connected. The attraction to Evan Delaney cancels out interest in everyone else, as if some giant masking mechanism has attached itself to all but this one man, obscuring every part and quality in every other person that would have, in the past, piqued my interest.

Sometimes I feel like I'm dying inside. Maybe another woman would be thrilled by all this but I have never felt so tortured. I can't focus on my work. I can't enjoy being with the kids. When I'm alone with Michael, I find myself in a constant state of agitation and annoyance. His smallest habits are magnified a thousandfold. The pursing of his lips every morning while reading the newspaper, the way he cracks his toes every night before switching on the TV, how he wears black socks with shorts and sneakers, the way he eats ice cream (one teeny tiny bit at a time, licked off the very tip of the spoon). I force myself to conjure what first attracted me to Michael but I can't seem to remember a single thing. When I squeeze my eyes closed and try to picture my husband, all I see is Evan.

[illegible]

every [illegible] find would move [illegible] the past [illegible] my [illegible]

[illegible] in [illegible] the [illegible] and [illegible] of [illegible] and [illegible]

[illegible] tip of the [illegible]

[illegible] and try [illegible]

[illegible]

Chapter TWELVE

I can't go on like this," I tell Annie. She says that she isn't sure she's qualified to advise me after my singing debacle, but we have agreed to meet again, this time outside the public library. "I'm an awful mother, the world's worst wife. For the love of God, Annie, you've got to help me." I absently run my hand over the smooth, cool haunches of a new limestone deer in the library's courtyard. Fake deer seem to be springing up around town while the real deer are killed off by new development. There are six wire deer outside the county courthouse, several topiary deer out by the mall, and now this, a trio of limestone deer in the library courtyard.

"Okay." She clasps her hands, and for a moment I think she's going to pray for my salvation. "At least give yourself some credit for catching this thing before it went too far. That's good, Julia."

I tell Annie that this "thing" has already gone too far.

"How far?"

"Far," I say.

"Very far?" she asks.

"As far as it can go," I say.

"You mean . . . ?"

"Yeah." I slump in my seat and throw my face into my hands. I try deep, measured breathing. I look up. "Now what?"

"It's not too late to back out," she says. "So, okay. You made a mistake. And you're obsessed. Addicted, maybe, you know? Hey. It happens. No shame in that. Now. If I were you, I'd try to replace this obsession with *another* obsession. Something healthy and productive. Something that will take your mind off the professor completely."

"Such as?" I am exhausted and hopeless. I already know that Annie's idea, whatever it is, will not work. I'm wasting her time and mine. I have a stack of work at the office. My laundry room is so stuffed with dirty clothes that I can't get the dryer door open. I haven't tended my garden in months; the only thing that isn't dying are the weeds. "What do you have in mind?"

"Well, such as exercising? You're always saying you don't have the energy to work out, right? So now you take all this, this *drive,* and you work it off. You could go to the Y. Hey, you could join my spinning class. Thirty minutes on that bike and you'll be too *tired* to think about this guy, believe me."

I look at Annie's earnest face and feel a wave of depression wash over me. "I hate exercise bikes."

"Okay, okay, spinning's not for everyone, I understand that. How about a hobby? You don't really have a hobby, do you? Have you considered a hobby? My sister bought herself a loom. She's making everyone blankets for Christmas. That's, like, twenty-nine blankets. She's insane. You think you could get into weaving? Or what about knitting?"

The last time I tried knitting I made a single sock big enough to fit a Rastafarian's dreadlocked head. I'd joined a knitting group for camaraderie and instruction but felt nothing but humiliation when it came time to "share" our projects. Some of the women were working on elaborate Fair Isle sweaters, a few were knitting up bulky woolen tote bags, which would be sent through the washing machine for "felting," a process that turns ordinary wool into soft and fuzzy felt. One ambitious college girl was designing a Mexican wedding dress. And there I was, with my gigantic Rasta Man sock hat. The knitters were polite enough to keep their mouths shut but I eventually lost my motivation and stopped showing up. Somewhere in my basement is a large cardboard box containing fifty-nine assorted skeins and knitting needles in twenty-three sizes and in every style, smooth bamboo to slick aluminum, double pointed to circular. I have needles as small as toothpicks and needles as long as my arm and I will probably never use any of them again.

"I've got it." Annie smacks the edge of the table. "Start a collection! Julie. Remember when we went antiquing in North Carolina? And you didn't buy anything? Remember you said you always wished you collected something."

"Yes, I remember."

"So that's it, then. You start collecting. My friend? Carrie? In Santa Fe? She collects penguins. She spends all her free time online, eBay, bidding on penguins. Ceramic penguins. Pewter penguins. Vintage penguins. Windup penguins. She's got a life-size penguin in her foyer, scares the hell out of me. It's like a full-time job, collecting those things, I'm not kidding. But *fun,* Julia, fun as all get out." She stops to catch her breath.

"Annie, I'm sorry. This is ridiculous. Are you hearing me? I am falling in love with this man. I want to be with him all the time. I'm fantasizing about my husband driving his car off a bridge so I can be with Evan for the rest of my life. I want to kill myself and you're talking about penguins?"

"Yes, I'm talking about penguins. An affair is a choice, Julie, and unless I've missed something here, it's not a choice you're prepared to make. So all I'm saying is, make another choice. Redirect your mental energy. It's a behavioral thing. Come on. Isn't there something you've always wanted to collect? I don't know, maybe those pretty cups and saucers? Or metal lunch boxes from the fifties? My sister collects anything to do with My Little Pony, though I don't get it, to be perfectly honest. Think, Julia, *think.* Isn't there something you could collect?"

Her question feels suddenly important to me, portentous, the kind of question a guidance counselor might ask, a question whose answer could change the course of one's life. "Well . . . I always thought it might be fun to collect cookie jars. My mother had a few." Trina couldn't afford an extensive collection, and had nothing as valuable as the retro chic jars in the window of Hazel's, the vintage housewares boutique on Beck Avenue, our city's two-block "arts district." She kept her cigarette money in an orange mushroom over the stove. On the Formica table in the center of our small kitchen was a jar made to look like a San Francisco streetcar in mustard yellow, a gift from a boyfriend in California. A smiling pig in a chef's toque held up the half-empty boxes of Alpha-Bits and Cocoa Puffs like a bookend. Trina thought this one might actually be worth some money, and tried to pawn it for cash but it turned out to be a cheap reproduction.

Annie claps her hands together with the earnest enthusiasm of a kindergarten teacher. "Perfect! See? Cookie jar collecting is in your blood. I knew it. Okay. So. When you get back to the office, go straight to eBay, go to the search box, and type in cookie jars. See what comes up."

"I can't use my work computer to bid on cookie jars, are you kidding?"

Annie gives me the kind of look you reserve for your kid, the one who can never seem to remember that the tag goes in the back. "Julia, Julia, Julia. What are we going to do with you?" She checks her watch, a slender gold-tone Timex her father gave her on her sixteenth birthday. "We've got a little time. Let's hit the antique mall. Come on, Julia. Don't make that face. It'll be fun!"

Nineteen minutes later Annie and I are pushing through the double doors of the Cambridge County Antique Mall, four cramped floors of old, overpriced crap and the unmistakable stink of mold, mothballs, and dead people's things. Naked rubber dolls, gaudy rhinestone jewelry, decrepit Fisher-Price toys, beaded dresses for flat-chested flappers, rusted old farm tools. One booth is devoted to small beady-eyed raccoons and possums, stuffed, posed, and mounted on varnished pine slabs.

Another is filled with delicate figurines manufactured in occupied Japan. There's a booth with vintage housewares from the forties, cherry-covered cotton aprons and metal cabinets and cat-head string holders.

"Oh! This one's a winner!" Annie is holding a cookie jar with two hands, like a trophy. "Today's your lucky day, Julia Flanagan. This one's a McCoy, and I believe it's worth at least three times what they're asking."

"Really?" It's a bloodhound, rump sticking straight up in the air. The tail serves as a lid handle. It's ugly, but the fact that it might have been dramatically underpriced stirs the prospector in me, and Annie seems so excited to have discovered it, I feel I'll be letting her down if I don't buy it.

Chapter THIRTEEN

Tonight while Michael is playing at a place called Little Pig's Tavern, and after I put the kids down for the night, I go online and register myself on eBay. When the first screen appears, I am overwhelmed by the myriad options. I could bid on everything from leather backpacks (starting at a penny) to Vespa scooters to time shares in Costa del Sol. I can bid on entire wardrobes of gently used clothes for every member of my family. Just for the heck of it I type in "kidney" and am relieved to see that human organs are prohibited by eBay, as are babies, animals, and Nazi memorabilia.

I could easily have spent the next six hours exploring the site, but I stick to my purpose. I register myself as DivineMissJ. I type "vintage cookie jars" into the search box and wait. There are nineteen pages of vintage cookie jar listings, three hundred sixty-three jars in all. At this point I calculate that I have gone thirteen minutes without thinking of Evan Delaney.

I scan the offerings. There it is. My mother's smiling chef pig cookie jar, but this one is authentic and currently going for $34. I match that price and enter a maximum "proxy" bid of $55 and stare at the screen. I reload the page. The cookie jar is now up to $57.50. Someone named I_Luv_Pigs had outbid me. I'll be darned. I plug in another bid and hit the button. Now I am the high bidder. Three minutes to go. I reload the page. I_Luv_Pigs outbids me again. Damn that woman. I am poised to place another bid, $99.75 this time. I don't hit the "bid" button. I wait and watch the clock. Two minutes left. One minute. Forty seconds. Twenty seconds. Now I place my bid. I've won! I realize that I'm sweating. I wonder if this is how it feels to play the horses.

Nineteen Evan Delaney-free minutes.

It is nearly two in the morning and I am staring at a ceramic crocodile. The seller, Uncle_Alberts_Attic, describes it as a "vintage treasure," and "a must-have for any serious collector." I click to enlarge the picture by two hundred percent. The crocodile is holding a dull yellow sign between spiked claws. EAT MY COOKIES. His mouth is gaping, not in a menacing way, but as if he's in the middle of a seizure. Stubby snout, big nostrils, long eyelashes. Actually, he looks more like a cockroach. According to my *Ultimate Guide to Vintage Cookie Jars,* "Cookies Croc" was made by Mandy's L.A. Originals, manufacturer of hundreds of "whimsical" cookie jars from 1947 until 1969, the year Mandy Millstein's son took over the family business and promptly destroyed it. The jar has received no bids. I study the crocodile's expression, which could be described as pained and trapped and possibly deranged. I offer five dollars. I am the sole bidder. Ten minutes later, the auction is over and the Cookie Croc is mine. I feel a momentary pang of buyer's remorse, then remind myself that I'm a collector now, and even the most hideous cookie jar is a vintage treasure, a must-have for every serious collector.

I am poised to log off when I hear the chime indicating that I've received e-mail. It is now 3:00 A.M. It's probably junk, I tell myself, yet one more invitation to GET OUT OF DEBT NOW! or SEE TEENAGE VIXENS HAVING SEX! or REFINANCE YOUR HOUSE TODAY! or TRY THIS PENIS ENLARGER, GUARANTEED! I move tentatively to my mailbox. The message is from edelaney. Moving slowly, as much to preserve the moment as to avoid it, I double-click on his name and hold my breath.

> *You mentioned that your son Jake likes motorcycles. There's a Road Rage expo at the convention center this Saturday. Thought Jake might enjoy getting up close and personal with the bikes. I'd be happy to serve as your personal tour guide. I'll be there at noon if you're interested. e*

Michael will be playing at a retirement party at Casino Bar on Saturday, and both girls, miraculously, will be attending birthday parties. And though I'd vowed to stay away from Evan Delaney, I feel comfortable accepting this invitation because it's really more of an invitation for Jake, not me. There could be no appearance of impropriety with Jake there. With Jake there, I was, above all and to the exclusion of all else, a Mother. A good mother, the kind of mother who seeks out enriching and engaging opportunities for her young son, even if it means giving up a Saturday afternoon, usually reserved for laundry and bill-paying.

I type: *Thanks for the invitation! Jake and I will be there. J.*

I replace the exclamation mark with a period, change the J to Julia, and then change it again to Julia Flanagan and send it off. This is fine, this is good, this will be just fine, no problem, it'll be fun for Jake, it'll be fun, it'll be fine.

I don't hear Michael open the door and saunter up behind me. "Couldn't sleep?"

"No, yeah, I don't know. It must be the nasal decongestant." A lie. "Non-drowsy formula. I'm wired." I know he can't possibly have seen the message from Evan, but I am nonetheless frozen with panic.

He kneads my shoulders slowly, with as much strength as a half-asleep man can muster. "I didn't realize you had a cold. Poor baby." My husband leans over to kiss my mouth but I put my hand up. "Don't. Germs."

He kisses me anyway. "I don't care." He kisses me again, touching his tongue to my lower lip. "Come back to bed. I miss you." He takes my hand and tows me gently to the bedroom.

"Hey. Will you teach me how to whistle?"

"Sorry, but I'm married."

"Lucky guy."

Michael holds me close but he is too tired for sex. As I float into sleep, with Michael's arm draped heavily across my chest, I can hear the computer's faint chime across the hall.

• • •

Like a dog show or Star Trek convention, a motorcycle expo is a closed society, a realm of experts and enthusiasts, of inviolable customs, charismatic personas, and a palpable thrill bordering on hysteria. And as with dog shows and Star Trek conventions, at the Road Rage expo I am an interloper. The last time I was in this exhibit hall was two years ago, for ASETE, the American Sexuality Educators Textbook Exhibition. Constricted like sausage in a somber gray suit and cramped black pumps, I staffed the Bentley booth from eight in the morning until six at night while Leslie Keen flirted with visitors and posed for the press alongside the giant penis we privately called Fred, after her boyfriend. Fred was made entirely of granite, six feet high from base to tip, eight and a half inches across, cold to the touch and dull from all the handprints. It took two men and a forklift to install the thing and even though I thought Fred was tacky and urged Leslie to leave him in the storage room, she insisted that we needed a gimmick to distinguish our booth from the rest.

Today it's a different milieu, same theme. The Road Rage expo is all about sex. The imposing bikes, the babes with big rumps and leather shorts, and the men, all tattoos and belt buckles, rippling muscles and heavy harnessed boots. The air is thick with pheromones, the floor covered in sawdust, Charlie Daniels thumping from speakers the size of my potting shed. Mullet heads in Confederate flag T-shirts mix uneasily with the J. Crew Sunday riders, and both groups stand in awe and admiration before Harley-Davidson's sleek FXDL Dyna Lowrider. I am amazed that I've made it to the convention center in time; I'd driven nearly the whole way behind a green minivan that crawled like a dung beetle and stopped for every yellow light and shuffling pedestrian. Jake is bug-eyed as I lead him around the Harley exhibit. He is wearing his Spiderman backpack, which I've stocked with grape juice boxes, a Ziploc bag of animal crackers, a disposable camera, and paper and pen for autographs, in case we run into anyone famous.

"Hey. You made it."

I turn slowly toward his voice. He is beaming.

"You must be Jake." Evan towers over Jake like a redwood, and realizing this, drops to his knees and extends his hand. "I'm Evan. I work with your mother."

Now that's a fine lie, I'm thinking. Evan Delaney does not work with me; the courtly love project doesn't make us coworkers. I don't correct him, just stand there holding Jake's clammy little hand, trying to look motherly and trying with all my might to forget what it was like to feel Evan inside me.

"Hi, Jake's mom." Evan rises to his feet and grins.

"Hi."

Damn my fair skin, these cheeks that flush and burn with the accuracy of a pregnancy test. "It's nice to be here. It's really . . . different. It's so, you know, bikerish." God, could I possibly sound like a bigger geek?

"That it is, Julia Flanagan. That it is." His eyes are twinkling. He thinks I'm adorable, I can tell. It seems like a long time since anyone thought I was adorable. Evan returns to Jake's eye level and gestures toward a 1970 customized Triumph Tiger, gleaming black with a fiery iron cross painted across the fuel tank. "How'd you like to sit on one of these choppers?"

Jake looks at me for approval and, receiving it, turns back to Evan. "Uh-huh." He smiles shyly and raises his arms so Evan can hoist him onto the Triumph's black leather seat.

Evan is gripping Jake with both hands. "Take a picture, Miss Julia."

I dig the camera out of the backpack, snap one picture, wind the hard plastic wheel forward, and take another. I am impressed by the fact that Evan is more focused on keeping Jake stabilized on the bike than posing for the camera. Jake is glowing like a Chinese lantern.

"Look at me, Mommy!" he calls out. "I'm a motorcycle guy!"

"You sure are, honey!" I resist but eventually surrender to the urge to compare my husband to the man who has just won my son's everlasting devotion. Michael, I guiltily acknowledge, would never take Jake to a motorcycle show because Michael doesn't like motorcycles and the idea of spending two hours in a room full of bikers would be unbearable. On the other hand, I quickly remind myself, his children are well fed, warmly dressed, and amply educated. When they are dirty, he bathes them without complaint. If they are tearful, he consoles them with stories of his own youthful catastrophes or tales of Joe Doody and the Planet Shmalla. He has taught them how to clean their rooms and why they should save their allowances. Michael is an excellent father, I remind myself. And I am happily married. I am happily married. I am happily married. I am happily married. I am happily married. I am happily married. I am happily married. I am happily married.

• • •

"Who's this?" Michael is standing in the kitchen in a ripped Dallas Cowboys T-shirt, holey underwear, and suede slippers. He squints at the photograph in his hand. I suppose I could have hidden the pictures, or picked out the ones that included Evan but I've left them scattered like playing cards on the kitchen table. I have nothing to hide.

"Who?"

"This guy. Here."

I don't look up right away. "You mean that person with Jake? By the motorcycle?" I'm aiming for a casual, disinterested tone. I am scrubbing a Jell-O stain off the kitchen counter. When plain dish soap doesn't work, I switch to the abrasive cleanser with bleach and stay focused on my task. I finally remove the stain with a Brillo pad and bleach and try not to think about the fact that this resistant red stain came from a food product.

"Yeah. The guy by the motorcycle. With Jake." Michael is dangling the picture in front of my face.

I remove my rubber gloves and study the photo as if for the first time.

"Oh. Yeah. Uh-huh. That's Evan Delaney. He was on that committee with me. You know, the Mendelsohn mural committee. Remember? Anyway, we're doing an exhibit. Leslie got some grant money." I resume my scrubbing though there's nothing left to scrub. "And, well, Evan knew that Jake's into motorcycles so he invited us to the expo. At the convention center. Two weeks ago."

"Cool. Did Jake have a good time?"

"I guess."

• • •

I wake in the morning and am filled with the singular knowledge that someone in the world thirsts for me. This simple fact propels me out of bed, informs my wardrobe choices, gives me the motivation to go to work every day even in the gloom. I carry Evan's desire with me like a secret jewel. It radiates and warms me. It keeps me perpetually on the edge of arousal. At odd moments—reaching for a teacup from the kitchen cabinet, correcting Caitlin's math homework, lacing up my sneakers—I find myself replaying incendiary moments: Evan's furtive smile during a Mendelsohn mural meeting, how his eyes linger on my lips when I talk. I lie in bed and imagine him standing in the door frame contemplating me with those sober eyes and every part of me aches to wrap myself around him. Evan Delaney, the fact of him, makes everything else in life bearable, not just my marriage but life's small injustices, the dry cleaner's failure to remove a mustard spot from my beige wool skirt, the fact that AOL continues to charge me a monthly fee even though I canceled my membership two years ago. Evan's desire for me is a gift, an affirmation, a refuge. I cannot, I will not, give up this drug.

But with this elation comes a sadness deeper than any I have ever known. When I break from my reverie I am filled with black, bottomless despair. Evan might as well be a gorgeous hologram: vivid, lifelike, out of reach. I am a married woman with three children and a husband who loves me. I cannot continue this affair.

I now have forty-seven vintage cookie jars. Most people spend a lifetime accumulating this many jars; I collected mine in twelve weeks, primarily during late-night eBay binges but occasionally during the day, on my lunch break, from the office, and always at those times I felt tempted to daydream about Evan Delaney.

My preferences are shifting rapidly and with no discernible pattern. First, cartoon characters: Dumbo, Mickey Mouse, Felix the Cat, Bugs Bunny. Then I feel myself drawn to elves: Elves on tree stumps. Elves in schoolhouses. Elves under mushrooms. Without warning, I suddenly crave cats and dogs dressed as clowns, with rosy cheeks, big frilly collars, wicker handles. Now I find myself powerfully attracted to animal jars made in Japan in the early 1960s. I have amassed an impressive assortment and decide that this must be my ultimate calling, to be the world's foremost collector of these friendly, big-eyed beasts. Some are wearing crowns, others beanies. Most are holding either lollipops or cookies. All are smiling. I cannot seem to resist them.

When Michael is working late at the office I log into eBay, immediately search "Japan vintage cookie jars" and up come the tigers, the pandas, the lions and rabbits. My fingers twitch as I scan the listings, enlarge the photos, look up market values in my cookie jar guidebooks. I study my rivals' bid histories with the diligence of an FBI profiler to predict whether my adversaries are likely to "snipe"—to outbid me in the auction's final seconds. I look at their past auctions to determine if they're bargain hunters or big spenders; how high will they be willing to go, and am I willing to go higher? I do a bidder search to learn how many auctions they're currently participating in. Does my opponent indiscriminately scatter lots of little bids among many different auctions in the hope that something will take root, the way I once tried to make a wildflower garden by tossing fistfuls of seeds on a windy day? Or does she focus her efforts on a single jar? I take all these factors into account as I post my bids and monitor my auctions. I discover a feral quality in me. The girl at Camp Wakkasee who'd rather sit alone on damp grass than play capture the flag is now a bloodthirsty competitor. I will not be defeated.

I am running out of space. I put the jars along the sideboard in the dining room and atop the Hoosier cabinet in the kitchen. I line them up like chess pieces on the entertainment center in the family room. I calculate that I can fit twelve of them on a baker's rack I found in the Pottery Barn catalog, so I buy the rack and install it in the front hall, though the dark green enameled steel doesn't really match the delft blue rug and goldenrod walls.

My new passion provides an unintended benefit. The cute UPS guy driver is at my door almost daily. He used to drop packages on my porch, ring the doorbell, then run like hell back to that truck, a technique I'm sure they learn in UPS school since they all seem to do it, even the chubby ones. Now he stands at the door and has to wait for my signature because these aren't place mats from Pottery Barn, these are vintage cookie jars, they are insured, and they always require my signature. The transaction should give me time to fully appreciate the beauty of his hindquarters. But the UPS guy's visits hardly raise my pulse now. It seems that I have room enough in my heart for only one extramarital fantasy and besides, I'm more excited about the thing he has for me, the wide-eyed panda swathed in newspaper and bubble wrap. I wonder if the UPS guy senses that something has changed between us. I don't even bother to wear makeup when I know he's coming. Sometimes I answer the door in my sweatpants.

Michael does not notice the jars at first, not even when I've placed one in the middle of our kitchen table. It is one of the dog clowns, more like a harlequin, really, and I use it to hold cellophane-wrapped peppermint candies, the red and white kind they give you with your check at the Italian restaurant. Michael also does not notice the elf-on-a-stump I've put on our bathroom vanity to hold cotton balls. Only when my collection has reached critical mass—for Michael that would be forty-nine jars—does my husband finally say something.

"Hey. Where'd these come from?" He has just arrived home and is setting his briefcase on the floor against a steel curlicue at the bottom of the baker's rack. I watch as he discovers my collection by degrees, first one jar, then two, then the shelf, then the whole rack. He steps back to take it all in. "How long have we had these?"

"Oh, a few weeks, I guess. I got them on eBay. I always wanted to collect something. I thought it'd be fun to collect cookie jars."

"Hmmm." Michael looks as if he's detecting a faint, disagreeable odor. He gives the jars a few more moments of scrutiny. "Why do they all look so . . . *scary*?"

"Scary? You really think so?" I hadn't considered "scary" as a possible descriptor. Tacky, yes. But most people would probably say they're cute. Surely someone must have thought they were attractive enough to mass produce. But the more I study them, the more I realize that Michael is right. Bulging eyes. Gaping mouths. Giant swollen heads. They are leering at us. And they are terrifying. "I think they're kind of cute," I say.

Michael tugs at his tie with one hand, unbuttons his shirt with the other. "If you say so." He kisses me on the mouth and reaches around to squeeze my rear. "If it makes you happy to collect these things"—he slips off his shirt and drapes it over the banister—"then by all means, honey, collect to your heart's content."

"Really?" I am startled by his support.

"Absolutely." He is already in the kitchen, aiming the remote at the TV screen. "Everybody should have a hobby."

All my friends loved my mother. She'd let them smoke Newports at our rented house and she'd let them make out with their boyfriends in the basement while I watched TV alone in the family room. This was six years after we moved away from Liberty; no one here knew my mother had been a check-bouncing drunk who did nine weeks as a trash picker on the side of the highway. By the time we'd settled into our new neighborhood, Trina had gotten mostly sober, found steady employment waitressing, and was going for her real estate license. As far as my friends were concerned, she was the coolest mom in the world, someone who knew about boys and sex and listened without shaming. My mother gave my friends pedicures, taught them to French inhale, let them try her beer, ice cold in a frosted Mickey Mouse mug from the freezer. We'd sit on the back porch and dangle our bare feet over the railing, Mom making perfect smoke rings and telling my friends about her failed romances, with Raul, who bilked her out of seven hundred dollars in a phony real estate deal, and with handsome Jim, the blond Unitarian pastor who said he'd leave his wife but never did.

Trina's mother Grace, who died when I was a baby, was a Mormon, rigid as cheap shoes, and she was a pincher.

"She'd grab a hunk of me and clamp down like lobster claws," Trina told us. "I went on a diet when I was twelve and lost all my baby fat just so she'd have less of me to get hold of."

A week has passed since Michael first noticed the cookie jars. I wonder when he'll notice that my heart is somewhere far away now. And I wonder when he's going to confirm what I've suspected, that he and Edith Berry are falling in love.

I am sitting with my mother at the round pine table in her small kitchen. The chef jar is still there, sitting on top of aluminum cabinets that have the color of a smoker's teeth. I vow not to mention Edith Berry, who is stuck in my head like a brain tumor, slowly growing in significance and threatening to affect my ability to function. I'm not in the mood to hear one of Trina's lectures on the ugliness of jealous women.

I'm not sure why I tell my mother about Evan Delaney; I've never consulted her before, not even when I was a newlywed trying to thicken gravy for Thanksgiving dinner, which she bailed out of anyway, in favor of going skiing with Theo, the Greek salesman she'd met at the craps table in Las Vegas.

"Is he handsome?" my mother asks, nibbling the end of her thumb the way she always does in the presence of, or when contemplating, a good-looking man.

"Very."

"Your father was handsome."

I wish she hadn't said that. I want her to either tell me every single thing about my father or nothing at all. She rarely talked about him and I knew enough to never ask. It was as if my mother had drawn a magic circle around herself, a nonpermeable membrane through which no information about my father seeped out and no inquiry dare seep in. I mentioned him only once when I was twelve, full of prepubescent self-righteousness and angry because my mother was out on a date and missed my solo in the seventh-grade choir's performance of "Dona Nobis Pacem."

"Dad was smart to dump you," I screamed.

Her slap landed on my cheekbone with a sharp crack. Four slim fingers left a scalding imprint. "Your father didn't leave me. I left him. And you should be grateful I did. He beat the crap out of me, Julia, and he would have done the same to you." I never mentioned my father again.

"Is he married, this professor?" my mother asks.

"No."

"That's not good," she says, frowning. "That means you have more to lose than he does. It'd be better if he was married. Then he'd have an incentive to keep his mouth shut."

I appraise the sixty-one-year-old Trina McElvy, tight jeans and high-heeled sandals. I don't think I've ever seen her without makeup, not even before bed. I notice a butterfly tattoo on her ankle.

"Is that new?"

"Nope." She raises her cuff and turns her ankle to give me a better view. "Got it when I turned fifty. Got another one on my sixtieth birthday, but I'd have to pull my pants down to show you that one."

"No thanks, Ma."

She's nibbling her thumb again. "So, Julie-bell, tell me about your beau."

"He's not my beau, Ma."

She raises her hands. "Ooooh. Touched a nerve. Sorry." She waits a beat. "Tell me about . . . the *professor.*"

I don't want to talk about this anymore. It was crazy to go to Trina for advice. What was I thinking?

"Oh, forget it."

Trina reaches across to the table to hold my hand. "Is Michael being good to my baby?"

"Huh?"

"Are you getting any?"

"Mother!"

She smirks. "I didn't think so." She grinds the cigarette butt in her coffee cup. "Okay. Fine. Here's my advice even though you didn't ask for it. If your husband isn't loving on you he's not much of a husband. It's a requirement in the Jewish religion, sex is, between husband and wife. I bet you didn't know that." She lights up again, takes a long, soul-satisfying drag, and cocks her head toward the cigarette. "I'm giving these up in two weeks."

"Sure you are." I know where this conversation is going. My mother never liked Michael. She thinks he's cold. Even when I was already engaged, Trina tried matching me up with single men she knew from work. Or wherever.

"You're a woman, Julia. You've got your needs. If your own husband can't satisfy you . . ." She shrugs her shoulders. "Why shouldn't you take care of yourself? You only live once."

Where have I heard that before?

"Just be careful. Don't get yourself knocked up, you know what I'm saying?"

I gather my things and stand. "Thanks for the advice, Mom."

Trina gives me an ostentatiously loud kiss on the cheek. "Anytime, sweetheart. Anytime you've got a problem, you just come to your old mom. I'll set you straight. I'm always here for my baby girl."

Chapter FOURTEEN

Ocean Isle is colder this time of year and a chilled fog shrouds the lovely sea, but that does not deter us from the shore. We arrange canvas folding chairs on the sand, set up our trusty blue cooler packed with tequila, beer, and Diet Coke. We are barefoot and wrapped in fleece blankets and we tilt our faces to the miserly sun. The weather is a disappointment but we're warmed by the alcohol and conversation. Except for a round old woman strolling with two Cavalier King Charles Spaniels, we are alone.

I dig my feet into the cool sand to elude the biting black flies and stare desolately into the fog. Annie is talking about the anniversary gift her husband gave her, a handmade coupon for "a night of undivided attention, including but not limited to a foot massage, a pint of Ben & Jerry's chocolate fudge brownie yogurt, the chick flick of your choice, and nookie." I stand up and move toward the ocean, the wind beating me about the head like a foam bat. The water is freezing, but I wade in a bit, soaking the bottom edge of my blanket. I look down at the gullies rushing between my feet, wedging shell fragments and tiny pebbles between my toes. I spot a piece of sea glass the color of amber, and as I bend to pick it up, another wave smashes against my shins and the glass slips away. The undertow is almost too powerful to resist.

Annie holds a match to her lips and extinguishes the flame with a quick Lamaze breath. She pushes the Candle of Truth across the table. "It's all yours, Francesca."

"Category: work." Frankie twists a curl around her finger. "I'm trying to get through to that asshole Gary Wallace," she begins. Gary Wallace owns the local *Star Gazette* and is notoriously resistant to giving free publicity. ("Tell 'em to take out an ad, for Christ sake" is his usual response to anyone requesting a blurb in the paper's "Neighborly News" column.) Burly and blond, with a round baby face and gold molars, Gary spent a million and a half on television advertising last year and wouldn't buy a box of Thin Mints from a Girl Scout if she was his own daughter. He has never contributed to a single community fundraiser, not the library expansion, or the new animal shelter, or the community kitchen. In his TV ads he's sitting on top of a silver rocket ship, screaming: "Read the *Star Gazette.* Our coupon pages are OUT OF THIS WORLD!" Riding the rocket like a bronco, he flies into a distant starry galaxy, which is where I think most people would like Gary Wallace to remain.

"I've been calling Gary to see if I could get some PR for my fortune cookies, right? And I keep trying even though he never, *ever* takes my calls. Well, I know how much the jackass loves rubbing elbows with big shots. So this time, when the secretary asks, 'Who should I say is calling?' I say, 'Please tell him it's Katie Couric.' Of course the jerk picks up right away. I can't believe it. I finally have Gary Wallace on the phone. The first thing I say is, 'This isn't Katie Couric it's Frankie Wilson and I've got this great new fortune cookie they're thinking of carrying at Bamboo Buffet please don't hang up.' "

"What did he do?" I ask.

"He hung up. *Obviously.* Then he calls Bamboo Buffet and registers a formal complaint against me." Frankie sucks on the lemon wedge and winces. "He can kiss my ass for all I care, cheap bastard. There'd better be a special place in hell reserved for men like Gary Wallace." She moves the candle to me. "Your turn, J."

"We're expecting big things from you, girl," Annie says.

"I think I'm having an affair."

I've said it low, all at once, and as fast as my lips will move, which defeats my purpose since no one actually hears what I've said and they insist I repeat myself slowly and clearly, which is exactly what I don't want to do. I close my eyes. "I . . . think . . . I'm having . . . an affair."

Annie makes a face. "What do you mean, you *think?* Wouldn't you know it if you were having an affair?"

"I met someone. A man. A professor." God, this is hard. Annie already knows about the affair but I decide against telling Frankie. I just can't handle her reaction right now. I feel too fragile. But I've got to give them *something.* "I can't stop thinking about him. We go on walks. He e-mails me. I e-mail back. I, I look forward to going to work in the morning. I think about him when I pick out my clothes the night before. If I don't see his car in the parking lot on campus I'm depressed for the rest of the day. And I have bought forty-nine hideous cookie jars just to take my mind off him. Oh, GOD, I don't know what I'm going to do."

I pause and wait for a response. "Say something. Don't just sit there *staring* at me."

Frankie is first to speak. She wants to know what he's like, and I feel myself buoy like a cork as I tell them about Evan's hair, his arms and hands, the long, strong legs, the way his eyes glitter when he smiles at me. I tell them about the day I met him, the Ovid poem, the Road Rage expo, and courtly love and the Kama Sutra and the look on his face when he asked me to "mark" him, so resolute, so carnal. Abandoning fully any reluctance to discuss him, I am now in my glory, racing to include as many details as possible, aware that I've got my audience completely enthralled. The flecks in his eyes. The single bulging vein traversing his forearm. His breath, always fresh and sweet. His upper eyelids, soft and a little baggy, and the chipped tooth that invites exploration.

"Holy *shit*!" Frankie says, looking genuinely mortified. "We've created a monster."

"No, no, we haven't created any monster. Hey. C'mon now." Annie reaches across the table to pat my hand. "This is normal female sexuality. This is *healthy.*"

"How can this be healthy? I'm so *miserable*!"

"And how are things with Michael?" Frankie asks.

"He's still in that band and no, I'm not replacing Edith Berry."

No one can understand why my husband had absented himself during my performance; I try to explain that Michael wasn't ready to play Captain to my Tenille. "And Edith still calls my husband Mikey."

"I say we kill her." Frankie tosses her lemon wedge across the table. "Wipe the little shit off the face of the earth. I mean it. I'm sick of these girls, shaking their little titties at married men—"

"—*Big* titties," I interrupt.

"Fine. *Big* titties. Even worse. Hello? Excuse me? He's *married.* Look elsewhere, *bitch.*"

I'm moved by Frankie's impassioned response. "I'm not going to kill her." I pick at the hardened wax at the bottom of the candle. "And I have no evidence that she and Michael are, you know."

"Of course they're not." Annie tugs her blanket more snugly about her shoulders. The fire we'd built in the fireplace had fizzled out some time ago and a damp chill has settled around our table. "Julia's husband isn't the cheating kind. Anymore."

"That's what I used to say." Frankie pulls her hood on and tightens the drawstring. "Damn, it's cold in here. I should do something about that fire." But instead of tending to the fire, Frankie brings her hands to her face and erupts in big, messy, heaving, clotted sobs. At first we all think she's kidding—Frankie had been popping Muddy Buddy mix only moments ago and anyway, she's not a crier—she didn't even sniffle when we rented *Beaches*. Frankie is the happy puppy, the ebullient, rosy-cheeked goof. Frankie likes to give gag gifts like farting rubber pigs and boxing nun puppets. She has a Scooby-Doo bobblehead on her dashboard. She floods our e-mail boxes with jokes. She believes that a box of Godiva chocolates is more effective than therapy any day. Above all, Frankie does not cry.

"God, Frankie, what *is* it?" Annie asks. "What's wrong?"

But I know precisely what is wrong with Frankie. It is Jeremy and that blubber-lipped receptionist. Now I feel guilty for not alerting her as soon as I'd spotted them together in Starbucks. I find a box of tissues on the kitchen counter and wedge it into her balled-up body.

"Frankie," I begin, gingerly, waiting for her sobs to ebb. "Is it Jeremy?"

When Frankie finally lifts and presents her face to us, it is no longer the round, girlish, mirthful face we know, but a deeply dented, haggard tableau of pain and betrayal. It was a face I knew intimately because it was my own face, five years ago.

"Uh-hungh." She honks sonorously into the tissue. "He's in love with his receptionist. *Miranda*." She twists her mouth and spits out the name like it's one of those nasty, shriveled-up green peanuts. "Can you believe it?"

"Frankie . . ." Annie asks, hesitantly, "what does Miranda look like?"

"What do you think she looks like?" Frankie snorts. "She's got big fucking lips like Angelina fucking Jolie!"

"Oh, Jesus." Annie slinks back into her chair and

yanks the hood of her white sweatshirt tighter around her head so all you can see is her nose and the dots of light in her black eyes. "I think I saw them together. About a month ago. At the two-dollar movie theater." Annie shuts her eyes and squeezes the bridge of her nose. "It was some stupid karate movie and the place was empty except for the two of them in the back. I was only there because I thought I left my umbrella under one of the seats. They never clean that place, you know."

Frankie is dabbing at her eyes and following Annie's story with some acrid combination of masochistic interest and roiling resentment. "And . . . ?"

Annie swallows, hard. "Oh, Frankie. You don't want to know."

"Yes I do."

Annie turns her eyes beseechingly toward me. I jump in. "Come on, Frankie. You really need to hear all the sordid details?"

"Uh-huh." Frankie is staring dully at a spot somewhere between Annie's brows. "Keep talking."

"I can't, Frankie." It is a rare moment for Annie, normally so forthcoming. This leaves the rest of us to conjure the possibilities. Were they kissing? Did he have his hand up her shirt like a middle-school kid on a date? Was she giving him a blow job? Or were they straight-out humping? Or, who knows, 69-ing?

"What-fucking-ever." Frankie tosses her soggy tissue into the white wicker and brass trash basket, then turns to face me with her swollen bloodshot eyes and an inflamed nose. "Don't do it, Julia." Her growly voice seems to be emanating from her bowels. "Michael's a nice guy. He loves you, Julia. Don't do it. It's so mean. It's just so fucking mean."

With Frankie's somber admonition lurking at the edges of my deteriorating conscience, I rededicate myself to steering clear of Evan Delaney. I let a graduate student take over the courtly love exhibit. But Evan remains a presence in my life. His e-mails come frequently, and they're always structured in a way that forces a response. (Considering a course on medieval sexuality curriculum. Any suggestions? Has Jake seen the latest issue of *Cycle*? If not, would you like me to drop it in campus mail?) I've diligently turned down his offers of Turkish coffee with every manner of excuse, but never with the truth. I have never said, for instance, You tempt me like nothing else has tempted me. I would sell my soul to have a single night with you, if I knew I could do it without hurting my husband. Never have I felt such turmoil. Sometimes I think I would rather be dead than live like this.

I know that I should be working on my marriage. After the square-dance debacle, I've been reluctant to ask Michael to try therapy again, but the grown-up in me knows that we must try again. I don't want gimmicks, I want a real psychoanalyst, a Freudian or Jungian, somebody smart and grounded in theories of the unconscious mind, someone who takes notes.

On my tenth birthday my mother tied a green and white Vera scarf over my eyes and took me on what she called a "mystery trip." Some indiscernible time later, it could have been fifteen minutes or three hours, she instructed me to remove the blindfold. We were in the parking lot of Toy Town on the west side of town, a rambling flat-roofed store, windows plastered with yellowed, oversized decals of dancing nursery rhyme characters. I remember feeling sorry for Mary because someone had peeled off almost all of the little lamb's head.

"Go ahead, Julie." My mother reapplied her lipstick in the rearview mirror. "Open the envelope." I did, and found it to be filled with bright, crisp money. I'd never seen so many ten-dollar bills in one place. I started counting. Two hundred dollars. It made me weep.

"What's wrong, sugar?"

"It's too much money. I can't . . . I can't take it."

"Aww, sure you can, sweetie. This money is all for you. I want you to buy whatever you want. Isn't there something you've always wanted, some toy or silly thing, some pretty little doll and a carriage, maybe?"

Two hours later, I'd filled the backseat and trunk with everything I'd ever seen advertised on TV and coveted for myself. A Lost in Space 3-D action game. A Barbie doll *and* a Ken with wardrobes. A doctor's kit, with a plastic stethoscope and candy pills in a black vinyl bag; five different paint-by-numbers kits including a black velvet one, a microscope with glass slides of wasp wings and silk strands, a badminton set with four plastic racquets, a pottery wheel, and a rock tumbler that made so much noise I was only allowed to use it when my mother wasn't home because she said it triggered headaches.

My mother forgot my eleventh birthday. But she made it up to me the following year by taking me and Katie Lender to Adventure Village, a small amusement park built into the depressed foothills of a southern Indiana town called Easterville.

It was like that my whole childhood; sometimes Trina remembered and sometimes she forgot depending on the ever-shifting circumstances of her fluid life: new boyfriend, new job, bad headache, lousy mood. I learned to regard my birthdays with detached curiosity rather than eager anticipation. At best it would be a rollicking celebration. At worst, forgotten.

All that changed when I met Michael. He believed that every birthday had to be a day-long homage to Julia. One year I walked in to find hundreds of photocopies of my face taped all over the house. Another year he put together a kind of "this is your life" party with my first flute teacher and the first kid I ever babysat. The birthdays became less inventive as our children were born, but the basic idea—a celebration of Julia—was always at the core.

Today is my forty-first birthday and Michael has made a point of *not* wishing me a happy birthday which suggests that I'm in for a big party. He did this when we were first married, inviting every friend and family member to our teeny apartment. It was kind of a surprise party in reverse. I didn't walk into a room crowded with people. I walked into an empty apartment, then one by one, everyone appeared at the door.

I'd better start cleaning.

6:00 P.M. The house is immaculate. I figure it's pointless to make dinner since Michael has probably ordered food, maybe even catered from Petit Plum, which makes an outstanding chocolate truffle cake. Oh, no. I hope he didn't order her lemon squares. Too sweet. Mine are better. I can't decide whether I should fake tears or not. I won't. I will cover my mouth in shock. That's what I'll do. I'll cover my mouth, maybe bite my knuckle. Oh, I suppose I could squeeze out a few tears.

8:00 P.M. The kids are starving so I microwave a lasagne. I guess I'll get them in their baths and start the bedtime ritual. Maybe Michael has a little private party planned, just for the two of us. I'd hinted about the lampwork necklace in the Trifles catalog. I have a strong feeling that he's got that necklace hidden somewhere in this house.

9:38 P.M. Michael is in his underwear, brushing his teeth. He smiles at me from the bathroom as white foam drips down his chin. He tells me I look beautiful and suggests I take off all my clothes and get into bed with him. "I'll give you a backrub—naked," he says, pronouncing the word "nekk-ed" like a hillbilly. "And then I'll give you a front rub."

So I let him. Maybe he has planned a different kind of birthday surprise, one that starts with sex and ends with cake. But as Michael's warm, strong hands make slow circles across my deltoids, he suddenly stops and gasps and I realize then that he did, in fact, forget.

"Oh, Jesus," he says. "Oh, God, Julie. Today's your birthday. I totally forgot. Oh, Jesus."

"It's okay." I can feel hot tears flooding my eyes. I blink them back and will myself to remain composed. I keep my face pressed into the mattress. "It's no big deal.

You've had a lot on your plate these days. With that antitrust case and your band and all."

"Oh, honey, oh, God, I'm so sorry. Oh, jeez. I can't believe I forgot your birthday. Things have been so crazy at work. I just. Look. Please. Tell me. How can I make it up to you? Please. I'll do anything. Name it."

"Just remember my birthday next year, okay?" I tell him. "That would be enough."

"I feel like such an idiot."

"Stop. Really. It's no big deal."

Now there is no way either of us could possibly continue the massage. I'm too bitter and Michael is too overwrought and remorseful. I sit up and reach for the clothes I'd left folded on the wrought-iron bench at the foot of our bed. "I think I need some fresh air."

"Can I come with you?"

I tell Michael that I'd rather be alone. I pull out of the driveway and start driving. I switch on the radio, find WAKC ("Ass-Kickin' Country"), crank it up loud, and head north on Kirby. I consider driving to Jupiter's, the pickup bar on the south side of town, but wind up in the Kroger parking lot. I turn off the engine, the radio, the lights. I am staring at the sign above the supermarket and notice that birds have built nests in the crevices along every single letter except the G, and wonder why they chose to reject this one letter. Perhaps there was a short in the wiring and one of them had been electrocuted while trying to establish its nest, so the others knew intuitively to stay away.

I am crying again and now my cell phone is ringing. "Michael?"

"It's Evan, actually."

"Evan. Hi. Are you, is something wrong?"

"No. Everything's fine. I just . . . I just wanted to, I don't know. I guess I wanted to hear your voice. I know I shouldn't have called. God. You're married."

"It's okay." I'm still sniffling.

"Hey, by the way, happy birthday."

He remembered.

"I wanted to call you earlier but I figured you were probably busy with some big family shindig."

I didn't say anything, just sniffled.

"Are you alright? You sound like you've got a cold. Or have you been crying?"

"My husband forgot my birthday."

Long pause. "Oh. I'm sorry."

"Me too."

Another long pause. "I have an idea. Just hang on a second."

Now I hear the sad, sweet wheeze of a harmonica. Evan is playing a melody I quickly recognize, that song from *Peter Pan,* which happens to be one of my favorites. He plays it mournfully and perfectly, and I find myself wondering if I'll ever find this treasure, this place where dreams are born, where time is suspended, where youth is eternal, and all one's deepest wishes are possible.

Two days later I find a box on my side of the bed. The box is wrapped in leftover Christmas paper, hastily, and taped in place with the self-stick address labels we got for free from the American Heart Association. I'm normally amused by Michael's childlike gift-wrapping style but today the sight of this package dressed in holly and berries in the middle of April makes me want to flush it down the toilet.

Michael steps quietly into the room as I finger the squashed red bow. "Ah," he says, clapping his hands together, "you've found it."

"I guess I have. Is this for me?"

"Who else would it be for, you little nut?" He wraps his arms around my waist from behind and nuzzles the back of my neck. "I'm sorry, Jules. I screwed up. Forgive me?"

I don't covet diamonds the way Frankie does, but now I find myself thinking that if this is an apology, there had better be something really expensive inside that box. I unwrap it quickly, lift the top off, and push aside the hard white tissue paper.

"Oh. Huh. A shirt." A polyester-cotton blend scoop neck in a dull blue, the color of cheap sidewalk chalk, the kind you get at the dollar store. An embroidered fish across the chest, yellow. I lift the blouse out of the box and shake it, expecting that a small velveteen box will drop from a sleeve.

"Like it?" Michael has his tongue stuck in his cheek and he's grinning, practically bouncing on the balls of his feet.

I am not an ingrate. I hate ingrates. "It's cute." I choke the words out.

"You do remember, don't you?" Michael cocks his head. "The fishy shirt? Door County? The gift store? Next to the pancake place? Come on, Jules. Work with me here. Fishy, fishy?"

"What are you talking about?" I remember a lot of things about that vacation in Door County—Michael getting the kids to bed early in the adjoining room so we could make love, the sweet honey powder he dusted across my breasts and between my legs, the hot bubble bath we took later, and the deliciously sensual way he washed my hair—but I have no recollection of a "fishy shirt." Michael holds the top up to his own chest and does a little dance. "Remember? Fishy, fishy?"

I watch my husband dancing with this ugly shirt, babbling nonsense, and I feel something like shards of glass shoot through my veins.

"Okay." Flop sweat appears across Michael's brow. He sighs as he resigns himself to the failure of his birthday surprise. "Think back. Last summer in Door County. We were in the gift store. Next to the pancake place. You looked at this shirt. I called the store. I had them FedEx it." He holds the shirt up and waves it. "*It was this specific shirt.* Jake liked the fish. You said, Fishy, fishy. I heard you. You loved this shirt." Then, with desperation, "Didn't you?"

"Not really."

"You didn't?" He drops his head in defeat. "Aw, honey. I'm sorry. I really blew it, didn't I?" Michael hugs me and his body feels like the lead apron the dentist makes you wear for X-rays. "Please, Julie, please let me make it up to you."

How could he possibly make it up to me, this man who routinely denies himself even the smallest pleasures? On second thought, self-abnegation no longer applies to Michael. Since he started playing with the band, my husband has spared no expense on his musician self. New sunglasses, a sleek black revolving shelving unit for CDs, expensive speakers. The guest room in the basement is now his music room. My gilt-framed cherub print has been replaced by a poster of the Allman Brothers. His old turntable, neglected since the advent of the compact disc, now sits on top of his grandmother's antique dresser, surrounded by stacks of classic rock LPs. I offered to help him repaint the room but he said it was fine the way it was, and I tried not to interpret that as a sign of rejection, a recoiling from my wifely cooties.

"Don't worry about it," I tell him, snaking out of his embrace. "It's a cute shirt. I needed a . . . fish shirt."

"You're just being nice."

"Yes. I am." Eager to take advantage of this small window of obsequiousness, I ask, "How's Edith?"

"Edith?"

"You know. Edith. Berry. Your paralegal? The girl who sings with your band?"

"She's fine," Michael says. "She seems to be getting better with every gig. She really has a spectacular voice."

And a spectacular body, I want to say. "Is she . . . dating anyone?"

"I don't believe so. Between work and singing with the band, I'm afraid that Edith doesn't have much of a social life."

In other words, you're the only man in her life, I am thinking. By day and by night, it's Mike, Mike, Mike. "I saw her at Borders. She told me you guys asked her to join the band."

"We did. A while ago. I . . . thought I told you."

"No." Say it, Julie. "You know, Michael, I've already been through this once with you. I don't want to go through it again."

He understands the reference immediately. "You won't have to, Julie. I love you more than life."

I toss the fishy-fishy shirt to the top wire shelf in my closet. It falls off the edge and lands crazily out of joint, like a woman who has jumped to her death. I pick up the shirt and jam it in between a pair of snow boots and a Hefty bag full of maternity clothes.

Have you ever probed your gums with a toothpick until they were raw and bloody, because even though it hurts like heck and you know it can't be good to dig at your teeth this way, somehow it also feels oddly pleasurable to pick and probe, even as you're bleeding? "Why didn't you tell me that Edith was an official member of the band?" I'm compelled to ask.

"Oh. I just, I thought you knew."

I keep picking away. "How would I know if you didn't tell me?"

"Maybe you would have known if you came more often to watch me play."

"For your information, Michael, there are three little things standing in the way of me becoming a barfly. They're called Caitlin, Lucy, and Jake. Remember them?"

"Julie, please, I don't want to get into this with you. Listen. I'm going out."

"Fine!" I throw the box on the floor. "Tell Edith Berry I send my regards!" I wait until I hear the garage door close, then go back into the closet, yank the fish shirt off the floor, and stuff it in the trash.

A half hour later Michael is home again clutching a bouquet of pearly pink roses, and unlike the cold, stiff roses you get in supermarkets, these actually have a lush, authentically rosy fragrance because they came from Louisa's, an old-fashioned flower shop downtown. Michael brought me a bouquet of these same pink roses when each of our children was born. He sets the flowers on my nightstand and drops to his knees.

"I adore you, Julia Flanagan," he says, reaching under the covers to hold my hands. He presses his face into my neck and I can feel his tears. "You can't leave me. I love you so much, Julie. God, how I love you. I'd be lost without you."

Michael has insisted we go to Primo for a belated birthday dinner. He is trying his best to engage me but all I can think about is the way Evan's jeans fit across his hips, how his forearms bulge when he flexes them, the crease of his eyelids, the subtle protrusion of his upper teeth, the way his lips curl at the corners, even when he isn't smiling.

My husband fills my wineglass and I feel like someone is stepping on my windpipe. My husband tries to make a joke—something about a misspelling on our menus—and I want to cry. I remember how it felt to look up from a book and see Evan staring at me, to be typing at my computer and feel his gaze warming the back of my neck, turning to find that he is, indeed, watching me.

My husband reaches across the table to spoon a bit of

raspberry sorbet in my mouth and I feel like I'm swallowing rocks. I shouldn't be here, not with Michael. I have nothing to celebrate tonight and neither does he. I feel only pity for the sweet, skinny, balding man across the table. He may be losing his wife. He just doesn't realize it yet.

Chapter FIFTEEN

"You have the weight of the world on your shoulders, don't you, Michael Flanagan?" Three weeks after the fish incident we're sitting with Dr. Tanya Walcowicz, bony and prematurely dowager-humped, sober in a gray tweed suit that is both out of season and out-of-date. Leslie Keen said Dr. Walcowicz was the best in the business. Then again, Leslie Keen is twice divorced. But I had to try something.

When I called to arrange the appointment, Dr. Walcowicz asked me what I hoped to gain from counseling. I told her that my husband and I weren't as close as we used to be, tried to describe as best as I could that the bond us between us now felt wispy, tenuous. I said that Michael spends too much time at work, and now he's involved with this band, and that he'd even forgotten my birthday. She said nothing but murmured softly. I assumed she was taking notes. I didn't, however, tell Dr.

Walcowicz what I felt deep in my heart and knew to be true, that I was inflating my husband's flaws to build myself an impenetrable pretext for leaving the marriage to be with Evan.

"You're the warrior who goes out into the world and slays the fire-breathing dragon to protect your family." It is our third session with Dr. Walcowicz. We are focusing on Michael's devotion to his work. She taps her sharp chin with the eraser end of her mechanical pencil. "Am I right? Are you a dragon slayer, Michael?"

"Yes." Michael is nodding vigorously, relieved and delighted that for once we've found someone who understands him.

I'm already a million miles away. I look down at my hands because I don't want to look at Dr. Walcowicz's gray panty hose, which gathers in loose wrinkles about her ankles. Resting lightly in my lap, my hands suddenly look small and ineffectual, dry as onion skin. I make a mental note to carry hand lotion at all times. In fact, I will buy a small tube for every purse so I never find myself without it.

"Michael, may I ask, when was the last time you felt babied?" Dr. Walcowicz doesn't wait for an answer. "Babies. Helpless, dependent. Tiny creatures, sweet and needy. Am I right? Michael Flanagan doesn't like feeling helpless, does he?"

Michael shakes his head and leans forward with his elbows on his knees. He wants to hear more. He thinks she's on to something. I'm wondering where she's going with this.

"Babies are helpless, Michael. They depend on us for food and clothes and all the rest, yes? And babies don't have to slay the dragons, do they? They don't have to work for a living. Babies don't have to be at the office every morning, or worry about getting the taxes in by April fifteenth, am I right, Michael? Little babies, little babies." She sings this last line and gestures as if she's cradling an infant in her arms. "So sweet, so helpless. Not a care in the world."

I hear a hissing sound and think something in the room must be deflating, like a pool float, then realize it's my husband, crying into his freckled hands. I hadn't seen this coming and all at once Michael is foreign to me, not just the crying, but every part of him, from the flushed bald spot to the ankle bones jutting through thin, olive socks. I realize that I never knew his ankles were so bony, had never seen those socks before, or noticed that there's a broken capillary on his bald spot. What else haven't I noticed about Michael Flanagan?

"I want you to take your husband in your arms, Julia."

"Me?" I am yanked from my musings. I hadn't expected to play a part in this.

Dr. Walcowicz smiles patiently. "Yes, *you.* I want you to take your husband in your arms."

My husband has stopped crying. I open my arms and Michael positions himself stiffly, with his face in my hair. I notice that he smells like a stromboli and I wonder whether that's another meal he shared with Edith.

"Good. Very good. Now turn the other way. Like a baby. There. Good. Julia, I want you to cradle Michael like a baby. You remember what it is to hold a baby, yes? Can you cradle Michael like a baby? Michael, can you just let go? Can you be a baby, Michael?"

My husband twists toward me and closes his eyes.

"Why don't you suck your thumb, okay? Did you suck your thumb as a baby, Michael?"

He already has his thumb in his mouth. "Umnh-mhh." My arms are beginning to ache.

"I thought so." Dr. Walcowicz checks her watch. "We have a few minutes left. Yesssss. Just sit there and feel this. Michael, remember how it feels to just *be.* To have all your needs met. Not a care in the world. You have your mommy, your thumb, your blankie . . ."

I can't hold it in a second longer. I am laughing now, big snorty hiccupping laughter that makes my whole body shake. And in the same moment I can feel something shift and now I am crying, but I am not crying with Michael or for him, or even for us. I'm crying because I am desperately unhappy. I am not yet willing to admit to my husband or therapist that what I really want is Evan Delaney, who makes me feel young and pretty and more important than his job. I want to be far away from this humpbacked woman and my thumb-sucking husband.

Three days later Annie and I are back at the Freedom Café, sharing a small slice of tofu cheesecake. She tells me that Frankie and Jeremy are in therapy and he claims to be done with his affair. As for Annie herself, everything's "copacetic" as usual; the only news is that she's taking water aerobics at the Y.

"That used to be my life," I told her. "When signing up for a water aerobics class at the Y qualified as a major life change. Before Evan Delaney."

"Okay. Here. How about this. Nonprofit work. Channel your energy into something productive and charitable and life-affirming."

"What do you have in mind?" Now that I've passed through the grotesque cookie jar collecting phase, I am open to almost anything. Doing life-affirming charity work seemed like just the thing to counterbalance the wicked thoughts and fantasies running through my head on a continuous loop.

"You know Serena Carmichael? The one whose husband divorced her two months after they adopted those twins from Guatemala? She's involved with the Cambridge County Wildlife Rescue. Wonderful group. They take in baby birds with broken wings, fix 'em up, release them into the wild. Or something like that. Very gratifying work, she says."

I'm thinking this may be Annie's best idea yet. I picture cupping a baby bluebird in my hands, releasing it into the clear sky over Cherry Hill farm, hugging my fellow rescuers as we watch the healed bird take flight. When I was a Girl Scout, our troop saved four baby possums whose mother had been hit by a moving van. Not only did we earn our animal care badges, but the district leader (the aptly named Eleanor Chesty) awarded us a special citation that I have to this day.

"And you won't have to worry about some hunky wildlife type coming on to you," Annie continues. "Because it's all women. Not a man in sight."

"Oh." I guess that would be a good thing. "This isn't some kind of Outward Bound thing for bored suburban women, is it? Because I don't think I have the upper body strength to chop firewood."

"Nobody's going to ask you to chop firewood. You can hold a baby bottle, right?" Actually, I breast-fed all three kids, as my southbound bustline proves, but yes, I assure her, I am confident that I can hold a baby bottle.

"Well, if you can hold a baby bottle, you can feed a baby coyote, or whatever. All they ask is that you commit to one day a month. That's doable, isn't it?"

"I guess."

Annie rips out a page from her DayTimer and scribbles something on it. "Here's Serena's number. Tell her I told you to call. Come on, Julie. Just take it. It'll be good for you."

I have driven the six miles to Cherry Hill farm and Annie is right. It's like another world out here, or at least another part of the state, where there are still big patches of trees and meadows and gravel roads.

"You must be Julia Flanagan. I'm Serena Carmichael. Annie told me you'd be stopping by." Serena's smile is fleeting, her eyes aren't unkind, just sober. Her long gray hair is woven into a thick braid and she's wearing faded denim overalls.

"You have any critters at home?"

"We've got a rat named Homer." I feel small and inadequate. I wish I could tell her we've adopted a three-legged goat or a blind fox or at the very least a cat. "The kids wanted a dog but my husband didn't so we got a rat and I told him it's a guinea pig." I was blathering now and knew it. "A dwarf Norwegian flat-coated guinea pig."

"I don't understand." Serena looks confused and I feel frivolous for mentioning it.

"Oh, it's a long story. My husband doesn't like animals. But when he was a kid there was this guinea pig . . ." I stopped myself. "Never mind."

"Husbands," Serena muttered under her breath. "Don't get me started on that topic."

We make our way to the main building, a low brick, windowless structure with multiple gates leading to outdoor kennels. We pass a slender deer resting on straw, its legs tucked beneath her. "That's Hester," Serena says, pausing to check the doe's water bowl.

"Hester?"

"You know, Hester Prynne. *The Scarlet Letter*?"

"Of course." The doe is small as a greyhound and surprisingly calm. "Hi Hester." I put my finger through the gate, expecting her to approach me but she doesn't, just stares at me with enormous, black, unblinking eyes.

That night I'm eager to tell the family about my experience at Cherry Hill. "You wouldn't believe this place. It's so *cool!* Serena, she's the woman who runs it, Serena Carmichael, she's so strong and tough, like Bonnie Raitt, or Jane Goodall, you know? And she's got these animals, these incredible animals, Michael, like this hawk named Hemingway with a broken humerus and—"

"What's a humerus?" Lucy asks.

"It's the leg bone," I say.

"The leg bone's connected to the hip bone," Michael begins to sing to the kids. "The hip bone's connected to the neck bone."

"The *neck* bone?" Lucy screams, and they all erupt in

giggles. Michael wipes the barbecue sauce from his mouth and takes a swig of beer.

"I ate a neck bone once," says Caitlin. "On Thanksgiving."

"Ewww." Jake screams. "Don't say that."

"*Any*way," I continue, trying not to sound as annoyed as I feel, "I got to hold a baby fox cub. His name is Finn and he's just as tiny as can be and so incredibly soft, Michael."

"He sounds sweet." He takes another gulp from the bottle. "Oh, hon, did you remember to pick up my dry cleaning?"

"What?"

"My dry cleaning. Did you remember to pick it up? Remember, I wanted to wear my blue suit in court tomorrow."

"Oh, no. I'm sorry. Darn. I totally forgot." I look at the clock by the stove. "What time do they close? I could go now."

"Hey, don't worry about it. I've got plenty of blue suits."

"No, I'll get it. I promise. I'll get it on my way to Cherry Hill."

"To where?"

"Cherry Hill. The wildlife refuge. You know, where I went today? Actually, it's *technically* called the Cambridge County Wildlife Rescue Society, but everyone just calls it Cherry Hill since that's the name of the farm that used to be there." Jesus Christ, has my husband heard a single word I've said? I'm expected to listen to every detail of every gig in every seedy dive—excuse me, *venue*—he plays in, and he can't remember the name of a place I mentioned five minutes ago? I want to scream.

"Sounds like a cool place." Michael pushes his plate away. "Sweetie, would you mind cleaning up tonight? I need to go back to the office and pull some things together for court."

"What? Oh. Sure. Okay. Go ahead. I'll clean up."

Michael kisses each of the kids on the forehead, then kisses me softly on the mouth.

"I think it's great, by the way. All this wildlife stuff. It'll be good for you to get some fresh air, meet new people. And if I may say so myself, they couldn't have found a better volunteer." He kisses me again. "I'm happy for you."

I squint at Michael and smirk. He is happy for me? I doubt it. This new volunteer job made me forget to pick up his dry cleaning. It isn't a source of pride but amusement, inspiration for a song about neck bones.

As if he can read my mind—which is impossible because as we all know, only wives possess that particular talent—Michael tells me later, as we're getting ready for bed, that he's proud of my new project. "Everything you touch turns to gold, Julia," he says, holding my shoulders gently and gazing into my eyes. "Think of what you've done at the Bentley. That place was just a mausoleum before you got there." He sighs deeply and steps back to look at me. "Are you okay?"

I awaken the next day with a blinding headache, my skin is scorched, and I feel like I've swallowed a paring knife. I call in sick, crawl back under the covers, and when Michael's alarm clock clicks to life—a smug NPR correspondent droning on about a combination laundromat/Vietnamese restaurant in SoHo—I croak out my plight.

"Michael. You'll have to get the kids up this morning. I feel terrible."

"What's wrong?"

"I'm sick. I think I might have the flu. I feel . . . horrible."

He kisses my head. "Poor sweetie. I'm sorry. Can I bring home something for dinner? Maybe that hot and sour soup you like so much from Beijing Kitchen?"

"Thank you."

He raises himself up on his elbows and regards me for a moment. "Go back to sleep. I'll take care of everything."

As Michael showers I drag myself to the bathroom for Tylenol and a glass of water. There are no Dixie cups left, so I use the red plastic cap from a can of shaving cream and try to ignore the "refreshing blast of menthol" on my tongue. I can see my husband's reflection in the mirror; he is lathering himself vigorously, according to the same sequential format he has used as long as I've known him. First the left arm, then the right, across the chest, now to the groin and legs, the right foot, now the left, onto his neck, butt, backs of the legs. He lifts the loofah brush from its suction-backed hook, passes the bar of soap over its webby surface, scrubs his back. There was a time when we would surprise each other in the shower. Are there any surprises left in this marriage?

I go back to bed and stay there until 11:45 A.M., at which time I get my first phone call of the day.

"Mom? They're serving Salisbury steak and canned peaches. I hate Salisbury steak and canned peaches. Can you drop off lunch?"

"Caitlin, didn't Dad make you lunch today?"

"No. He told us we should just get school lunch. But I hate Salisbury steak and canned peaches. Can you bring me lunch? Please? I didn't eat breakfast either and I'm starving to death. I feel like I'm going to faint."

"Didn't Dad give you breakfast?"

"There wasn't enough time."

I look at the clock. Caitlin's lunch period ends at 12:30. If I move quickly, I can make her lunch and drop it off by 12:15, giving her just enough time to gulp it down before literature circle.

"Thanks, Mom! I love you so much, Mommy. Are you feeling better?"

"Yes, sweetie. I feel so much better." My eyes are sizzling like a couple of fried eggs in my skull. As I pull together Caitlin's sandwich—peanut butter and honey on whole wheat, no crusts—I see today's newspaper scattered across the kitchen table.

Braless in a stained sweatshirt and hoping my black drawstring pajama bottoms will pass as workout pants, I make my way through Twin Pines Elementary's double glass doors and shuffle toward the main office. My hair is matted, my eyes are smudged with yesterday's mascara, and as I glance down at my feet I realize I'm wearing a gray New Balance running shoe on my right foot, and a red-striped Reebok cross trainer on my left. Predictably, I see every single person I'd hoped to avoid. Geneaology snob Kelly London. Matt Helms, the cute divorced dad who picks his son up every other Monday and Wednesday for lunch. Kristine Haywood, president of the PTO and former *Glamour* magazine cover girl. The hated and heavily lipsticked Shari Tabor, who bought our first house, then told everyone that my family had left behind the gift that keeps on giving—silverfish. Neva Brubaker, crisp and blindingly clean in a Talbots ensemble, size four. Mr. Marker, the gym teacher who flirted with me at the science fair last year, right next to a simulated tornado.

Though Michael has promised to be home by five, it is 6:40 when I hear the garage door rumbling and by then the kids have already helped themselves to dinner: Pop-Tarts, string cheese, barbecued potato chips, cold white rice, and Pecan Sandies. I haul myself downstairs and watch him hang his jacket in the front closet.

"Do you feel any better?" He sets his briefcase down and slips off his shoes.

"Not really. You were supposed to be home early today. Don't you remember?"

"Oh, Jesus, I'm sorry, Julia. I was almost out the door when Scott Haines called and the guy would not stop talking. He tells me his father was diagnosed with lung cancer. Poor guy was beside himself. I couldn't just hang up on him, you know how that is. Then I realized that I had to go back to my depositions and check on this one thing, and then—"

"I was *sick,* Michael. I'm *still* sick."

"Oh, honey. Can I make you some tea? Or chicken soup?" He steps into the kitchen and freezes. "Jesus Christ. What happened in here?"

"Hungry children, Michael. That's what happened."

"Shit. What a mess. I'm so sorry."

"You've been saying that a lot lately."

"What?"

"Nothing. I'm going back to bed. There's a lasagne in the freezer downstairs. And there's probably enough romaine lettuce in the fridge for a salad."

"I already ate." Michael pats his paunch. "We ordered in Chinese and worked through dinner."

" 'We'?" I prop myself against the wall for support.

"Me, Curt, Joe, Edith. It's that same damn antitrust case I've been working on for half the year. It's a killer." He pushes another chip into his mouth and it cracks apart at the corners of his mouth. "I would have rather been home, taking care of my baby."

I believe him but I also want to kill him.

A friend of mine said that every married man is destined for a midlife crisis, and it is our job as wives to hold on tight like a rodeo cowboy and try to stay in the saddle. Jumping off is always an option too but if our goal is to stay married, we'd better hold fast. At some point in a married man's life, my friend had said, usually sometime in his forties but it can happen earlier or later, the man considers the years behind him and the years he has left, and suddenly realizes every single thing that he may never again experience, all the flirting and fucking, all the women in all their diverse physical forms and sexual styles. He remembers what it was like to just take his car and drive with no destination in mind, to throw his dirty socks wherever he likes, throw them on the kitchen table if he felt like it, he could play poker all night and come home stinking of beer or not come home at all. No one bitched at him, no one implored him to talk about feelings, no one complained that he wasn't attentive enough or affectionate enough or nurturing enough or "fully present" in the relationship. He was a free man. And the fact that he may never be free again overwhelms and horrifies like the diagnosis of a terminal disease. "So he panics and does something really stupid," my friend had said, "like asking his secretary out for drinks. And then, well, you know the rest."

The only way to avoid the rodeo is to marry an older man. A *much* older man. "I mean, a man who's in his seventies. One who's done with his stupid changes," she said. Which is what she did. Her second husband is seventy-two.

When I consider my friend's insights I can't help but feel guilty because I am the iron ball and chain that stands between Michael and the life he'd prefer to lead, a life without the demands of children, breadwinning, and wife. But what about my midlife crisis? Isn't it possible that I, too, stand at the median of my life full of disappointment and despair over dreams unfulfilled?

As I've said, I don't make a fuss about my dreams, but I've had a nightmare I can't ignore. I'm on an elevator with Edith Berry. The elevator is claustrophobically tiny, mahogany paneled, and musty. The elevator is moving up slowly, creaking as we pass the second floor, then the third and so on. Somehow I know that Edith and I are both on our way to the same job interview. Edith is wearing a tiny pink Lilly Pulitzer dress and pink heels, and I'm barefoot, in my underwear. Edith's legs are lean, bare, and bronzed and mine are stubby, lumpy, and pale. Her hair is long and lustrous. Mine is a gigantic mass of tangles sticking straight out from my head. The elevator stops abruptly on the fourteenth floor and suddenly there is a deafening alarm, like a tornado siren. The doors open and a handsome young security guard appears. He points at me, scowls, and says, "You." He gestures toward to a sign on the wall. MAXIMUM LOAD: 600 POUNDS. He jerks his thumb backward. "Off."

There's Andy Warhol's Fifteen Minutes of Fame, and there's Julia Flanagan's Fifteen Minutes of Thin Thighs. Every woman who has struggled with her weight is granted fifteen precious minutes where she can bear to see herself in shorts. Maybe she gets her fifteen minutes in college on spring break, or maybe on her wedding day, or just in time for her ten-year reunion. She can have several of these fifteen-minute segments at various points in her life, but they're always time-limited, always on the verge of negative reversal, like Cinderella's coach. I had my fifteen minutes of thin thighs at my wedding, again after Caitlin was born (joined Jenny Craig and bought a treadmill that, when folded flat, makes a great crafts table for the kids), and yet once more for Michael's company picnic (Weight Watchers and six months of brutal Thai kickboxing).

Until Edith, I didn't worry about my body, just tried to cope gracefully with the extra pounds that come with motherhood, age, and a desk job. But last month I bought a girdle to compress my belly so I could wear a great pair of low-slung pants I found at Nordstrom. The tag said it was a "body shaper" but I know a girdle when I see one. My mother wore a girdle. In my case, all the "shaper" did was redirect the flubber to my thighs.

Rather than delude myself into believing I'm destined for lifelong sveltitude, I have resigned myself to serial fitness, the sporadic disappearance and inevitable reappearance of fat. The elevator dream has me convinced that it is time yet again for Julia Flanagan's fifteen minutes. Because I never start a new project without first assembling all the appropriate accoutrements, I drive directly to the Wayfield Mall to buy myself a new scale. Actually, it is a solar scale. It never needs batteries. The scale's accuracy, according to the earnest young salesman at Brookstone, is guaranteed within one-sixteenth of a pound. State of the art, he tells me.

After four days of eating nothing but eggs, cream cheese, baloney, and beef jerky, I remove everything I'm wearing including my wedding band and step gingerly on my new solar scale. I peek at the reading. It says LOW. I have a hunch that this can't be a reference to my weight, so I check the user's manual and discover that "a reading of 'LOW' indicates insufficient light levels." I switch on the exhaust fan over the shower, which has its own built-in light, and try again. LOW. I put on all the lights over the sink and one more in the foyer. LOW. Now I'm beginning to wonder what kind of moron came up with the idea for a solar scale? Why would anyone need a solar scale? So they can weigh themselves on the beach?

Wrapped in one of the kids' Flintstones beach towel, I carry the scale into my bedroom, switch on my overhead light, the two bedside lamps, and the halogen torchier. My bedroom is now as bright as a tanning booth. I step on the scale. LOW.

I try the kids' bathroom, Michael's study, the upstairs hallway, the laundry room. LOW, LOW, LOW, LOW. I find a flashlight in the utility closet and shine it directly onto the scale. LOW.

I stamp downstairs in the Flintstones towel and set the scale besides my front door, the brightest spot in the house, the one place plants will thrive because of the direct southern exposure that floods the windows framing the door. I drop the towel and step on the scale. Finally, a reading. Very nice. I weigh eighteen pounds.

I am standing naked on a defective state-of-the-art solar scale, and I now have the creeping sensation that I am not alone. In fact, I'm certain that I'm under observation. The children are in school, Michael is at work, and Homer is in his cage upstairs. Out of the corner of my eye I realize with horror that there is someone at the window. I make myself look and find Evan Delaney looking back.

I have several choices.

(1) I can scramble into the coat closet (but do I run backward or forward?).
(2) I can bend over (already a bad idea) and retrieve my towel.
(3) I can pretend I don't see him and go about my business.
(4) I can answer the door completely naked, like it's the most natural thing in the world. I look again and see that Evan is enough of a gentleman to have

turned away from the window. I choose the third and first option. I retrieve my towel, shut myself in the coat closet, then reemerge wearing the mink coat I've been storing for my mother.

The man I've assiduously avoided for weeks, the subject of every daydream and sexual fantasy, is now standing on one side of my door while I'm on the other, naked beneath my mother's mink coat. It seems hard to believe that only months ago the most newsworthy thing in my life was serving jury duty on a shoplifting case.

As I reach for the door I pray that I don't look as deranged as I feel. "Evan. Hi. How are you? What brings you to this neck of the woods?" I'm steaming underneath the coat and I can feel myself splotching.

"I stopped by Bentley to drop off some books and your boss told me you were home waiting for a refrigerator to be delivered. She also mentioned that you were behind on the Japan project, and asked if I'd mind dropping this off." He hands me a bulging interoffice envelope. "So you could work at home." He eyes the coat and smiles wryly. "Do you always dress like this for delivery men?"

"I lied about the refrigerator. I just needed to take a mental health day. Leslie Keen is driving me crazy."

"Listen. Julia. Is everything okay? You just dropped out of sight." He passes his hand through his hair. "I was beginning to think I'd imagined you. Are you alright?"

"Yes. Of course. I'm fine. I've just been, you know, busy." And I'm avoiding you, I scream silently to myself, because I don't want to have an affair, I want to be a good wife and good mother and keep my family intact and just the sight of you makes me weak and I don't want to be weak. It's my own fault that Evan Delaney is standing here now. I could have been explicit in ending the affair. I could have said, outright, Evan, it's over. I never want to see you again. No visits, no calls, no e-mails, no nothing. I could have slammed the door on Evan and his beautiful green eyes and amazing body and delicious smell and the way he made me shimmer like a new penny but I didn't, did I? No, I had left it open, just a crack, just enough for him to get back in.

"Busy," he repeats, squinting at me. "I have an idea. As long as you're playing hooky, why don't you change into something normal. Have you ever been to 611 Worth Street?"

"No. What's that?"

"I'll show you. You'll love it. But maybe you want to change first."

"I don't think I can go. I mean, now that I've got this Japan project."

"You wanted a mental health day, remember? Come on, Julia."

I'M HAPPILY MARRIED. I'M HAPPILY MARRIED. I'M HAPPILY MARRIED. I'M HAPPILY MARRIED. I'M HAPPILY MARRIED. I'M HAPPILY MARRIED. **I'M HAPPILY MARRIED.**

"Give me five minutes."

611 Worth Street turns out to be a medievalist's vision of heaven, an underground emporium of swords and axes, suits of armor, forged buckles, brass and gold garters and girdles, quatrefoil lanterns, herald's trumpets,

gothic triptychs. I must have passed the corner of Worth and Second a thousand times and never knew this store was here. There is an incense cone burning on a glass gargoyle, patchouli, intoxicating, arousing.

I point to a long sword on the wall. "Is that real?"

Evan lifts the sword from its stand and touches his finger to the blade.

"The Marshall sword. A replica of Sir William Marshall's own weapon of choice. Marshall served faithfully under Richard the Lionhearted." He offers it to me.

"No, that's okay."

"Here. I'll help you."

He encircles my arms with his own but the sword is very heavy and it droops in my grip. Evan puts his hands over mine and now is closer than he has ever been, and I can smell the sweetness of his breath on my neck. "Thirty-three-inch blade, perfectly balanced, central ridged fuller, full-length distal taper." I have no idea what he's talking about and I find it all very arousing. He turns the sword in our hands, first one way, then the other, then pushes me gently forward as he jabs. "Magnificent weapon."

I don't want him to let go.

"Please don't take this the wrong way, but the thought of you in that mink coat, Julia, I mean, the thought of you underneath the coat . . ." He still has his arms around me, holding my hands as I grip the sword, "I'm sorry. I shouldn't say this."

"It's okay. I want you to say it."

"I can't. I won't."

• • •

I have cooked dinner and I have done two loads of laundry and now I am writing Caitlin's report on the Salem witch trials. She thinks she is dictating to me as I type but her dictation only provides the basis for a far more engaging and sophisticated report and as far as I'm concerned, I should have done this for my daughter long ago. Every kid in that class gets help from parents. Last week they brought in their pioneer village projects, and each one was more professional than the next. Ashley Cain's village had running water and a stone fireplace with electric wiring to give the illusion of real burning logs. Chaz Bennett's was so big that his parents brought it in on a rolling cart and used the handicapped elevator to get it to the class. Caitlin's project, on the other hand, actually appeared like the work of a child. The whole thing was constructed from Popsicle sticks and looked, frankly, like crap. As the other kids and their parents, the real architects, brought in their projects and I watched Caitlin's crestfallen expression, I vowed that I would give my daughter every academic advantage, and if that meant my direct involvement in homework, then so be it. *So be it.*

Four words in five hours, unless "ah" counts as a word, in which case he's averaging one word every hour. Upon arrival, he says "Hi." During dinner, the word of the hour is "Fork?" At 9:00 P.M. he asks, "Where's the remote?"

I am now on the bedroom floor with my dresser drawer, determined to get it organized in one night. I find three-year-old Target receipts, junky gum machine trinkets Lucy forced me to buy, then promptly abandoned, loose change, twelve different shades of foundation (all wrong), tangled necklaces, a million bottles of hotel body lotion (always take them, never use them). Occasionally I try to engage Michael ("Wow, I wondered where that Dave Matthews CD went") but he doesn't respond.

When I cannot endure the silence another moment I blurt out, "For the love of God, Michael, would you please just tell me what's bothering you?"

He is in bed with his head propped against the giant denim-covered PrimaLoft-filled "reading wedge" I bought for him last Christmas from the Company Store catalog. His reading glasses are perched on his nose so he can alternate between watching the game and perusing the paper. He clicks the mute button on the remote and turns wearily toward me.

"I'm not sure I want to get into it because it's going to open up a whole can of worms and you look so content there, organizing your drawer. I don't want to bother you."

The famous and familiar Julia-and-Michael tango begins. "But you've already brought it up and I can't relax knowing something's bothering you. Please just tell me what it is."

He removes his glasses and rubs his eyes. "Maybe later, hon."

"Now."

"It's nothing."

"It's something."

Michael bolts upright. "Okay." He takes a deep breath. "Do you realize that your daughter is scavenging your drawers for clean socks? Have you seen the mountain of dirty clothes in the laundry room? Isn't it just a little ironic that you're spending all this time cleaning out, I don't know, beaver kennels when your own house is such a . . ." He waves his hand. "Well, you know. I'm sorry, Jules. I really didn't want to have to talk about this.

"Julia, I'm sorry. I hate this. I tried to ignore it. But it's been building up. And you're the one who's always saying we need to talk things out."

"So talk."

"Look. Julia. I rely on you to keep things moving smoothly on the home front. I'm not asking for anything extraordinary. Just the basics. Food, laundry, keeping up with the kids. Did you know, for instance, that Caitlin got a thirty-one on her math test last week?"

"Yes, I know. And I'm hiring a tutor."

"Well, a thirty-one is pretty serious, don't you think?" My affable Michael, a man who would sooner eat moldy bread than confront me with his grievances, seems to be gaining steam. I can hear Homer spinning in his wheel across the hall and the sound is amplified by anxiety, grinding my skull.

"I know how happy you've been at Cherry Hill. And that's great, Julie. I'm not trying to be in a fight with you. I love you. But I just don't get it. Honey, you used to *care* about this family. But the kids can't eat frozen pizza for dinner every night. We made a deal, remember? I'd take the job at Wellman only if you could cover for me at home."

I wish I could say that I volleyed back a brilliant retort, vindicating myself and all working mothers who struggle mightily to care for families, earn a living, and do some good in the world. Why hadn't I documented all the times this week that I'd wiped runny noses, made nutritionally balanced lunches, played Candyland until I wanted to kill Queen Frostine, cleaned footprints off the white tile kitchen floor (Michael doesn't even know where we keep the mop). I wish I had asked him why can't he do the laundry once in a while, and how come he gets to play in a band in bars until one in the morning but if I spend a little time at Cherry Hill I'm tampering with our domestic equilibrium?

But somehow I know that this isn't about dirty laundry or Caitlin's thirty-one or my volunteer work. Something else is going on, and with dread in my heart I force myself to ask, "What's really bothering you, Michael?"

"Nothing."

"Tell me."

Michael doesn't say anything right away and his pause compels me to look at him, and when I do I can see that his face is no longer animated by moral indignation. Now it holds only sadness. Sadness and fear.

"I saw you. Today. On Worth Street. In that medieval store."

I feel a lump the size of an avocado rise in my throat.

"Ohhh-kaaay," I say, proceeding cautiously. "And?"

"And you looked like you were having a grand old time, Julie. With some guy who had his arms around you." Michael looks as if he's about to cry. "Who was that?"

"That was Evan Delaney. A colleague, Michael. He's a medievalist. And he was showing me how to hold a sword. That's all."

"Why weren't you at work?"

"I took the day off."

"To be with him?"

"No, to be at home. Evan stopped by with some files. He suggested I take a break." This account of my afternoon is so spare and devoid of significant detail that it easily ranks as the biggest lie I have ever told.

"That's all?" Michael asks.

"That's all." I go back to reorganizing my drawer and Michael goes back to clicking channels and by the next day it is as if the entire conversation never took place.

"It occurs to me, Julia Flanagan, that we've already engaged in three critical rituals of courtly love." Evan and I are sitting under the magnolia tree outside the Bentley, the first time I've seen him since our visit to 611 Worth Street. Evan had called to invite me for a walk and I surprised him by accepting. I saw no reason to deprive myself of the pleasure of being with this resplendent man who actually wanted to be with me.

"How do you figure?"

"Well, let's see." He counts on his big fingers. "One, I've serenaded you. Okay, maybe I should have used a lyre instead of a harmonica but as far as I'm concerned it qualifies. Don't you think?"

I nod groggily, already drugged by the tacit intimacy in his words. This was a declaration. I had not prepared myself for it.

"Two, I've sent you poems."

"Yes, you have." I wonder what will come next and brace myself for something genuinely loving and irreversibly frank.

"Three, I've made you the center of my universe."

I feel myself shining inside; his words fill me like fresh water. Evan has taken the next step, articulating the feelings that have filled his heart. I want to, but cannot, do the same. I am afraid. All I can manage is: "So what haven't we done, Sir Delaney?" His answer surprises me.

"Well, I haven't challenged anyone to a duel."

"I don't think that will be necessary."

"Oh, but I must. Now, who would you like me to fight? I suppose I could kill Leslie Keen for making your life a living hell. Or I could have it out with your husband."

"Not funny," I say but my heart is spinning like a gyroscope.

"I'm sorry. That was out of line."

I look at him. "What is this?"

"This what?"

I gesture with my hands, gathering up the air between us. "*This*. This *thing*. What are we doing? What are we?"

Evan gazes at me with those impossibly green eyes, reaches for my hand and kisses it. "We are colleagues, and we are friends, Julia. This thing we have is called friendship."

"Is that all it is?"

"Is that all you want it to be?"

"Yes, Evan," I force myself to say. "That's all I want it to be."

"Then I guess we're good, my friend." He drops my hands and I feel the air cool the spot he'd kissed.

I must have looked as disappointed as I felt.

"Isn't that what you wanted to hear? Or was there something else you wanted me to say?"

Friendship isn't enough for me, Evan, I am thinking. I

want to know how it feels to fall asleep in your arms and awaken in your bed.

"No," I finally say. "There's nothing else I wanted to hear."

"Okay, then." I watch as Evan rises from our spot under the tree, brushes off his pants, and makes his way back to his office. I want to grab the leg of his pants and pull him back to me but all I do is sit there and watch him leave me.

Tonight I will call Evan Delaney's office just to hear his voice on the answering machine.

The beach house is beginning to feel familiar, not nearly as breathtaking as the first time I stepped through the beveled glass doors. Even the elevator is now just another utilitarian construction detail: How else would one transport coolers from kitchen level to beach level? I have been spoiled.

I've been assigned the corner bedroom this time, the "Swedish Room," with its view of the bay to the west, and the Atlantic to the east. I feel guilty taking the largest room, but Frankie insists on it; everyone else has had a turn in this room except me. Crisp and fresh in white, blue, and young grass green, all solid colors except a single pillow in the middle of the full-sized bed, a primitive green leaf print. The bed is a pristine antique, with a simple carved headboard in solid alder painted white dating back, Frankie told me, to the Gustavian period of the late 1700s. Two white nightstands flank the bed, a squarely built table with a single drawer, and a round pedestal with no drawer. Fresh white geraniums in a small painted blue bucket, a white plaster dove sitting atop an old leather-bound Bible. Fifteen paces beyond the bed is a sitting area with a white wicker and wood rocking chair, rolltop desk, sturdy white wooden coffee table, old Norse maps in blue frames, and a pewter tree-of-life candleholder. The only concession to modernity is the Macintosh computer, a seventeen-inch active matrix flat-screen monitor, Internet at the ready, so guests can check e-mail and surf the Net.

I could live in this room. I must live in this room. I want Frankie Wilson's parents to adopt me and let me stay in this simple, lovely, orderly Swedish room for the rest of my life. I would read the Bible every night and plot imaginary journeys on the Norse maps. I flop across the goose feather comforter and wonder how my friends would react if I simply refused to go back to Indiana with them. Surely there is some obscure legal loophole to protect me. Squatter's rights? Possession is nine-tenths of the law? How could I return to my life in Larkspur Estates and behave as if nothing had happened? How could I go back to putting the trash out on Wednesday nights like a regular person? Would I look any different, pulling out of my driveway, squinting into the sunlight, and flipping down the visor? Decorating my mailbox with the seasonal mailbox covers I'd bought through the Lillian Vernon catalog, the rosy hearts in February, the penguins in Santa costumes in December? Christmas parties, bulb planting, garage sales, gutter cleaning, retrieving the mail, putting out the trash—I feel as if I am no longer entitled to these rituals of domesticity. I should be living in a house on fire. In fact, I should be ablaze myself.

When the Candle of Truth is passed to me tonight, my friends watch with voyeuristic anticipation but they feel guilty because they bear some culpability in the mess that has become my life, having challenged me to commit bigger, darker, and more daring misdeeds. I'm no longer the dork, the baby, the novitiate. I've outdone them all.

"Michael was working late again. With Edith Berry. Who's still singing in his band, by the way," I begin slowly. "And, as you all know, I was still mad at Michael for forgetting my birthday, and he's always working late or playing with the band, and I never really recovered from The Rock Barn thing, when he walked off the stage that time." I checked for empathic nods and clucks that were, as expected, forthcoming. The context is critical. The context is *everything.* I need to remind myself and my friends that none of this would have happened if Michael hadn't started with the band, with Edith, the late nights, the forgetting.

"I arranged for a sitter and phoned Michael to let him know I'd be working late too."

My friends look like Girl Scouts around a campfire, wide-eyed and bracing themselves for a heart-stopping tale.

"And at first, that's all I'd intended to do, just work. Leslie Keen was leading another one of her Sex on the Seas cruises. I was supposed to do her PowerPoint presentation. 'From the Kama Sutra to *The Joy of Sex.* Sex manuals through the ages.' But I couldn't focus. I was restless. Usually, I just churn it out. I might as well be writing about mayflies. But tonight, I don't know, it was different. All those naked people having sex in all those weird positions. It was making me, you know . . ."

"Horny?" Annie is perched on the edge of the sofa, elbows on knees, her sneakered feet planted firmly on the sisal rug.

"Yes." God, this is hard. "So I decide to take a walk. To clear my head. I'm outside now, on the quad, and I'm all alone. I look up and there's one light on in Volk Hall. Second floor, third office from the left."

I pause, remembering how I'd stared up at Evan's office and wished on it like the evening star. I had never felt this way, so full of sadness and yearning and desperation. I wanted to be held and kissed and I wanted so much more than that, and yet I knew that these basic pleasures, which I have come to believe are the *entitlement* of every living creature, were out of my reach, which only made me feel more despairing. Star light, star bright, first star I see tonight . . .

"And then Evan appears at the window. He just stands there, looking at me. And somehow I know that I have no choice but to be with him."

Annie is smiling. Frankie is twisting the fringes on her blanket and doesn't look up.

I take the stairs two at a time quickening my pace with every landing. Evan opens the door just as I raise my hand to knock. My heart is hammering wildly against my ribs as his eyes meet mine, and he says nothing as he takes my hand and draws me into the room. There is no cautionary inner voice to quell my driving desire, no conscience, not a single rational thought in my head. Just pure, raw hunger, a visceral force unlike any I've ever experienced.

Evan reaches to remove the fake ponytail and drops it to the floor. "Your husband is a fool," he whispers.

His kisses are hot and hard and deep. My skin feels scorched against his, and I decide that if I am to die for my sin, let me die burning in Evan Delaney's arms. In an instant our clothes are in heaps at our feet, and I am staring at the top of his beautiful head as he runs his full lips and hot tongue over my breasts and belly, then between my legs. My body arches as he probes and strokes, the softness of his mouth against my body feels like my first taste of pawpaw, the tropical-tasting fruit that grows wild in Midwest shade and yields sweetly to teeth and tongue. He brings me to an intense climax not once, but twice, then hoists me onto his desk, and now he is standing before me, Evan Delaney, full of heat and blood. We fit together perfectly.

He keeps his gaze locked on mine as he moves and whispers, "Oh. Julia. What you do to me."

After a while he shudders and sighs and is done. I keep him inside me for a few moments, holding him close, feeling his chest heave against mine.

"So, you're having an affair?" Frankie asks.

"Actually, yes."

Frankie throws her hands up to her mouth and gasps, then notices that Annie doesn't look particularly surprised. "You knew?"

Annie nods.

I explain to Frankie that I hadn't felt comfortable telling her because I knew she was raw from Jeremy's affair and thought it was unlikely she'd offer the kind of support I needed at the time. "You're probably right," Frankie admits.

I continue. "Evan and I had arranged to meet again at

his apartment the following Saturday. He had prepared dinner but we never made it to the table." The evening unfolds as I'd expected, clothes torn away and tossed to the floor, hungry pawing and hot kisses.

But this time, Evan says, "Excalibur and I have been waiting for this moment."

I am sure I heard wrong. "Excuse me?"

He smiles at me. "Excalibur."

I realize he's talking about his penis and suddenly it is as if someone has switched our soundtrack from Barry White to the Chicken Dance. My desire is draining away. I try to get myself back in the mood, try to focus on the heat of his stare, the enormous erection that probes urgently between my legs, the delicious scent of his body, the way his hard butt feels in my hands. I kiss his soft mouth and try to get the feeling back. But the naming of his penis makes me feel silly and embarrassed and, as Eve must have felt, shamefully naked.

I let Evan kiss me a few more times, then push my hand down between us, blocking his entry. "Evan. I'm sorry. I can't do this."

"You said what?" Annie is staring at me.

"I told him I couldn't go through with it. I just couldn't do it. The spell had been broken. I had to get out of there."

"Good for you," Frankie whispers.

Annie shakes her head. "So you ended your affair? All because he gave his penis a name?"

"Yes. No. I mean . . ." I search for words that might explain my sudden withdrawal from the man I had craved for months. "The fact that he gave his, you know, a name, it sort of broke the spell. It gave me the time I needed to really *see* what I was doing. Really *consider* about the consequences. So then I started thinking about Michael and how great sex used to be and how much he loves me and that I want to be his wife forever. I know it sounds corny."

"It doesn't sound corny," Annie says.

"I just couldn't go through with it. I pulled back and thought about what I was about to do, and whether I was ready to deal with all the turmoil and pain and loss that comes with an affair." I pause here to glance significantly at Frankie.

"I thought about my kids, and what it would be like for them to not have Daddy around, to shuttle back and forth between two households. I knew it would destroy them. But most of all I thought about Michael back home, who isn't perfect but he's my husband and you know what? He's really trying. The man is trying."

As I watched Evan between my legs I had something like a near-death experience, scenes from my marriage passing before my eyes. I saw how Michael proposed to me, on one knee, dressed in his volunteer fireman uniform with the truck outside my house, lights flashing. I remembered the look on his face when each of our children was born, the way he cried and the way he kissed me. I saw the two of us laughing and screaming as we sledded down the hill behind the house after the kids decided they were too cold and tired to endure another moment in the snow. How he carried me downstairs and to the car when I was pregnant with Jake and suddenly started bleeding, how scared he was about losing the baby. I thought about the dinner he made for me when I got the job at the Bentley, how he'd sent the kids off to their grandparents and lit the dining room with what seemed like a thousand candles. I even saw the Fishy Shirt episode, Michael desperately trying to please me with his birthday surprise.

"I couldn't go through with it, Annie, I don't know how else to explain it. So I put my clothes on, I apologized, I explained that I wanted to work on my marriage, gave him one last kiss, and ran all the way back to my van. I haven't seen him since."

"Wow," whispers Annie.

"But you know what? Honestly? I don't regret a minute of it. Not a single second." And it was true. The affair had unlocked something in me. Something wild and beautiful. Joie de vivre.

I go on to tell them about when I get home from Evan's apartment, and I find my husband sitting at the kitchen table alone eating cold cereal. My goal is to get up the stairs to the bedroom without talking to him but he stops me.

"Jules?"

"Yeah?"

"Can I talk to you? Please?"

I'm sure he knows something. I'm sure I must smell of sex. I keep my distance. "Sure. What's up?"

"I'm so sorry, Julia. About everything. About working too much, and forgetting your birthday, and spending too many nights out with the band. I've been a lousy husband, Julie, and I want to make it up to you. Please. Tell me you'll let me make it up to you."

"Where's all this coming from?" I remain at a distance, still convinced that Michael would detect the scent of another man on my body.

"I had a session. By myself. With Dr. Walcowicz."

"You did?"

"Yes, I did. And Dr. Walcowicz made me realize something. She made me realize that I haven't been straight with you. I haven't told you the truth."

Uh-oh. Here it comes. My husband is having an affair with Edith Berry. Okay. I can deal with this. Stay calm. Breathe. It'll be fine. In fact, it could be very nice. I can convert his office into a sewing room. I can take showers and not worry about running out of hot water. I'll never have to hear his snoring again, not the Popper, not the Asthmatic Pug, none of it. Lots of men have affairs, lots of women are divorced. I'll get a good lawyer. I'll get Alexis Merriweather's lawyer and leave Michael without a pot to piss in. But what if I can't cope? What if I lose my mind and become one of those bag ladies outside the public library, pushing all my worldly possessions in a stolen Kroger supermarket cart?

"The truth is, I've been miserable. I hate my job. The hours. I hate being away from the family. I hate being away from you, Julia." He takes a deep breath. "I want to go back to Legal Services. I want to be able to leave work at a humane hour every day. I want to be a husband to you, Julia."

"What about the house?" We couldn't possibly pay the mortgage on his Legal Services salary and what I make at the Bentley.

"So we'll move into a smaller house. I don't care about the goddamn house, Julia. I care about us."

There's something so reckless and exciting about his proposal that it makes me almost giddy. A smaller house, a new job, our old life. But then Michael's face is overcome with such gravity, I expect him to announce that he is dying of prostate cancer and wants to make the most of whatever time he has left. But that's not it at all.

"When I saw you with your . . . your colleague in that shop, I knew in my gut that there was something going on. Between the two of you. I could see it. For all I know, you're having an affair."

My body goes rigid. I wait but say nothing.

"And, honestly, I wouldn't blame you if you did."

To my husband's credit, he doesn't ask me if I did, in fact, have an affair with Evan Delaney.

"But, Julia. Whatever it is you're doing, I need you to come back to me. You are my wife and I cannot imagine my life without you." Michael stands up, shoulders slack, arms beckoning, palms up, all defenses down. As my husband hugs me, I can still feel Evan's tongue between my legs. I am tired and confused. I go upstairs and take a scalding shower. I am asleep by the time Michael comes to bed.

"Jesus, Julia." Annie passes me the bowl of M&M's. "So, are you ever going to tell him? About Evan?"

"Are you crazy?" Frankie looks at Annie in disbelief. "What's she going to tell him? 'Darling husband, I thought you'd be happy to know that I had sex with this hunky English professor but I couldn't do it again after he called his penis Excalibur. Aren't you proud of me?' "

Actually, I *had* considered telling Michael some version of the truth, not only to clear my conscience, but to initiate a broader conversation about the state of our marriage and his murky relationship with Edith Berry. And, frankly, I wanted Michael to know that another man—a real man, a charming, articulate, passionate man—found Mrs. Julia Flanagan, rapidly aging suburban mother of three, intensely desirable.

"Don't tell him," Frankie says softly, staring into the candle's flame. "It's over. Just leave it alone."

"I disagree," says Annie. "I think you should put your cards on the table, Julia. This could be a transformative moment in your marriage. Your pain. Longing. Loneliness. Put it all out there. You could have continued an affair. But you chose to walk away. I think your husband needs to know that."

Along with four catalogs, a few bills, and the usual low-interest credit card offers, I find a pink envelope in the mailbox, recognize my mother's loopy script, and slide my finger under the flap. "This birthday greeting isn't late. It's just early for next year!" A smiling cartoon chef wearing oven mitts withdrawing a three-tiered birthday cake from the oven. Inside, a yellow Post-it note. In the careful and heavy-handed print my mother reserves for important messages, Trina has written: Charlie Gillespie. (317) 631-3182. He is your father.

Now that I finally know, I realize that I no longer care. I slip the note in between the pages of the Hammacher Schlemmer catalog and toss it with the rest of the junk mail into recycling.

• • •

Thirty-six days since I left Evan Delaney and Excalibur Michael and I are still in counseling with the terminally unfashionable Dr. Walcowicz, whose techniques no longer make me laugh because they work. She instructed us, for instance, to go back to our old neighborhood in Ann Arbor and stand outside the house on Skerwin Avenue where Janet Hobart died on the bathroom floor while her husband lay oblivious in the next room.

"Don't say anything," Dr. Walcowicz told us. "Just stand there and stare at that bedroom window and remind yourself of all the reasons why you promised yourselves you would never wind up like Janet and Harry."

Something profound and elemental has shifted in our marriage. We are kinder to each other, and we've managed to relocate the companionability as well as the physical attraction that first brought us together. Michael moved back to Legal Services and his life is no longer consumed and defined by his job. He still plays with the band, but not as frequently. He is my lover again and he is my friend. We've put an offer on a house downtown, a sweet yellow bungalow that needs a little TLC.

There is one question remaining, though. Did Michael have an affair with Edith Berry? I may never know.

I'm working late tonight, the kids are sleeping at their grandparents' house, Michael and his band are playing at a fundraiser for the Boys and Girls Club.

I am cataloging erotic French stereoscope pictures, picking at my salad, and drinking a flat Diet Coke. A storm is gathering to the west; the wind whips through the stand of sycamore trees outside the window, a high, dead branch comes loose and smacks against my window. I stare at the postcard in my hands, a mostly naked woman in garters and stockings perched like a Pekinese on a floral ottoman in a Victorian room.

I look out the window across the quad. For a moment I wonder if Evan is in his office now, then I remember he's no longer here. After all his efforts to be a good citizen of the academy, he was denied tenure and is now teaching at Sarah Lawrence. I know this because he told me in his very last e-mail to me, the one in which he said he misses me, thinks of me, even dreams of me, but understands and respects my decision to stay married. I wished him well and haven't heard from him since.

I look at my watch. There's still time. I shove the stereoscope cards in the drawer and find my purse. Eighteen minutes later I'm pulling into the cramped gravel parking lot of the Boys Club. I push through the door and can hear the dull thud of the base and faint din of a party and as I get closer I can hear Michael's sax rise above the music as he takes a solo on "New York State of Mind" and, actually, he sounds like a real musician. I slip into the room and see my husband onstage, wearing my favorite jeans and his Superdad T-shirt. His face brightens like a halogen lamp when he sees me. I move deeper into the crowd and watch him from the floor. He watches me as he plays, as if every note in that transcendent solo is meant only for me.

The band plays the opening bars of "Color My World." Michael puts his sax on its stand and jumps off the stage.

"Shouldn't you be up there?"

"I'd rather be here with you." He slips an arm around

my waist. "I want to dance with you," he says, pulling me very close to him, and I remember how much I'd enjoyed dancing with my husband and how much I've missed it. He dips his head to kiss me, and gives me a lover's kiss, moist and deep. He holds me tighter and I can feel his arousal.

"This will probably sound strange, under the circumstances, but I really want you right now."

"Did you fool around with Edith Berry?" I whisper, bracing myself for the answer. "Did you? Are you?"

"What? Are you kidding?" Michael stops dancing and gives me the look he reserves for my least feasible propositions (adopt a monkey instead of having a third child, turn the backyard into an organic vineyard, buy an old school bus and convert it to a guest house). "Absolutely not." He spins me around slowly and kisses me on the tip of my nose, then softly on the mouth. "I have been an inattentive husband. I've been a workaholic husband. And I've been a forgetful husband. But I will never be a philandering husband again. I have never wanted anyone but you, Mrs. Flanagan."

I believe him.

Now as we move around the dance floor I find myself oscillating between relief and disappointment. If he'd been fooling around with Edith Berry, my desktop escapades with Evan would have seemed virtuously self-restrained, planting me firmly on higher moral ground. Instead, I'm a strumpet. I flirted with Evan Delaney, I played hooky with Evan Delaney, I had sex with Evan Delaney. I remember Annie's entreaty to lay my cards on the table. There is no telling where a full confession might lead. It could help us create a fresh new relationship. It could also end everything. What would I say? Michael, we're finally even. You had Susie and I had Evan.

I look up at the kind, open, handsome face of the man I love. "Michael?"

"What is it, sweetheart?"

"There's, uh, something I need to tell you. Something you're entitled to know."

"Tell me, honey." He brings my hands to his lips and kisses my fingertips. "You can tell me anything."

"Michael . . ." I can hear my blood roaring in my ears. I take a deep breath and shut my eyes. This is it. "Michael?"

"Yes?"

"It's about Homer."

With or Without You

Carole Matthews

When Jake tells Lyssa it's not working, she knows he's not talking about the toaster. What she doesn't realise is that he has been seduced by another woman.

Lyssa's immediate reaction is to sob into her pillow and wait for Jake to come home with his tail between his legs. But slowly she understands that's not an option. In a bid to escape, she embarks on a trekking holiday in Nepal. Her sister teases her that she'll meet a hairy-arsed yak shepherd – but it never occurs to Lyssa that in the Himalayan foothills she might fall in love . . .

When it's time to go home – back to reality and a very sheepish Jake – Lyssa has to face the hardest choice of her life.

Praise for Carole Matthews' previous bestsellers:

'Matthews is one of the few writers who can rival Marian Keyes' gift for telling heart-warming tales with buckets of charm and laughs' *Glasgow Daily Record*

'A feel-good tale . . . fun and thoroughly escapist' *Marie Claire*

'Will have you giggling from the start . . . hilarious' *OK!* magazine

0 7553 0993 6

headline

Amazing Grace

Clare Dowling

Grace Tynan's life is terrifyingly planned: her career in property, the school car pool, her marriage to a man whose head is like a sieve. So when a college dropout called Adam knocks the side mirror off her BMW with his anti-nuclear placard, the last thing Grace expects is to fall in love.

Anxious friends soon notice an alarming change – Grace gives up work, she shuns dinner parties and, most disturbing of all, she stops highlighting her hair. Has the Grace they know and love turned into a Rainbow Warrior, or has she simply decided that her grey life needs a bit of colouring in?

Praise for Clare Dowling's previous novel, EXPECTING EMILY, also available from Headline:

'Commercial fiction at its most entertaining' Marian Keyes

'Very funny and original' Cathy Kelly

'Sparkling and witty . . . a great beach read' *Irish Tatler*

'Very warm, very funny . . . witty and refreshingly honest' *Irish World*

0 7553 0368 7

headline